JUST DESSERTS

A NOVEL OF LOVE, ADVENTURE, AND
CONFECTIONS.

JONATHAN DANIEL

JUST DESSERTS
TIER 1 OF A THREE-TIERED CAKE

A novel of love, adventure, and confections.
By Jonathan Daniel

For Kinley.
You are my Kupcake and I'd go to the ends of the world and brave the most vile dangers for you.

Even yogu-- I must not say its name.

1

Jerome had pretty much decided to get his berries frosted - and why not, he asked himself, since it would make him look cool and edgy - when he learned that his true love had been abducted. His fingers paused in the act of sprinkling flour on the exposed berries for a trial run as the gossip drifted through his window. "They took her? What was Princess Kupcake doing out there?"

"Who knows? But they must have been waiting in ambush near the Oreo Bridge. I heard they killed one rock candy guard and knocked the others out. Her assistant Peggy barely escaped with her life. I heard they even had you-know-what in a cage."

"What?"

"*You know.*"

"Would you make sense, you cracked pile of dough?"

There was a pause, and Jerome held his breath in anticipation with flour trickling from his fingertips. "Yogu-"

"Shut up, right now! Don't say that name in front of me, Great Mother Baker anoint me."

"I'm just saying. They jumped the guards, knocked her personal assistant down, and made off with her."

"Where do you think they took her?"

"Are you losing your chocolate? Did someone fill your head with candied cherries? Since German Chocolate Cake led the raid, they must have taken her to the Black Licorice Castle. It's the only thing that makes sense."

"I don't know, they could have taken her someplace else. To the Mint Cookie Mountains, or to the realm of the French Toast folk. You know those savages will buy anything."

"You really think they would have sold the princess? They'd get so much more for her through a ransom."

"Look, I'm just saying that Kupcake had no business being outside of the castle grounds like that. She's always been impulsive. Hey, don't get mad at me – I love her, too. I'm just saying that she has a wild streak in her and would be better off if she'd hurry up and marry some proper prince."

Jerome didn't hear the rest, as a cold spike had been driven through his cake. Throwing open his door, he stepped out and confronted the pair of sweets.

"Kupcake has been taken?"

A chocolate nougat bar and a cinnamon cookie gaped at him, their surprise at his sudden appearance quickly giving way to narrowed eyes and grimaces of disgust. "The hell do you care, muffin?" the nougat bar sneered. "Oh, don't tell me. You're in love with the princess? Think you may grow up one day and marry her?" He laughed, the cookie joining in. His eyes fell on the flour coating Jerome's blueberries. His laughter rose another notch. "Holy Rolling Pin, were you trying to frost your own berries? Sal, get a load of this guy, trying a home frosting kit."

Sal the cookie just shook his head pitifully, his sugar coating catching small flashes of sunlight. "Pathetic. Why don't you clean an oven while it's on?"

Next to him the nougat bar scoffed. "Dude's wearing a wrapper from six seasons ago too."

Jerome ignored them; he'd heard worse before. "Are you telling the truth, that she's been taken?"

Finally, the laughter died and the cinnamon cookie said, "Yeah. Just a few hours ago, she was out and German Chocolate Cake took her."

"Was he acting on his own? Or did Devil's Food Cake send him?"

The pair stared at Jerome as if he'd suddenly coughed up a wad of cotton candy.

"Who else would have sent him?" the cookie asked mockingly.

Jerome's mind spun. "And you said they're at the Black Licorice Castle? When is King Red Velvet sending the Fudge Army?"

The pair of sweets stared at him, their mirth gone. "How the hell would we know?" the nougat bar spat. "What do we look like, personal assistants to the king? Besides, what good would the Fudge Army be? They haven't been a fighting unit in years – everyone knows that. They're just used for show around the Lemon Icebox Castle. Now, how about you not worry about things above you and focus on not being a walking piece of shit? Come on, Sal. I need a mug of extract." The moved past Jerome, the cookie taking an extra step out of his way to put a shoulder into the muffin as they passed. Jerome stared after them, not wanting to believe what he'd heard. Kupcake had been cakenapped.

And did they really make home frosting kits?

But as the day wore on and word spread, the truth began to settle in like a heavy mix of dry ingredients seeping into waiting batter. Kupcake was gone, having been spirited away to the Black Licorice Castle under orders of the nefarious Devil's Food Cake.

Now, standing before his spun-sugar fireplace, Jerome clenched his fists in anger, heedless of the crumbs that shook from his body and littered the floor of his small home. His mind was reduced down to a single thought as he turned and retrieved his toothpick sword from its perch above his mantle. He held it before him, admiring its blade. In his whole life, he'd only drawn this sword once, when a band of chocolate bunnies had invaded his yard in search of scraps. Of course, he hadn't killed them – he'd never killed anything. The sword had come out only after his screaming, waving of arms, and stomping of feet had gained him only sleepy stares. And the toothpick sword had fared no better, as the bunnies had regarded it for just a moment before deciding that it wasn't edible and continuing with their conquest of Jerome's yard.

Jerome knew that even if Red Velvet sent the Fudge Army it could be days or even weeks before they managed to gain access to the Black Licorice Castle. The nougat bar was right that the king's army hadn't fought since the last Cookie War. No, Jerome thought, he couldn't trust that they would move quickly enough.

He vowed he would get her back, or he would die trying.

2

After sending word to Stan, his boss at Stan's Fix-it-All (We repair what your husband crumbled.) that he wouldn't be back to work for quite some time, Jerome made a quick sandwich (no sense in storming the Black Licorice Castle's gates on an empty stomach). His stomach full, Jerome prepared to be off in search of his love. As his hand reached for the doorknob, his eyes fell on a drawing he'd made of the princess. It showed her smiling as she read to cakelings and gumdrops, her perfect peanut-butter buttercream frosting shining in the light. Her eyes were a little too close together and one was significantly higher than the other; and now that he really saw the picture, he noticed that for some reason he'd only given her one ear – and that was down near her elbow. But at least he'd gotten her crooked smile right.

He loved her with everything he was, and for some reason, she felt the same, despite his horrid drawing skills and the fact that he was a muffin. Jerome took a deep breath and pulled the door open.

The reality of the length of the trek ahead of him came to him with a suddenness that stopped him in his tracks. Jerome had spent his life in the small village just outside the gates of the Lemon Icebox Castle where Kupcake lived. He'd never visited any other town or

land in the cakedom of All That's Good (But Never Goes To Your Hips
Or Butt) in his life. Now, he realized, he would be travelling - alone -
through lands he'd never seen before. Additionally, he would be
attempting to sneak into - again, alone - the Black Licorice castle and
rescue his love.

"What am I thinking?" he marveled. Getting to the Black Licorice
castle might not be that hard, considering everyone knew where it
was. All Jerome had to do was point himself directly north and walk
until he came to it. Of course, he wasn't crazy; he still had all of his
unfrosted blueberries and crumbs about him, and knew there would
be dangers along the way. But, he thought as he glanced at the
smooth blade of his toothpick sword, he would handle them when he
had to.

Not that he'd had a lot of practice with the sword, truth be told.
He'd only always fancied himself as a wild adventurer, hacking and
slashing his way through rabid hordes of cherries jubilee and discov-
ering treasure in the highest peaks of the Mint Cookie Mountains.
Other than the bunny assault that he'd failed to thwart, the only practice he'd gotten had been waving the sword in the backyard whenever
he'd had too much extract or felt really bored.

His movements had never been good, but every once in a while
he would land a good blow. The feeling of the blade slashing across
practice dummies filled with whipped cream was always satisfying.
The dummies were molded to look like the jawbreaker guards who
Devil's Food Cake was known to employ – partly because round was
the easiest shape for Jerome to make. He'd drawn on faces - mostly
straight - in black icing and begun attacking them with wild, adven-
turous abandon.

Standing in his doorway, he felt that he could dispatch most
anything that came his way, especially if it were round and filled with
whipped cream. Or at least not much bigger or menacing than a
rogue gumdrop. As long as it wasn't a chocolate bunny.

But getting into the castle and back out would require a massive
amount of luck and skill served atop a bed of pure chance, with a side
of 'Holy Rolling Pin, did I really just do that?' and covered in gravy.

Not necessarily lucky gravy... gravy was perfect just by itself. Jerome looked around his simple home. This was crazy, he thought. A simple muffin who had never ventured beyond the borders of the town, who spent his days repairing walls with icing and melting sugar for windows, would most likely be killed the moment he stepped into the Red Vines Forest. There was no telling what kind of horrors awaited someone out there.

No. Jerome flexed his fingers around the hilt of his sword and shook his head, scattering his fears. He would do anything for Kupcake, and if that meant braving the dangers of the lands, untold confections, gummy monsters, sour straw guards, and any other nightmarish delicacies, he'd do it. He would climb inside the searing walls of the Great Mother Baker's Oven happily if it meant seeing Kupcake safe again – seeing her cake and buttercream frosting as she smiled at him with her slightly crooked smile and two perfectly symmetrical eyes.

But, he thought, with a small crumb of an idea growing quickly in his mind, there was one confection he could visit first who may be able to give him guidance and possibly equip him with the tools he needed to succeed. It would be a long shot, though, as this particular confection hadn't been seen by anyone in a long, long time. Plus, the last time he'd been seen, he'd made a promise to stay out of the affairs of other confections.

As a young muffin, Jerome had read about the catastrophe that had led to the last Cookie War and the subsequent self-imposed isolation. Yet, Jerome had to try. It was the only real chance he had at succeeding. Bolstered by this thought, he left his house and stomped down the street to the stables.

It took him quite a while to wake his closest friend and trusted mount, Cleetus. The large green gummy bear had been sleeping – something he was well and truly good at doing – with his legs splayed skyward and his wide belly rolling up and down with each deep, snoring breath. Jerome managed to lure the bear not only out of slumber but also into his riding gear with the promise of a large bowl of simple syrup. Mounted, Jerome turned his eyes skyward. The clear

blue sky seemed to mock him. Its cloudless perfection hung overhead as a reminder that, across the land, life went on as usual.

With a scowl, Jerome urged the bear forward.

The Red Vines Forest lay several miles away from the center of
town and wasn't on the direct path to Devil's Food Cake's lair, but
Jerome's detour for aid required him to enter the dark and dangerous
wood. Even so, he wasn't exactly sure where this particular confection
lived. Still, finding him was imperative if Jerome was to have any
chance of reaching his foe, let alone making it past all of the guards –
sour straws, jawbreakers, dark toffee squares, and, if the fables were
true, atomic fireballs. He pushed aside the thoughts and focused on
the long ride ahead.

As they rode through the streets, past storefronts and homes,
Jerome could feel others' eyes on him. Confections of every make
stared at him from doorways and through sugar glass - some of which
he himself had made - with scorn and not a little distrust. He ignored
them as best he could.

Muffin hate had been the soup du jour for centuries, ever since
muffins had migrated to the land of All That's Good (But Never Goes
To Your Hips Or Butt). Now, these same confections who had for
generations hated muffins – for reasons as simple as the fact that
muffins lacked frosting or that they were mixed in a different manner
than cakes – stared out in silent judgement of him. *It wasn't like they
were trying to do anything to save Kupcake.* No, they were content to sit
behind their walls and wait for King Red Velvet's Fudge Army to
bring her back. The sound of sobbing drifted out from behind several
doors and open windows. *At least they feel bad,* he conceded.

A chocolate-coated marshmallow used a broom to push trash
from in front of his shop and spat white goo into the street in front of
Cleetus. The bear paused and lowered its nose to the small puddle.
Jerome dug his heels into Cleetus' springy sides and grumbled a
command, never taking his eyes off the threatening look coming from
the marshmallow. Jerome sighed as they moved past. He'd shopped
in that store. Had even helped the mallow repair one of his windows
after a cold night had sent a jagged crack from one edge to the other.

Giggling floated down from the other side of the street. High above him, on a sagging balcony, small gumdrops were huddled together, laughing and staring as he went by. "Does he think he's a hero?" one of them tittered in a tinny voice. The others shook with their own mirth.

To combat the heavy press of sadness he felt at their words and stares, Jerome forced Kupcake's face into his mind. He remembered their first outing together. She'd told him she was supposed to be practicing her sewing, but felt that learning how to fashion a rope and repel down a wall without being detected was much more fun. There'd been a gleam in her eyes, a glint of mischievousness and excitement. He'd known right then that he'd never be the same... that he could never live without this perfect baked good in his life. Smiling, Jerome let that memory and the slowly shifting gait of the gummy bear take him through the rest of the town. He barely noticed when they moved through the small, unmanned gate into the wide expanse of the fields beyond.

The orange sun was reaching its midday position as he approached the edge of the Red Vines Forest. Reining Cleetus to a stop, Jerome dismounted and stretched. A small stream of simple syrup flowed nearby, and Cleetus, snorting and grunting happily to himself, stumped to it. The bear lowered its head, and soft slurping sounds soon drifted over to Jerome.

The Red Vines Forest had stood for hundreds of years. Some of the trees within it were close to two hundred feet tall and so wide that no one could wrap their arms around the large, red, twisted trunks. As a young muffin, Jerome had heard stories of the forest from his uncle Gregor, who'd gone in on hunting trips for animal crackers. He had managed to kill a bear and a zebra, and Jerome's mother had been pleased to see that Gregor had only bitten the head off of the zebra before getting the cookies home.

But there were worse things in the Red Vines Forest, he knew. Gregor had talked about one particular day in the forest, with his eyes dark and his tone low as if he'd even then been afraid that the things would hear him and come for him. He'd described tracks and

scratches deep within the gummy bark of several trees. Once, he'd
said, as he'd finished his lunch, a scream from something large had
torn through the trees deep in the forest. Hearing his uncle describe
the experience had made Jerome's butter run cold, and he prayed to
the Great Baker Herself that he never saw what had voiced the sound.
With any luck, he thought now, he would avoid it and find what he
was looking for before the sun clocked out and turned in for the
night.

Stupid celestial unions, Jerome thought. One didn't want to be deep
in the Red Vines Forest after dark by themselves if they could help it,
Gregor had always cautioned.

Jerome whistled sharply and Cleetus shuffled over, taking his
time and sniffing an occasional blade of grass as he came, clearly not
happy about having to abandon the syrup stream.

"Stop that," Jerome commanded. The green bear just looked at
him out of the corner of his eye and pretended not to hear him.
Jerome climbed back into the saddle and urged Cleetus on.

Jerome's attention was so sharply focused on the forest before
them that, as they entered, he didn't notice the thing that had been
following them from above drop down soundlessly and land on the
far bank of the syrup stream. It regarded them with cold, unblinking
eyes as they disappeared into the twisted and gnarled rows of Red
Vine trees.

Among the trees, the air grew chilly and Jerome pulled his cloak
tighter about his body. Cleetus grumbled again in irritation, but
Jerome paid him no mind. Gummy bears could withstand fairly cool
temperatures, though if the air reached freezing, the bear would
become useless. But there was no danger of that in the Red Vines, so
Jerome ignored the complaints and dug his heels into Cleetus' flanks
again.

The faint chirping of butterscotch candy birds guarding their
chocolate eggs filled the air, and the spaces between the trees were
gloomy pools of shadow. As Cleetus plodded along, Jerome stared
into the dark places until the even darker shapes within came into
focus as simple undergrowth – and not some contorted confections

lying in wait for him. Overhead, the sky winked with cheerful patience through the thick, twisting red limbs. More than once, Cleetus slowed his pace to less than a crawl, just above the speed of molasses on a cold winter's day, so that he had to be prodded and threatened before he would continue.

They traveled for several hours, and the further they pushed into the depths of the forest, the more Jerome began to fear that they were lost. The fear was spurred on by the softening of the light as the sun - refusing to work beyond its allotted shift - headed for the far horizon.

A deep growl rose from behind them. Cleetus stopped and Jerome twisted in his seat, his hand going to the toothpick sword's handle. The forest behind him was as still as the rock candy guards Kupcake's father employed. And the rapidly fading light made it nearly impossible to see anything.

The growling came again – closer this time, and to the right. Jerome dismounted slowly and drew his sword. He held it with both hands before him, ready for whatever would come. His brow furrowed as he stared into the gloom, trying to see his would-be attacker.

A pair of glowing eyes, low to the ground, faded in from the blackness. Behind Jerome, Cleetus gave a scared grunt and shuffled several steps away.

Jerome tightened his grip on his sword.

3

Kupcake lay on a silicone baking mat bed in the darkness of her room, staring into the blackness around her. Like wet batter, her mind shifted with questions. Why had she been taken? When would her father send the Fudge Army to rescue her? What about Jerome? Did he know she'd been cakenapped? Oh, and why would anyone put raisins in food? And what were raisins, exactly? Just geriatric grapes. Raisins gave the impression that they were always wondering if there would be pudding at dinner or if this would be the weekend their children would visit.

But mostly she thought about Jerome and how she was glad he wasn't a raisin. Or had raisins. That would be gross. She was supposed to have met up with him later in the morning, and had been plotting her escape from her armed escorts when the ambush had overtaken them.

The fact of the ambush still surprised her. It hadn't been common knowledge that she planned on going out. Nobody other than Peggy, Kupcake's small attaché of personal guards and their commanders, plus Mike the stablemaster and his assistant - a cross-eyed but absolutely horrible chocolate-covered cherry named Chet – had known that she'd be leaving the grounds. Holy Rolling Pin, she'd not even known she was leaving until right when she'd looked at her day's schedule and seen that her parents had slotted curtsey practice in during the time Kupcake had planned on seeing Jerome. The thought of dipping and holding her wrapper 'just so' in order to please the sugared orange-gummy instructor had filled Kupcake with dread. So, she'd thrown her day planner across the room and considered her options for getting out of the castle. In the past, she'd ridden out in a laundry cart with piles of old linens layered atop her. Another time, she'd disguised herself as a plumber and, after being asked to fix a split in a sink drain - which she'd done handily - strolled right past the front gate guards. Kupcake smiled at the memory of the fake moustache she'd employed in that disguise.

Of course, not every one of her escapes had been to meet Jerome. Many of those occasions had been for her to go into town and do the charity work that brought her such joy. Reading to gumdrops and baby candy canes and visiting those confections who were too ill to leave home made her heart swell with love.

But, this time? She shook her head. What had gone wrong? How had those sour straw guards gotten so close to the castle? She thought back to seeing them emerge from the shadows across the Sweetwater River, nocking honey straw arrows as they advanced. She heard the ghosts of the impacts of their shots on her guards, and heard Peggy's cry of alarm and pain as an arrow... well, Kupcake assumed an arrow had struck the oatmeal cookie, as she'd not ever actually looked. Instead, her attention had been focused on the sour straws who'd violently pulled her from her animal cracker horse and clamped their rough hands over her arms and mouth; she'd also been focused on the form of German Chocolate Cake approaching, a malicious smile on his face as he said triumphantly, "Got you, bitch."

The grating sound of something sliding broke her reverie and she lifted her head. The room remained dark, but through the gloom, she could make out that the spy-hatch had been opened, allowing guards in the hall to look in on their prisoner. Kupcake's cake crawled as if dozens of gummy spiders were dancing across it as she heard a deep voice say, "Perfect." The grating sound came again as the spy-hatch was closed once more. Kupcake laid her head back down, confused. Her bewilderment shifted, though, changing into irritation at that word. *Perfect.* She'd heard that word most of her life in reference to herself - often from the confections in town, but also from members of the royal court.

She sneered against the thought of it. *Perfection.* She was so sick of hearing about it. She was not perfect. Far from it, in fact. Her smile was crooked, and she wasn't positive, but she thought one of her eyes was higher than the other. Of course, that could have just been the mirror she'd looked into that one time. Yet, being a member of the royal family and the only princess in the land meant that you had to put on the mantle of perfection at all times.

That was one of the things she loved so deeply about Jerome. When she was with him, she could truly be herself. He never judged her. He didn't revel in her perfection. When they were together, she felt the weight of duty and image being lifted from her, and she was free to speak crassly, and even - on occasion - expel gas around him. In the darkness, Kupcake allowed herself to think that if things continued the way they were going with the muffin, she might actually be able to go to the bathroom when she was with him, rather than holding it until she got back to the castle or slipping behind a Red Vine tree. And she meant really going to the bathroom, for things other than the dainty, princessy draining of excess syrup.

No, she wasn't perfect. Jerome was perfect. Perfect and all hers. But he'd be so worried by now, she thought. He'd have nobody to talk to about this, nobody other than Cleetus to lament his loss with. Her heart ached at the thought of her love feeling alone and helpless. Had he gone to the Oreo Bridge and waited, or had he learned of her cakenapping before making it that far? *Great Mother Baker, Jerome, I'm so sorry, I -*

The sound of a latch being thrown crashed through the silence of her dark room, sending her thoughts of Jerome scattering like a cookie that had been smashed under a boot. Hinges turned with a loud screech and she winced as she sat up. Amber light spilled into the space, and Kupcake squinted in the sudden glare.

Dark figures shifted in the light and, as her eyes adjusted, three sour straw guards moved into the room, their skinny, arced bodies moving with smooth power. They stood impassively, not looking at her.

"What's going on?" she asked them. To a confection, none replied, their sugar-dust eyes only being fixated on the opposite wall. She took advantage of the light and really looked around her cell for the first time. She'd felt her way around it before, but now it was nice to see the objects clearly. It was a small room with a brick floor and walls. A single window containing thick black licorice bars coated in hardened caramel sat high in the wall. Through the bars, she could see the stars like edible sprinkles on the blackness of the night sky.

The bed was a thin silicone mat perched atop four narrow metal posts. Higher on the opposite wall there jutted a bracket for a torch. In a corner stood a shabby two-drawer dresser that looked as if it had recently been in a nasty fight with a thug who had a hatred of dressers born of some childhood trauma. A handle for the bottom drawer hung limply, clinging to the wood by only one screw. *I can do something with that*, she thought before turning away from the dresser, lest her captors see her interest in the handle.

The sound of feet on licorice stone echoed beyond the door. The guards moved deeper into the room to stand only a few feet from her.

Shadows shifted, and then the light in the room increased. Standing in the doorway, holding a torch in one gloved hand, was Devil's Food Cake.

"What do you want with me?" Kupcake demanded. Devil's Food Cake didn't respond. He merely stood there, staring at her with his gaunt, dark features and light icing softly illuminated by the torchlight.

"My father is going to destroy you and this castle when he rescues me! Don't think for one second that you can actually–"

"Shut up." The command came so suddenly and softly that Kupcake felt like she had been punched. She'd never been told to *shut up* before.

"What did you say to me?"

"I said, 'shut up.' I'm not interested in your empty bravado about your father and what he can and will do to get you back. Your father is a weakling, a coward and a pathetic excuse for a leader. He can't do anything and is most likely afraid to even try."

"He is no coward! He has knights; he has his Fudge Army."

Devil's Food Cake laughed, and it was a thick, grating sound that made Kupcake's frosting crawl. "The Fudge Army is a joke. You know as well as everyone in the cakedom that the Fudge Army is merely for show and has been for years. Sprinkles, if you will. It's been so long since they've been utilized, they have no real fighting ability anymore. If your father sends them here, they will die."

Kupcake stared at her captor, her will and ability to respond as dried up as a cookie left in the hot sun for days. She swallowed hard and forced her mind to clear.

Devil's Food Cake moved deeper into the room. Kupcake's nose twitched at the acrid smoke coming from the torch as he drew closer. "So, Princess, you are here for as long as I want you here."

"What about a ransom? My father has plenty of brown sugar that he could pay you with. Candied gumdrops? All-purpose flour? Specific purpose flour? Flour that is still searching for its purpose, but has a suspicion that it has something to do with accounting? Name your price, and he will pay it for my safe return."

Devil's Food Cake stared at her, a wry smile playing across his face. Slowly, he shook his head. "You don't get it, do you? I don't want your father's worthless sugar or flour struggling to find its place in the world. I don't want any riches in exchange for your safe return. There is nothing material that your pitiful, lying father could offer me in exchange for you."

She ignored the insult to the king. Devil's Food Cake was most likely trying to goad her into some outburst. She wouldn't give him the satisfaction. "Then, why did you take me captive?"

"I have my reasons."

"What are they? Surely, something can be done to negotiate my release."

"I will not consider your release at all. However, there are some things that can happen which will ensure that you continue to receive care, food, and simple syrup, and that you are allowed to stay here in my most luxurious of rooms."

Kupcake glanced around the room. "*Luxurious*?" she asked. "I read a book about a stable boy who had to live with the horses he looked after. He slept in a corner opposite the one they used for their personal business, and those lodgings were better furnished than this." She looked back at Devil's Food Cake and saw that her response had had no effect on him. If anything, he seemed more imposing, more threatening. Kupcake swallowed hard. "Fine. What things?"

Her captor stared at her for a long time. "First, you will become my wife. This won't happen until the coward has left the Lemon Icebox Castle and come here, as I want him to witness the marriage. As my bride, you will come to me and do whatever I want, whenever I want, with no hesitation or complaints."

Kupcake pushed back the thought of his disgusting cocoa hands touching her wrapper and the spongy cake beneath. She shuddered.

"Second, I must be named Extreme Ruler over all of the cakedom of All That's Good (But Never Goes to Your Hips or Butt). All regions of the land will fall under my sole rule. Anyone who defies me will be immediately put to death by milk."

"My father will never bend to you."

"Which brings me to the final condition. Before I am named sole ruler of the cakedom, your cowardly father must draft a declaration of my complete rule. Once that's done, I will exile him to the borderlands, where he will live out the rest of his days penniless and embarrassed. He will be lucky to get employment scraping week-old batter off of a spoon. That is unless I change my mind and have him reduced to crumbs."

Kupcake started, shocked and horrified by her captor. Holy Rolling Pin, he couldn't be serious, could he? Week-old batter? Who left their spoons that dirty for that long? Barbarians? Lemon squares? Worshipers of the Gluten Free God?

"I'm very serious," Devil's Food Cake said, as if he had read her thoughts. "Your father must sign the cakedom over to me. Then, he will be sent away for the rest of his miserable life. You will become my bride, and I will rule this land."

"Why are you doing this?" she managed after a moment.

Devil's Food Cake sneered down at her. "Your father knows why this is being done. It's long overdue."

Her father knew? What did that mean? Surely, it couldn't be that King Red Velvet had made some arrangement with this foul confection, could it? *No*, she dismissed the thought immediately. She and her father had never been exactly close, but even on his worst day, King Red Velvet wouldn't give his own daughter away. "And if I or my father refuse?" Kupcake's voice broke as she spoke now, butter tears flowing from her eyes.

Devil's Food Cake moved further into the room. "If you or your father refuse any of my conditions, you, my dear, will fall to the same fate as the previous occupant of this room." With that, he thrust his torch into the far corner, dispelling the shadows that had remained there.

A scream erupted from Kupcake's throat.

Scattered about the brick floor were nothing but a few small crumbs.

4

Jerome flexed his fingers, trying to improve his grip on the suddenly slick and heavy sword. His entire cake seemed to hum with fear as he waited for the approaching beast to break free of the shadows. Around him, the air had grown thick and the Red Vine trees loomed like eager spectators crowding forward to witness carnage. Behind him, Cleetus had retreated several yards, and Jerome knew without having to look that the gummy bear was poised to flee.

Ahead the beast's eyes glowed a dark orange from out of the deep gloom. They remained where they were, however, the creature seemingly content to stare at its prey for the moment.

"Come on," Jerome growled.

"State your purpose," the voice drifted from the shadows, several feet to one side of the floating eyes.

"If that thing comes closer, my purpose is to kill it." Jerome hoped his words sounded more confident than he felt.

"You wouldn't have time to even raise your sword higher than it is now, sir. That is a fondant tiger. You know of the species?"

Son of a bitch. A fondant tiger? Jerome clenched his teeth in frustration. "I thought those were extinct. The last one known to be seen was on the border of the Peanut Brittle Badlands over a hundred years ago."

The voice chuckled. "Quite so. But just because that was the last one 'known to be seen' doesn't mean that it was the last one to exist. Now, again, what is your purpose? Why are you here, this deep in the Red Vines Forest?"

Jerome stared at the glowing eyes of the tiger and sighed. "I am seeking the Moon Pie Wizard. I need his help and counsel. He knows the land and the citizens of all the far reaches of this world, and he is my only hope of reaching and getting inside the Black Licorice Castle."

There was a silence in response, and then: "And why do you want to go there? Are you selling cookies? I can assure you they won't buy them. I know of some Snickerdoodle Scouts who went there once to sell cookies. The few who did return did so only as doodles, if you know what I mean."

Jerome saw no reason to lie or withhold the information. "Do you not know of the recent cakenapping of Princess Kupcake?"

Again, a chuckle. "Yes, I know of it." The voice deepened, almost to a mutter as it continued, "So, he's finally gone and moved to get his revenge, eh?" The voice continued to grumble for several moments before the owner cleared his throat and said, "So you think that you alone will be able to, what, storm Devil's Food Cake's castle and slay all his guards, and kill the German Chocolate Cake and rescue the princess? All by yourself?"

"I have Cleetus to help me."

"I suppose Cleetus is the rather large gummy bear cowering behind you? The one who seems to have wet himself?"

Jerome took a moment to turn and glare at Cleetus. The bear was hunched over and half hidden behind a Red Vine tree. When Jerome's gaze met Cleetus', the bear hung its green head.

"Basically," Jerome said, turning back to face his questioner.

"Then, you absolutely need my help and counsel." The speaker moved forward and stepped into the light. The Moon Pie Wizard was one of the oldest living sweets in all of All That's Good (But Never

Goes to Your Hips or Butt). In most parts of the realm, he was but a legend – someone told of in stories that started with "Once Upon a Time." Few confections had ever seen him. Even fewer had tried to find him. Most seemed content to believe that he was but a legend, a wizard who had been great at one time, and who had actually created the Pop Rock people, but who was no more. Most who had come into contact with the lunatics who were the Pop Rock people felt glad to be rid of him.

Especially after the last Cookie War.

The Moon Pie Wizard walked with the aid of a staff, but didn't seem to need it much. His step was light as he moved around a marshmallow stone, his deep blue robes adorned with yellow half-moons fluttering gently with each step.

The fondant tiger followed its master, and Jerome watched as the creature – a low, slinky, light blue beast – padded into the clearing. The sunlight that filtered down through the Red Vine trees showed the faint orange stripes along its body. It looked once at Jerome, sniffed the air, and then turned its head and continued walking.

The Moon Pie Wizard strolled casually past Jerome and Cleetus, not even looking at them. He'd moved several feet past when he called over his shoulder, "Well, are you coming or not, Jerome?"

"How did you..." But Jerome just shook his head instead of completing the question. He looked back at Cleetus with a scowl and waved his hand. "Come on, you big sissy."

The Moon Pie Wizard walked ahead, weaving between the trees and turning randomly as if he were following a path only he could see. The fondant tiger walked a few feet to the right of the wizard, seeming to mind its own business. It occasionally stopped and sniffed at something before continuing on. Only once did it look back. In its eyes, Jerome felt he could see the hint of hunger. Or it could be gas. Jerome could never really tell the two looks apart. Just to be safe, his hand drifted to the hilt of his sword and rested there for the remainder of the walk.

Finally, the wizard stopped and muttered, "Here we go." Jerome saw no hint of a house, only the Red Vines Forest stretching far into the distance in every direction. The wizard walked a few steps more and stopped before the largest Red Vine tree Jerome had ever seen. The trunk, where it sprouted from the ground, had to be at least thirty feet wide.

"Here we are," said the wizard.

"Here we are... where?"

The wizard looked back over his shoulder at Jerome and winked. Then, he took a step towards the tree and vanished. A soft rustling pulled Jerome's gaze away from the tree. The tiger scratched in the dirt, pushing leaves and dirt around as if to cover something, and finally trotted forward and disappeared in the same spot its master had.

Jerome stood rooted to the spot, waiting for something else to happen. When nothing did, he looked back at Cleetus, who was sniffing the air in the area of what the tiger had been covering up.

"Are you coming or not?" the wizard asked, his disembodied voice causing Jerome to jump.

Jerome looked at Cleetus again. "What do you think?"

The green bear simply looked at Jerome and blinked, which for most gummy bears was an act of extremely profound meaning. Jerome sighed and stepped forward towards the tree.

He stopped when his face connected solidly with the spiraling red trunk. He heard the ghostly chuckling of the wizard. "A bit more to the left, my boy."

Jerome stepped back and rubbed his nose. He took a step to the left and tried again – more slowly this time and with one hand outstretched. There was a blurring of his vision, as if he were passing through a gentle syrupfall. He pressed forward and stepped into a large, welcoming room. The floor was of grey stone, the walls the same. Ahead of him was a long bench made from a Red Vine tree. Beyond that stood a pair of double doors, partially opened. Cleetus' soft chuffing behind him told him that the bear had found the opening more easily than he had.

"Please remove your shoes," the wizard asked from beyond the doors.

Jerome hesitated, not wanting to remove his boots.

"Look, you're only wasting time. I'm not trying to trick you; I simply like a clean house. You've been traipsing through the woods, so you have dirt and muck on your shoes." Jerome slipped off his boots and placed them near the bench. He then moved towards the doors. "Stay here," he told Cleetus. The gummy bear looked at him as if insulted, and then moved off to find a comfortable corner.

Jerome noticed the faint scent of spiced tea and cinnamon drifting from beyond the doors. His stomach growled in response. The doors opened to reveal a short set of stairs which led down to a large, cozy common room. There were several pieces of overstuffed furniture in the room, as well as a few tables and a large fire burning warmly in the fireplace. To the right of the common room was an expansive kitchen. It was there that he found both the wizard and the source of the smells.

"Would you like some tea? Maybe a spiced cake?" The wizard flitted about the room moving items and stirring things that hung from a rod mounted over a fireplace.

"I'd rather talk about my quest to save Kupcake."

The wizard smiled and filled two mugs. He placed several small, round cakes on a plate and, with an almost dismissive wave of his hand, sent the food and drinks floating through the air to land on a thick, heavy wooden table to the left of where Jerome stood.

"We'll get to all of that. There's plenty of time."

"How can you say that? How can you think to eat at a time like this? Kupcake is in danger. Her life is at stake. She—"

"She is perfectly fine for the moment, I can assure you. Oh, now, don't look at me like that! I'm not in league with Devil's Food Cake. No, no, no, nothing quite so diabolical. I just know things."

"If you're so all-knowing and powerful, why can't you rescue her now? Surely, you can summon a spell that would pluck her from that hideous place."

The wizard smiled and sipped his tea, smacked his lips in satisfaction as he looked at his guest.

"It's true that I'm wise and powerful. I'm sure most of the rumors you've heard about me are true. Except that one that I once turned myself into a large gingerbread man and roamed the Gumdrop Fields with nothing, not even icing, covering me."

"I'm not interested in the stories."

"It wasn't a giant gingerbread man, to be honest." The wizard smiled and winked. "It was a large chocolate bunny. I've always liked bunnies. Don't you like bunnies?" He popped another spice cake in his mouth and frowned as he chewed. "Although, I have to admit, that business with the Pop Rocks people – that..." he shook his head. "That was unfortunate."

Jerome slapped his hand on the table, causing the cups to rattle and spill some of their contents. "I said I'm not interested in the stories!"

The wizard made a quick motion with a finger and a rag floated over from across the room. He plucked it out of the air and cleaned up the spilled tea. When he was finished, he leaned back, affixing Jerome with a stern look.

"Listen to me, boy, and listen well. You're talking about a one-man assault on the Black Licorice Castle. Do you not remember the wars of the past? All three of the Cookie Wars? The Lady Finger Crusades?"

"I have read of them. I also read that you were responsible for the last of the Cookie Wars."

The Moon Pie Wizard's face clouded. "Yes, I know the rumors you're talking about." He raised a finger and pointed it at Jerome. "I'll have you know that I played only a small part in that. I had no way of knowing the fig bars would turn out to be so evil." He waved a hand at the room around them. "That's why I've spent the rest of my life here, hidden away from the rest of the cakedom. But if you know of those wars, then you should know that several times during each of those wars – and countless others – entire armies have tried to lay siege to that vile place. And all of them - every single one – have been turned away. We're talking entire armies here. Thousands of sweets! What hope do you really think you have of making it inside and then out once you've found your true love?"

Jerome started. "I never said... I don't... I can't. It's not proper for me...."

Moon Pie Wizard laughed. "Relax, boy, relax. Your secret is safe with me. Besides, who would I tell? Fangus?" He gestured behind Jerome to where the fondant tiger lounged. The tiger looked up and regarded Jerome, licking its lips before it laid its head back down.

"I'm just saying," Jerome said. How could he admit it? The mixing of cupcakes and muffins was forbidden, had been for centuries. He'd heard of muffins being exiled for simply sitting too close to a cupcake. He didn't want to think of what would happen to one who was actually in love with one.

"You're just saying without saying it directly that you love her deeply."

"Yes."

"But why? What is it about her that moves you so?"

"She is the most beautiful in all the land. She is kind and sweet and loving."

"Yes, yes, we know all of that. But what is it about her that moves you?"

Jerome looked at the wizard thoughtfully. "*She* moves me. She raises me up. Most people look down on me because of who I am, what I am. Not Kupcake. Before her, most confections wouldn't give me the time of day. I spent all my time working or reading on the banks of the Sweetwater River near the Oreo Bridge. When I met her, of course I knew who she was, but I had no idea how—" he searched for the right word, found it, and continued, "—normal she was. Sure, she's deeply good, and sees the good in everyone, but she's just a normal confection. When I met her, she was splashing chocolate mud on a chocolate frog. Her frosting was all messy and she didn't care. At that moment, she was just happy, playing with a frog. She and I spent the next couple of hours talking about the book I was reading and some of her favorites.

"She's impossibly brilliant. I can't keep up with all the things she thinks about, all the experiments she does, all the inventions she creates. Did you know she figured out a way of repairing fellow cupcakes' wrappings, using a method of melting sugar down into caramel and pairing that with cream cheese? Don't ask me how, it's very, very complicated. She's not your garden variety princess who spends her days sitting on thick cushions and being doted upon. She's a doer!" Jerome felt his throat constricting, and he took a moment to calm himself. The Moon Pie Wizard sipped his tea and waited for the muffin to continue.

"Since then, I have never felt alone; I have been able to forget that I'm a mere muffin, something that everyone else looks down on and blames for events so far in the past they don't even matter anymore. It is because of her that the skies are always clear for me. Because of her that the wind through the trees is always a gentle, loving song. Because of her, everything I eat tastes like a feast. It is because of her that, anytime my thoughts wander to her, my heart races and swells to bursting. It is her who I love and because of her that I love."

The wizard regarded Jerome for a long time. "Good. That's what I wanted to hear. You sound like Hoyt the stable boy." The wizard shook his head wistfully. "Damn good books, that Campor series. I don't even mind the half-naked men and three-fourths naked women on the cover," he mumbled. Then, in one fluid motion, he pushed back from the table and stood up. "Come on, I need to show you something."

Jerome followed the old wizard out of the kitchen, through the common room, and down a short flight of stairs. The wizard touched a section of the wall, and a hidden door swung in. He led Jerome into a large space with an old, creaky wooden floor. The wizard snapped his fingers, and torches mounted to the walls around the room sprang to life, flooding the space with flickering amber light.

Around the room were various tables and bookshelves, all full to spilling over with books, papers, scrolls, more than a few stuffed dolls in the shapes of fried pies, and other items that Jerome couldn't quickly identify. Things floated in jars, and wooden boxes sat here and there. In the center of the room was a large dais which held a large double boiler.

The Moon Pie Wizard walked to the boiler, reached into his

robes, and produced a rubber spatula. "Come here," he said as he inserted the spatula into the upper chamber of the boiler and began stirring.

Jerome walked carefully across the room to stand next to the wizard. He saw that the spatula stirred a light grey slurry mixture.

"Oatmeal," the wizard said in answer to the unasked question. "I found that oatmeal gives me the best results."

"What kind of results?"

"In order for you to reach the Black Licorice Castle, find your way inside, make it past all of the guards and into the room where they're keeping the princess, you're going to need massive amounts of luck and skill, with a dash of 'How the oven did he manage that?' thrown on top. Probably with a side of 'I thought for sure he was going to die.' I can tell you how to get to the castle and warn you about some of the areas you may have to travel through in order to get there. But to defeat the guards, to destroy German Chocolate Cake and to vanquish Devil's Food Cake, you're going to need a weapon much more powerful than that toothpick sword."

"What's wrong with my sword?"

"Nothing's wrong with it, if you want to use it to spear the occasional chocolate pearl or gumdrop. And I'm sure that it would be quite handy if employed in a fight against the occasional sour straw guard. But beyond that, it won't do you much good."

"Then, what? What do I need?"

The wizard was silent for a moment, concentrating on stirring the oatmeal. Finally, he smiled and said, "This."

Jerome looked into the oatmeal and saw that it had thinned out, but instead of the bottom of the boiler pan, he was seeing something else... the rough shapes of dark walls, and the hint of a stone floor. "What is this?"

"It is a place far away."

"How does that help me?"

"Just wait."

Moments later, an object floated into view. "Is that...?" Jerome asked, breathless.

"Yes," came the wizard's soft response. "The magical Piping Bag of Ganache."

Jerome stared at the bag and its silver, spiked tip. "Where is this?"

The wizard looked away from the boiler and fixed Jerome with a hard stare. "Deep in the Land of the Danish Wedding Cookies."

"How do you expect me to get in there and back out alive?"

The wizard chuckled. "Come now, the odds of you even making it there are at least seventy-thirty."

Jerome blinked. "That's not bad, actually."

"That's against you, son. But I may have something that will help bump those odds a bit higher. You have to go retrieve it though."

"What are the odds of me even getting it?" Jerome asked morosely.

"Eighty-twenty, easily."

"For or against?"

The Moon Pie Wizard's eyes twinkled as he smiled.

5

Jerome tightened the straps on the new saddle the wizard had given him and patted Cleetus on his shiny rump. He'd spent the night comfortably ensconced in a tea towel near the Moon Pie Wizard's hearth and he felt energized as his breath plumed in the cold air. Cleetus grunted in response to Jerome's gesture, but largely continued to ignore him. The bear gave an "I'm not happy about this shit – it was warm in there" grunt and blinked slowly in irritation at Jerome.

"Are you ready?" the wizard asked from the invisible door of his Red Vine tree home.

Jerome nodded, one hand going to his toothpick sword to ensure it was secured to his waist. "I think so. But why are you helping me? You said you're happy living here, away from other confections and their troubled lives. Why help now? I asked you last night several times, but all you wanted to talk about was eggnog."

The wizard shrugged. "Love," he said simply. "I don't know much... well, that's not exactly true, I know damn near everything, one bit of which is that eggnog is astonishingly good for your libido. But also that there are few things in this world which are important. Love, the kind of love you and Kupcake have for one another, is to be cherished above everything else. I don't believe for a second that muffins are as bad as people say they are. I know your ancestors had a crumb in that nasty business with the Burnt Ones, but I also know what your people did to stop it, even if history has forgotten.

"Now, of course, you'll probably die before you even get to your destination, and you most certainly will die if you reach the Black Licorice Castle, but I think you and your love for the princess should be given every chance. Besides, you asked." Jerome gaped at him. "I don't suppose I could ask you a favor, could I?" the wizard went on. When Jerome didn't answer, the wizard continued. "I really do love those Danish Wedding Cookies. I know they're bad for you, but if you could find a way to bring some back, I'd appreciate it. From what I hear, they are scattered everywhere."

"You want me to bring you back cookies?"

"If you don't mind. If it's not too much trouble."

Jerome stared at the confection for a while longer and then shook his head. "Fine, I'll see what I can do." He turned and swung up into the saddle atop Cleetus. The bear grunted again and shifted under the weight. Jerome tapped his heels against the bear's flanks. Cleetus threw a single dirty look over one shoulder before he began walking, grumbling softly to himself.

The day wore on as rider and gummy bear trundled slowly through the giant stalks and deep shadows of the Red Vines Forest. As they moved, Jerome scanned the shadowy depths as much as the gloom would allow.

He twisted in the saddle, hoping to see the fondant tiger slinking along behind them. Instead, all he saw were shadows, Red Vine tree trunks, and the ground they'd just crossed. He shook his head and returned his gaze to the front. *A fondant tiger. What next?* A small thrill coursed through his cake at the thought of it. Nobody he knew had ever seen one. Until the day before, he'd thought they were just legends – fiction, really.

And the Moon Pie Wizard, another legend. And having found the wizard, or rather the wizard having found him, Jerome felt he had a direction now; a course that would give him the advantage when he ultimately reached the Black Licorice Castle. To the monotonous rhythm of Cleetus' slow gait, Jerome felt himself lulled into a semi-trance as his mind floated back to the conversation held over the double boiler in the wizard's home.

"You expect me to..." he'd started, and then shaken his head. "Great Baker, that's a suicide mission. No confection has ever gone into the Land of the Danish Wedding Cookies and come out as more than just crumbs."

The wizard had smiled and winked at him. "Sure, sure, there are those who say that the Danish Cookies are wicked, tart creatures who lay waste to anything that is not themselves. Truth be told, they will lay waste to themselves also if left to their own devices."

"So, how is it you expect me to get in there, find this—" he gestured at the image of the Piping Bag of Ganache floating in the oatmeal, "and still be able to infiltrate Devil's Food Cake's castle?"

"Well," the Moon Pie Wizard said, stroking his chin, "You're going to have to go about it the long way. I'm not going to lie to you... it won't be easy. But if you can make it, I can tell you where to find something that will help you slip into the Land of the Danish Wedding Cookies and out again without ever being detected."

Jerome thought about it. Without being detected. Holy Rolling Pin and the Great Baker Herself. This cookie had let too much creme filling go to his head. Then again, he thought, looking at the fondant tiger who lay a few feet away, maybe someone who was able to tame something like that creature knew a couple of things.

"Okay, what is it?"

The Moon Pie Wizard stepped away from the double boiler, and the image of the piping bag vanished like smoke. He walked deeper into the room and settled into a large chair, and which point he reached over and plucked a candy cigarette from a pack on a table next to him. He held the cigarette up, sniffed it, and then bit half of it off. "Out there," he pointed vaguely with the remainder of the cigarette, "there's a bag of never-ending powdered sugar. Get that and coat yourself in the sugar, and you can walk right into their land, find the Piping Bag of Ganache and get out, and none will be the wiser."

Jerome walked across the room. "Are you out of your mind? That bag is another fairy tale! I once read about it in stories about the Eleven-Day Pretzel War."

The wizard grunted and ate the remaining half of the candy cigarette. "I heard that, too. Nasty business, that war. Some horrible stuff happened during those eleven days."

"So I read. And that's not counting what Yogu-"

The wizard held up a hand and closed his eyes. "Do not invoke that name. Bad things happen when one mentions that stuff." He retrieved another cigarette. He held it to his mouth and said, "But, yes, I see what you're saying. However, you'll be happy to know that the Bag of Never-Ending Powdered Sugar isn't a myth. It's real, just like Mister Davenforth here," he added with a nod at the fondant tiger.

"I thought his name was Fangus?"

"Hmm?" The Wizard blinked and looked at Jerome, his brow wrinkling in confusion.

Jerome opened his mouth to ask again, caught the wizard's eyes, and promptly closed his mouth. Some things, you just didn't ask about. He sighed. *Great Mother Baker, help me*, he prayed.

"If it will help me get in and rescue Kupcake, I'll do it. Where do I find—" his voice cut off, his throat suddenly dry and flaky. He shook his head. "No."

The wizard's face made a "sorry to tell you this" expression, and he shrugged. "It's the only way. It's kept deep in a cave there, guarded by some really nasty things." He brightened slightly as he went on, "But I'm sure you'll have no problems at all."

And, now, riding his bear, Jerome found himself moving at a glacial pace through a place he'd never wanted to be in to start with, heading somewhere he wanted to be even less, all in order to find something that he wasn't entirely certain even existed, only to then plan on traveling someplace worse to find yet another artifact that, as far as he knew, existed only in the icing-addled mind of the Moon Pie Wizard.

He kicked his heels into Cleetus' flanks again and urged the gummy bear to speed up. Lingering would only make them easy targets for flying wax lips or the Reject Jelly Beans. Old Man Nougat, the town cobbler, swore he'd once had a run-in with a band of Reject Jelly Beans out in Trifle Town. He said they were the reason he'd lost his caramel coating. Jerome had only heard him tell the story once, and once had been enough. As he'd told the story, something deep in his eyes had said that there was more to it he wasn't saying. The look had spoken of unforgettable horrors.

Jerome scanned the twisted trunks and branches of the Red Vine trees, his eyes lingering on the dark pools of shadows between and behind them. Any one of them could hide untold dangers, Reject Jelly Beans being the least of them.

Cleetus plodded onward, and Jerome found his thoughts shifting to the ambush and cakenapping itself. Why would Devil's Food Cake have taken the princess? What good would it do him? What end would it serve? The questioning thoughts brought back a memory of something the Moon Pie Wizard had said in the forest... something about 'He finally moved to get his revenge.' Jerome cursed himself for not having asked about that.

He tightened his hands on the reins and focused on the road ahead. There was only one way to find the answers to his questions, and by the grace of the Great Baker Herself, he was going to get there, come the Oven or No Flour.

His body rigid, he continued to guide Cleetus towards their destination. Towards the Bag of Never-Ending Powdered Sugar.

Towards the Pudding Swamp.

6

King Red Velvet paced in his chambers, his face lined with worry. His path took him from the door around his bed and past the large fireplace, and then beyond the table, atop of which lay a pile of sprinkles and edible gold leaf, before he moved on to one of the large windows that stretched to the ceiling. He stopped and placed his hands on the cold glass, his eyes taking in the southern gate and the rolling hills beyond it. Leaning forward, he fixed his gaze on the expanse of woods in the distance.

"Kupcake," he whispered, his breath fogging the glass. Saying her name aloud brought a ripple of fear, a series of worrisome flutters through his cake. It had now been two full days since his daughter had been taken. The king's frosting colored a deep burgundy to match his cake at the thought of those vile creatures touching his daughter. His color deepened even more as his anger turned to the guards assigned to her, for not protecting her better. If they had done their job, this never would have happened. Yes, he told himself, it was their fault she'd been taken.

He thought of the message his daughter's personal assistant Peggy had whispered through her bruised lips as she'd lain in the infirmary. "He said 'One for one.'" That was what German Chocolate Cake had told her to relay to Red Velvet just before dealing the oatmeal raisin cookie a final blow which had sent her spiraling into unconsciousness. "He said that's what Devil's Food Cake wanted you to know." King Red Velvet had only been able to stare down at the terrified cookie – seeing beyond her, seeing years into the past.

Great Mother Baker, we were but young cakes back then. How could he...? It wasn't my fault.

Leaving the infirmary, King Red Velvet had called an assembly of his inner circle of sweets. Then, keeping Peggy's relayed message to himself - there was no way any of the confections around him would have understood it or found it useful - he'd demanded they explain to him why this had happened. They'd all stammered and speculated, a few bringing out charts and graphs; one had even done an interpretive dance, but nobody had had the vaguest idea of why Devil's Food Cake might have attempted such a bold and brash move. Certainly, it was common for the king's own armies to clash occasionally with sour straw soldiers and other disgusting sweets who owed their allegiance to the Bitter One. But for the dark delicacy to have staged such a raid, coming deep into Red Velvet's lands and stealing away his very child? It made no sense. Perhaps he was looking to extend his rule beyond the Black Licorice Castle, and felt that keeping the princess captive would give King Red Velvet the incentive to negotiate.

Then again, he thought, allowing his mind to brush once more across the surface of that long-hidden memory, maybe there was a reason, even if it came from a place of misunderstanding and grief. *It wasn't my fault, however,* he thought. *I did everything I could. But he never believed me... always blamed me for the way things went.* Red Velvet slammed his fists against the window. *It wasn't my fault! I did nothing wrong! If the others had executed the plan properly, everything would have gone perfectly!*

The king sighed and pulled himself away from the window, resuming his pacing back to the door. It didn't matter what had happened in the past, as Kupcake was still gone.

One for one. The cryptic message tolled in his mind like a cake timer. The king thought of the Cookie Wars, those bloody conflicts that had raged across the entire cakedom. The third had been particularly nasty, with the involvement of the fig bars. *The most insane of confections*, the small voice in his mind reminded him. *But that was a good stand against their villainy. You and he once stood together.*

Through the door, a knock sounded, soft but insistent, and for a moment he assumed it was Queen Peanut Butter Cup. As a way of distracting herself from her own anguish over her daughter's cakenapping, the queen continually checked on him to ensure that he was eating and caring for himself. This also gave her the opportunity to nag him about what his plans were for rescuing the princess.

"Yes, what is it?" he called, his voice tired and irritable. If she was coming to him with talk of consuming food again, he wouldn't hear anything of it. How could he be expected to eat, something he normally took great pleasure in, at a time like this? Indeed, only a few years ago, he would have charged across the land by himself, armed only with a sword and six thousand of his personal guards – and possibly some siege machines and enough sprinkles to nibble, as sieges required a lot of snacks - and stormed the Black Licorice Castle to rescue his daughter. A few years ago, he would have fought every sour straw and despicable confection in the land in order to have his Kupcake home safely, or at least not in too dire need of therapy. But that would have been years ago. Such thoughts were the fancies of young chocolates still growing their candy shells, or of young cake pops yearning for their own frosting. Not the thoughts or actions of mature cakes.

Not to mention that he'd grown rather soft in the past few years. There'd been nothing of note to keep in shape for, and sprinkles and simple syrup were oh so delicious.

The door opened slowly, and one of his guards peered around the corner. The guard saluted and said, "Your Highness, pardon the interruption, but there is a visitor for you."

The king scowled. "I'm not receiving anyone right now. Everyone in the cakedom knows what's befallen us. How dare someone call for an audience with me?"

"Sir, it's a gummy pickle."

The king froze. "A gummy pickle?"

"Yes, sir."

"I'll receive him in the Cake Stand Room." The king followed his guard out the door, his jaw now set in anticipation of meeting an emissary of Devil's Food Cake.

The pickle stood in the middle of the Cake Stand Room, its bent, knobby, and shiny body starkly out of place among the finery of the throne room. It held itself as straight as it could, but the king could see its eyes darting nervously around the space, taking in the towering ceiling, the immense windows, the flanking rows of rock candy guards, and, of course, the Cake Stand Throne.

The Stand had been around almost as long as the Land of All That's Good (But Never Goes to Your Hips or Butt), and throughout the years, many leaders had perched atop it, basking in the light that was positioned just so in order to highlight the ruler's majestic frosting.

"Speak," Red Velvet commanded.

The pickle stared coldly back at him. "I come with a message." Its voice oozed sourness.

"What is it?"

The pickle took a short step forward. Instantly, there was an accompanying rustle as every rock candy guard stepped forward in unison. The pickle stopped and glanced at the encroaching guards. "You should tell your men to hold their position."

"I'll do no such thing. You are a subject and emissary of Devil's Food Cake, and it is known to all of us that he's responsible for my daughter's disappearance. It's this 'message' you claim to have that is the only reason you're not being melted down into goo. Now, speak. What is it that you've come to say?"

The pickle licked its lips and grinned. Cold gelatin gleamed through the split that was its mouth. "Lord Devil's Food Cake requires your presence, King Red Velvet. He commands it."

"Nobody commands the king!" barked Stuart, the king's personal assistant. The pickle's eyes shifted to the glaring peanut butter cookie.

Even the king felt rather surprised at the sudden appearance of his assistant, but he nodded in agreement.

"Nobody tells me where to go," he said.

"Even if that person is the one holding your daughter? Even if that person is the one who is responsible for her treatment? Are you really willing to risk something happening to her?"

The king leaned forward, his hands gripping the sides of the Stand. "Is that a threat?"

The pickle chuckled, its slick body undulating as it did so. "Lord Devil's Food Cake requires your presence," it said again. "You are to come to his court no later than a week from today. Once there, you will remove your crown and kneel."

The king scowled. "Your lord is a fool to think that I would agree to such a thing."

"That's not all my lord requires, but the rest you will learn once you are presented to him."

The king leaned back on the Stand and stared at the emissary. What kind of idiocy was this? What was that bastard's plan? *One for one.* Wasn't it bad enough that he'd taken Kupcake? That he saw keeping her locked away as some way of balancing the scales from so long ago? Was that even what he was attempting? Red Velvet took in a deep breath. It had to be so; otherwise, why the message? *One for one.* Words clearly meant to have no meaning for anyone but himself. And, now? To retrieve his daughter, he was expected to come and kneel before this disgusting confection? Surely, Devil's Food Cake wasn't looking for simple humiliation... not if he'd carried his grudge this long.

"I will consider it," he said, slipping off the perch. Immediately, Stuart was by his side, ready to assist in any way. The king turned to leave.

"Sire, what of the pickle?" Stuart asked.

King Red Velvet stopped and regarded the messenger. For a moment, his rage returned over the creature's boldness, in the way in which it had spoken to him. Its very presence in this castle of sweets was abhorrent. In that span of seconds, Red Velvet almost condemned the miserable wretch to listening to his mother-in-law drone on and on about her collection of classic whisks, or to rub the bon bons in her feet, either of which was truly a punishment worse than death. But just as his mouth opened to issue the command, Kupcake's face surfaced in his mind. Her smile, and her gentleness and concern for every creature, be they confection or hard candy. All were worthy of life, preferably one without the tedium of hearing about the differences between the eight-tine whisk and the twelve-tine, Kupcake would have said, even if that life disagreed with you.

The king sighed, fighting back tears and swallowing the lump in his throat. He waved a hand. "The... thing... is dismissed. See that it is escorted from the grounds and sent north to its master."

"And what should I tell my lord?" the pickle asked as rock candy guards closed in around it.

King Red Velvet stared back at the pickle. "You can tell your master that his request has been received and is being taken under advisement."

As the king left the Cake Stand Room, Stuart whispered at his side, "You're not really going to go through with that request, are you?"

The king, his voice low, replied, "If he thinks I am going to stand in front of that cake and bend my knee, he's nuttier than a fruitcake."

7

"I don't want to go in there, either," Jerome said, giving Cleetus' reins another tug. The gummy bear's feet dug into the ground and he leaned back against Jerome's insistence. With a heavy sigh, Jerome threw down the reins and stared at the bear. Cleetus blinked slowly in response before he shambled a few feet away. He lowered himself down into the nook of a Red Vine tree and promptly began snoring.

"Are you kidding me?" Jerome asked. They had reached the end of the Red Vines Forest and now stood at the edge of the Pudding Swamp. Ahead of him, solid ground wound haphazardly around pools of the thick, swampy ichor that - if he landed a single misstep - would drag him down into a saccharine tomb. The swamp stretched out with only an occasional rotting candy stick tree to give any sort of reference point. But even those eventually faded into the gloomy distance.

As Jerome stood there contemplating the inevitable foray into the swamp, the air was cut by a chilling scream. The creature - Jerome knew it had to be a creature, as no normal confection would make a noise like that - was something hidden by the far-off darkness and scattered dead trees of the Pudding Swamp. The scream seemed clotted with a thick mixture of pain, hunger, and hatred.

A pain in Jerome's hand pulled his attention away from the shadowy depths of the swamp. He looked down and saw that at some point he had drawn his sword, and now he gripped the pommel so tightly that it had left indentations in his hand.

"Cleetus, get your big green ass up," Jerome said. Within seconds, Jerome heard soft grunts and shuffling, and then Cleetus' smooth, cool green nose bumped his free hand. Jerome climbed into the saddle, and they followed the twisted path.

All around, scattered like chocolate chips across a kitchen floor, were pools of pudding. Jerome watched them closely as Cleetus picked his way between each one. Some were a solid color – chocolate, vanilla, tapioca – while others were a hideous miasma of flavors, a multi-colored ooze that churned his stomach at the sight of them, never mind all the smells that wafted up. He knew that one single misstep would find them caught in one of the pools, where the pudding would eagerly swallow he and Cleetus both. Drowning in pudding was not a good way to go.

On a rare wide expanse between puddles, Jerome stopped to stretch. They'd been picking their way through the swamp for over an hour now, and he estimated that they'd only made it a half-mile. But the good news was that he'd begun seeing a more clearly defined path, the pools of pudding spread out more evenly despite having grown in size.

There were no signs of life in the warped and twisted candy stick trees. The trees had long ago bent and been half-melted, their striped colors running together in a horrible tableau. *Melted* was not the right word, perhaps. It was as if the trees were giving up, their colors draining away and bodies slumping as they resigned themselves to their fates here among viscous pools of death. Sighing against the sadness he felt at the observation, Jerome took a sip of syrup from his canteen. As he returned it to his pack and secured the straps, the same scream he'd heard before tore through the land once more.

It was closer, he thought, but sound travelled strangely in the

Pudding Swamp. It was impossible to know just how far off it was, and worse, from which direction the cry had come. The sound sent shivers through his cake, and he once again drew his sword and guided Cleetus down the path.

The attack, when it came, came soundlessly from above and behind him. Jerome was on the ground, his sword having been knocked several feet away even before he realized what was happening. Pain seared across his back as he scrambled to his feet. Again, he was impacted, and felt the heat of the wound and tasted dirt as he landed flat on his face. He heard Cleetus chuffing in fear.

Jerome rolled over, grabbing a handful of dirt and throwing it upward just in time to see it hit the falling sour candy. The sour let out a shriek that sounded more like an angry whistle, and then twisted and impacted the ground a few feet away. Jerome leapt up and, in one fluid motion, kicked the attacker away. It flipped and rolled, still screeching, and landed at the edge of a chocolate pudding pool. Jerome watched in horror as the dark semi-solid bubbled and then lurched upwards and out, stretching beyond the confines of its pool in order to lock onto one rounded edge of the sour. The candy's screeching intensified as the pudding began devouring it.

Swallowing a hard lump, Jerome pulled his attention away and looked for his sword. Hefting it, he turned to face the next wave.

The sours, four of them in all, were lined up in a rough semi-circle around him, blocking the path. *Must have hidden in the trees*, he thought. All four moved gently in the dirt, as if conferring with one another about the best way to attack a foe who was now aware of them, and armed and standing in front of a large green gummy bear.

"Well, come on!" he shouted. "Let me check to see that you're done!" Two of the sours rushed forward, their bodies undulating across the mud.

Jerome slashed at one, his toothpick sword cleaving neatly through the gelatin of the sour's body. The creature screeched and collapsed. "You want some? I got some for you! All day, son!" Jerome pivoted and thrust, the sword's tip piercing the second charging sour. The small sour slid a few centimeters closer, but then shuddered and died. Jerome flicked his sword, and the sour flew off and collided with one of its two remaining companions, both going tumbling across the ground. The last sour standing considered its fallen brethren and then, with one final look at the panting Jerome, turned and wobbled away as fast as it could go.

"I guess all that slashing at cream puffs taught me more than I thought," Jerome said through gasps for breath. He looked back at Cleetus sitting on his haunches, idly cleaning one of his legs. "Is this boring you?" Jerome asked the bear. Cleetus paused and glanced up as if to say, 'Well, of course.'

Jerome rolled his eyes and moved to the heap of fallen sours. The one on the bottom of the pile struggled weakly to get out from under its slain brother. Jerome looked down at them both. The surviving sour stopped its struggles and hissed at him. Jerome's brow furrowed. He still had no idea how these damn things were making noise. It didn't matter, though. With one smooth motion, he reared back and kicked both sours into a mixed pool of chocolate, vanilla, and strawberry pudding. They sank immediately, their hissing cries dying out like steam from a kettle removed from flame.

He sheathed his sword, the motion bringing a fresh round of pain to his back. He'd forgotten about the initial attack by the sours, those little shits having come falling from a tree and using their sour coating to scorch his cake. Retrieving a jar of icing salve from the supplies the Moon Pie Wizard had given him, he spread the concoction gingerly on his wounds. Relief seeped into his cake immediately. But as he returned the jar to the pouch, the scream he'd heard on the edge of the swamp ripped through the air again. The cry was so loud that it seemed to vibrate the air around him. It was not, he knew now, coming from the sours, but from something much larger and worse. Jerome looked down at Cleetus, who was busy gnawing on one of his feet.

"Quit chewing on yourself, man. We gotta get out of here." Reluctantly, Cleetus lifted his head and stood up, ready to move on. Jerome climbed into the saddle and, with another nervous glance around the Swamp, spurred Cleetus into motion.

8

Captain Talton leaned back against the smooth black stone wall of the Black Licorice Castle and forced his breathing to slow. Beside him, his sergeant applied a thick coating of powder made from a specific mint candy to the hinges of a heavy wooden door. Above this she placed a small plastic container of dark, sugary liquid. When triggered, the container would burst and spill its carbonated contents along the strip of powder – resulting in a violent reaction which would in turn blow the door off of its hinges.

Talton was counting on there being no sour straw guards on the other side, this being a remote door near the rear of the castle. According to the best intelligence they had, which came from the gummy pickle who'd had the extreme misfortune of being the messenger delivering the ransom notice - if you could even call it that - from Devil's Food Cake, this door was the prime point of ingress. Talton had been shocked at the quickness with which the pickle had given up the information, but then again, gummy pickles had never been the bravest or most loyal of confections.

The sergeant nodded that the mixture was set before stepping away and drawing her plastic toothpick sword. Talton took another look around, his eyes taking in the distant woods and rocky terrain they'd crossed to reach this specific point along the castle's walls. He saw no signs of movement, and nothing to indicate they'd been spotted or were currently being observed.

He grinned again. They were the best of the best, after all. Of course, nobody had seen them. Within minutes, they would be inside and Kupcake would be secure, safely on her way back home where she belonged. It had been foolish of her to leave the immediate castle grounds with only a couple of guards and that simpering servant of hers. Anything could have happened to her, and anything had. And because of her recklessness, she'd put herself, her father, and the security of the entire cakedom at risk. War could come of this, and there hadn't been war in a long, long time. Would the king even be up for it? The Fudge Army certainly wasn't. Those lazy doughboys hadn't had a reason to stay in fighting shape in three generations.

Not like his team. The Baker's Dozen Rock Candy Attachment included the most elite of the candies, and he trained them daily to ensure peak readiness. Just in case something like this happened. They'd practiced this exact maneuver of entering and clearing a multi-floor dwelling more times than he could count. And they'd only messed up once, early on, when one of the troopers had gotten distracted by a lemon blueberry bundt cake changing her wrapper, as seen through an open window a few houses down.

That trooper was now assigned to cleaning up the chocolate chip droppings in the barrack's bathrooms.

Satisfied everything was ready, Talton nodded to the sergeant. She returned the nod, then backed away and placed herself flat against the wall. The others in the squad flanked Talton and the sergeant. There was a brief moment of hesitation, but then he heard the soft pop of the container followed by the sound of liquid rushing free.

Almost immediately, the door flew inward with a roar. The sound had barely faded into the early morning air when Talton, followed by the rest of his squad, rushed inside with their swords at the ready.

They pushed deeper into the castle, meeting no resistance along the way as they cleared each room quickly and efficiently. Part of Talton's mind thought it odd that nobody had come to investigate the clamor, but he decided it was more a testament to the low sugar in their heads and pure laziness. Most everyone would be asleep at this time, he thought as he paused at a large door, stopping just long enough to determine it was unlocked.

The door opened into a wide, round space. On the far side, he saw two other doors, both of them closed. To the right was a staircase that hugged the curved wall and rose to meet a metal catwalk which encircled the entire room. Talton and the squad, seeing no one, pressed forward.

The sound of the door they'd entered slamming shut behind them resounded louder in Talton's ears than the explosion they'd used to enter the castle. The deep booms of heavy bolts slamming home filtered through the thick wood as he whirled to see one of his troopers straining to pull the door open again.

The loud clatter of dozens of feet on the catwalk above filled the room, pulling Talton's attention upwards. Thirty sour straw and jawbreaker guards stood at the railing, their faces impassive and their eyes focused on their quarry below. Every one of the guards was armed with honey stick arrows, and each arrow was trained on Talton and his men.

The sergeant continued to the far side of the room and tried both doors, only to find them - as Talton had expected - locked. She turned and stared at him, panic mingled with resignation in her hard eyes.

"What do we have here?" a voice floated down, echoing slightly off the curved walls.

Talton searched for the source and found it. German Chocolate Cake stood between two tall sour straws. His coconut and pecan filling glistened grotesquely from between the three layers of his cake. He leaned forward and placed his hands on the railing, looking down at them with a wry smile on his face and the overhead light glinting off the nuts embedded in his frosting.

Talton took a long, slow breath before he answered. "Captain

Talton, leader of the First Batch of the Baker's Dozen Rock Candy Guards. Where's Kupcake?"

German Chocolate's smile widened. "She's here. Resting. I won't say *comfortably*, all things considered, but she's here."

"Come down here and fight me like a proper confection!" Talton demanded.

German Chocolate laughed. The sound was pinched and nasally. "Are you really going to throw cliched bravado at me? I thought you were better than that. Look, here's how this is going to happen. You and your people are going to die. We have the advantage in every way. Trust me when I say that I won't lose any sleep over it. I'm going to leave and go find something to eat since the petit fours I had earlier just aren't cutting it. After that, I'll probably go slap that insolent confection around a little, just to remind her not to get too comfortable here."

"I'll kill you—"

"No. No, you won't, Talton. After you're dead and I find something decent to eat, the only thing left will be for your pathetic, cowardly master to trundle his rotund self over here and bend his knee to the proper lord and master of this cakedom, Devil's Food Cake. He will bow before my lord and master, and he will - well, I won't say he'll be shown mercy because what my lord has planned for King Red Velvet couldn't be considered mercy by any stretch of the recipe. Afterwards, there won't even be crumbs left. I'm sure you can guess what I'm talking about. I won't say its name, but you know what I mean." From the corner of his eye, Talton saw a couple of the guards take a hand from their respective bows and make the sign of the Great Mother Baker at the vague mention of the vile concoction German Chocolate referenced.

Talton said nothing, only staring at the horrible figure above him.

"This is where your pitiful story ends, my dear captain. And all for nothing. Kupcake will remain here for as long as Devil's Food Cake wants. And believe me, she'll be badly mistreated for the rest of her days. And I will love every moment of it."

"I'll—" Talton boomed, but the words died in his mouth as German Chocolate waved a dismissive hand and turned to leave.

"Goodbye, Captain Talton."

Talton heard the thwang of bowstrings, but then all he heard were the screams of his men.

9

We were brothers once. Not in butter or syrup, but in bond and duty. The truth of the words stung Devil's Food Cake as brightly now as it had forty years before. Now, as then, the words tasted like soured milk, like flour overmixed and burnt. His fingers twitched, tracing patterns in the frosting that filled the massive mixing bowl tub.

Yes, he thought bitterly, *brothers once but no more. Not after what he did. Not after what happened.* Red Velvet hadn't even had the scones to deliver the news personally, and had instead sent a foot soldier to tell Devil's Food Cake that his own son wasn't coming back. No, the pitiful cake had locked himself away in his private quarters and refused to face Devil's Food Cake. Red Velvet had been called back to the Lemon Icebox Castle and his own father soon afterwards. The fucking coward.

"Sir, the emissary has returned."

The statement scattered his thoughts. Devil's Food Cake's eyes opened slowly.

"Show him in," he announced, his voice echoing in the large room. As he waited, he leaned back and let his arms float to either side of him. His fingers continued to play silent notes in the lard and powdered-sugar-frosting bath. The soft scuffling of feet on black licorice stone brought his attention to the doorway.

The slumped, misshapen form of the gummy pickle filled the space, the creature keeping its eyes cast towards the floor. Devil's Food Cake lay still, his eyes taking in the pickle. "Well?" he snapped. The word ripped through the chamber like a knife through mostly softened cream cheese, and the pickle jerked in response.

"I delivered your message as instructed," the pickle said, its voice low and quavering. When Devil's Food Cake didn't respond, the pickle continued in earnest. "I met with the pseudo-king. It pained me to do so, to stand there before someone who held the throne you so rightly claim. It took every ounce of my strength to keep from ripping the cherry crown off his head and-"

"Yes, I'm sure you would have kicked his ass thoroughly, what with all of your obvious musculature. It's a miracle you didn't slay every living candy in the palace. But, your own delusions of strength aside, what was his response to my demand?"

At this, the pickle seemed to cower even more, drawing in on itself. Its hands wrung around each other, and Devil's Food Cake understood that the answer wasn't going to be to his liking. Devil's Food Cake allowed the tension to grow and the silence to stretch. His fingers continued to wave back and forth in the frosting as he stared at the pickle messenger.

"He... he said that he would consider it."

Devil's Food Cake brought one hand out of the bath, considered it, and then slowly licked the sticky substance from his fingers. "Do you think he will?"

"Sir?"

"Do you think he'll consider it?"

"I... I certainly hope so. I was very clear in that it was your wish that he—"

"My wish?"

The gummy pickle staggered backward even though Devil's Food Cake had asked the question casually. "Sir?"

"Are you suggesting that you presented my demands as a request?

That it was a favor I was asking? That if it didn't inconvenience him too greatly, would he please be willing to come for a visit?"

The pickle twisted its body in a movement that Devil's Food Cake took to be the shaking of its head. "No, absolutely not. I made it very clear that under no circumstances was he to refuse. I told him that grave danger and injury could befall Princess Kupcake if he were to remain there and not take an audience with you."

"*Made it very clear*, did you? Well...." Devil's Food Cake stood out of his bath and waded to the edge of the pool. Frosting sloughed from his body in thick clumps, splattering back into the larger collective. He reached for his robe where it lay in a soft pile at the edge of the tub. "I can only assume that he should be here any moment then, what with your strong language and the threat of imminent physical harm, right?"

The pickle looked over its shoulder, unsure of how to respond. "My lord, please." No other words escaped its mouth. Instead, its body jerked and, with saucer-wide eyes, it looked down to where a cocktail toothpick sword impaled it. The pickle's gaze traced along the hilt to where Devil's Food Cake stood at the edge of his bath, his hand still outstretched after having sent the killing blow.

"I want your last thoughts to be of this fact. If King Red Velvet does not appear in front of me as instructed, I will personally kill every last gummy and gumdrop in your entire family, in return for your arrogance and failure." Devil's Food Cake then climbed the rest of the way out of his bath, shrugged on his robe, and stepped over the now collapsed gummy pickle. As he passed two sour straw guards, he gestured over his shoulder. "Have that cleaned up and send for German Chocolate Cake. Tell him to meet me in my chambers."

By the time Devil's Food Cake arrived at his personal bedroom, German Chocolate Cake was already waiting by the door. His head of security bowed quickly. "You summoned me?"

Devil's Food Cake pushed past the other pastry and into his room. "It seems that the imbecile you sent to fetch Red Velvet failed in conveying the seriousness of the summons."

German Chocolate Cake inhaled, held the breath a long moment, and then slowly let it out. "I feared that would happen. You know the pseudo-king is stubborn; his pride rules over his mind, over even common sense. How would you like to proceed? Shall we send another messenger?"

Devil's Food Cake poured a glass of simple syrup from a pitcher and sipped it, his eyes never leaving German Chocolate Cake. "Another messenger, yes. That much is certain." He hesitated, the glass half-raised. "What of that other business?"

German Chocolate Cake stiffened, his chest puffing up with pride. "Just as you expected. The pickle relayed the information about the door and Red Velvet sent a detachment of his special forces, the First Batch of the Baker's Dozen Rock Candy Attachment. We saw them coming a mile away. They've been dispatched." He smiled wickedly. "It was messy."

Devil's Food Cake sipped his syrup and thought, with his eyes staring beyond his head of security. This was going perfectly. *That old crusty crumb is doing everything I expected him to. It's as if he's read it on a recipe card somewhere. Time to up the stakes.* "We'll send another messenger, but this time I think they will carry something a little more meaningful than words."

"Sire?"

Devil's Food Cake smiled coldly. "This time, I don't think we'll send him with just empty-worded demands and idle threats against that little wretch we're keeping locked away. No, we have to send something considerably more substantial to Red Velvet, and let him know that I'm absolutely serious and will see him bend before me."

"What do you propose, my lord?"

Devil's Food Cake paused with the cup just before his mouth. "We'll simply send him a piece of his daughter."

10

"Come on, you goober. That thing is gaining on us!" Jerome grunted and pulled harder on Cleetus' reins. The gummy bear moved sluggishly, his feet dragging through the loose dirt that comprised the path which wound between pools of pudding. Cleetus was tired, Jerome knew – both of them were.

The screeching ripped through the twisted trees again, this time even closer. Jerome felt the scream, his body seeming to vibrate from its force. It was a sound full of hunger, hatred, and - he thought – excitement, in that its prey was so close.

Cleetus froze in place at the sound, but then, to Jerome's surprise, unlocked his feet from their dirt moorings and hurried forward. Jerome fell back as the tension he'd been maintaining on the reins evaporated. He hit the ground hard, the breath flying from his body. As he lay on his back, rocking back and forth with trying to retrieve air into his sponge, he watched Cleetus vanish into the shadows ahead.

When he was able to finally draw a breath, Jerome picked himself up and looked in the direction in which his bear had vanished. He called, but the gummy bear was either beyond hearing or so scared that Jerome's words meant nothing. Jerome dusted himself off and assumed it was the latter. His stomach knotted, sending tendrils of discomfort through him as worry set in. Traditionally, gummy bears weren't particularly brave or adept fighters. They were loyal, kind, and gentle, but not always the cookie with the fewest crumbles. An image of Cleetus caught in a pool of pudding swam through Jerome's mind, and he felt the knot in his stomach tighten even more.

Several yards deeper along the path, Jerome paused and scanned the surrounding swamp. Pools of pudding bubbled, the twisted trees bent and dipped, and shadows covered everything. He called out after Cleetus again. His voice fell flat in the thick air.

Ahead, the path grew narrow, and Jerome had to pick his way carefully around several large pools of pudding. He inspected the dirt in front of him for any signs of the bear's passing, but found nothing. Where had that green gelatinous ass gone?

He heard a grumbling that dissolved into a high-pitched squeal and whirled around looking for the source. As he moved, however, one foot brushed against the edge of a pool of tapioca. The pudding grasped eagerly at his boot, and he felt himself shift across the ground a few inches as more pudding pulled his foot deeper.

A disgusted cry flying from his mouth, Jerome reached for his sword. Yet, even as his hand gripped it, he realized that if he struck at the muck below him, he would also lose his only weapon. Instead, he twisted away from the pudding pool and shook his foot, working it free of his boot. The ground was cold beneath his stocking foot, and he watched helplessly as the pudding sucked down its leathery prize.

"Choke on it," Jerome growled. He returned his attention to his surroundings and the horrible noise. Whatever it was, it was closer. The darkness seemed to press in against him as if trying to hold him in place for what was coming. Another shriek filled the air, and Jerome turned and began to run.

He had made it only a few feet more when an ear-splitting crash forced him to stop. Whirling around, Jerome pulled his sword and saw a massive tree resting across the pool that had consumed his boot. Beyond it, still shrouded in shadow, was an immense hulk.

There were no protrusions, nothing to indicate arms or legs; only a bulk that rose in a sort of dome.

Jerome cast a glance behind him, but realized that there was no point in running. Whatever this abomination was, it would keep following and eventually catch him. No, he would make a stand here and put an end to this. He widened his stance and gripped his sword in both hands, ready to defend himself. Or die trying.

The creature hesitated within the shadows, just out of clear view, as if it were assessing its prey now that it'd caught up. Jerome's palms sweated, and he flexed his fingers around the handle of the sword.

"Come on, you pile of yogurt!" Jerome shouted, oblivious of the horror whose name he'd just invoked. "I'll slice you up and feed you to..." his voice died on his lips as the creature pushed out of the darkness and into the dimly filtered sunlight. Jerome's sword tip dropped as the enormity of what had been chasing him presented itself.

The congealed salad sifted and pushed along the ground, its body quivering with every movement. "Oh Holy Rolling Pin," Jerome whispered. His eyes roamed the salad's body. He could see the pieces of fruit suspended in the gelatin. Worse, there were other things trapped within it. His sword dropped even lower as he saw the partially digested remains of several cookies and pastries, their limbs twisted and surprised looks on their faces. There were even a few gummy birds and smaller creatures in the beast's pink bulk. Jerome fought down his breakfast, willing himself to focus on the threat at hand.

A low slithering noise drew his attention to the ground, and he saw that the congealed salad was pushing its body outward in the form of transparent pink tentacles. The tentacles extracted matter from the salad, and were snaking their way across the space between them. Jerome cried out and slashed at one with his sword, the toothpick cleaving the tip from the appendage. With a squeal of pain, the tentacle retracted and was reabsorbed by the body. Three more erupted and moved more boldly towards him. Two approached from his left, and the third joined with one of the original tentacles and circled to his right.

Jerome twisted back and forth, struggling to keep the arms in sight while also keeping an eye on puddles of pudding. He slashed and darted towards one pair, only to turn at the last second and drive the other two away. As he struck one, splitting it lengthwise, he felt a searing burn across the back of one of his legs. He looked down and saw a tentacle slapping against his leg, working to wrap itself around him. The pain was excruciating. Jerome screamed and stabbed the feeler, his sword driving deep into the pink substance. The congealed salad shrieked again and pulled the tentacle back. But the movement wrenched the sword from Jerome's hand, and he watched, helpless, as his only weapon was absorbed into the creature's body. The sword settled, floating suspended near what he thought had once been a strawberry and the remains of a chocolate chip cookie holding onto a milk pail.

Terror flooded him in a cold wave as the cookie blinked at him.

Great Mother Baker, they're still alive in there! he realized.

More pain erupted along his other leg as one of the remaining appendages grabbed at him. Jerome kicked it away, pushing his body backwards and landing on his rump. Sensing that their prey was now on the ground and vulnerable, the feelers shot forward eagerly. Jerome rolled, ignoring the searing pain in both his legs as he twisted and turned along the dirt path until he was several feet away from the outstretched arms of the congealed salad.

He pushed up onto his feet and sprinted into the swamp. But he heard the oozing shifting behind him as the salad took up pursuit.

11

Jerome ran blindly through the swamp, leaping from side to side in an effort to maneuver around the random pools of pudding. The path rose and then dipped sharply away, and he stumbled over the decline, the pain from the wounds in his legs flaring brilliantly. Behind him came the popping of branches as the congealed salad charged after its prey. Jerome willed himself not to look back, knowing that it was close and gaining on him every second.

The gelatinous horror screeched again, startling Jerome so much that he lost his footing, tripped over a tree root, and went sprawling down an embankment. When he blinked away the dirt and confusion, he found himself in a natural depression. The dirt walls of the hole towered over him, reaching several feet above him; however, the wall angled down to being a manageable three-feet high in one corner. Hope flared and died just as quickly as he saw the large pudding pool beneath it – a mix of what seemed to be chocolate, orange, key lime, and cranberry filling most of the space against the shorter wall. Jerome wouldn't be escaping that way.

More branches gave way with loud cracks as the congealed salad pushed closer. Jerome stared up at the lip of the hole, waiting for the massive, slimy pink bulk to appear like a perverse sun rising over a desiccated land. The noise of his approaching death - or would he not die, only to live the rest of his life trapped in that hellish gelatinous body? - manifested as small trickles of dirt that ran down the right-hand side of the hole. They were followed by the first tips of several tentacles.

Jerome staggered away, putting his back against the farthest wall and watched helplessly as the salad moved closer, its tentacles snaking their way down into the hole. Within seconds, he could see the top of the creature's body looming over the edge and its eager appendages gliding across the bottom of the floor.

His sword floated out of reach inside the beast's form, and Jerome stared at it, willing it to pull itself free and fly across the hole to him. Instead, it remained suspended in its gelatinous grave. The cookie trapped near the sword only blinked feebly at Jerome.

Jerome, his breath coming in fast hitches, searched for anything to use as a weapon. *It can't end like this*, he thought. *I can't go down like this.* But his eyes fell on dirt and more dirt. There was nothing in the hole with which he could defend himself.

The tentacles were ten feet away and moving slowly now, as if they knew their prey was trapped and there was no reason to hurry. Jerome pressed himself against the dirt wall and felt something slap at his shoulder. He ignored it, his attention focused only on the probing appendages advancing towards him. The thing that had bumped him brushed against him again, however, and he broke his attention away and looked up to see a wide, flat rope of white- and pink-striped gum extending up and vanishing over the edge of the hole.

Jerome gave one last glance at the tentacles. The congealed salad monster pushed itself over the rim and began following its arms into the hole. Jerome turned and gripped the gum rope, and he began climbing.

More than halfway down the slope into the hole, the congealed salad saw its victim escaping and let out a scream of rage. Jerome climbed, terror propelling him as he pressed his feet into the dirt and pulled on the gum rope with all his strength.

At the top of the hole, he went to his knees, his chest heaving from the exertion. *Gotta get to the gym*, he thought wryly. A scream from behind and beneath him jolted him, and he took off at a sprint, following the gum rope as it extended through the swamp and into the creeping shadows.

After several minutes, he slowed to a brisk walk, casting nervous looks over his shoulder. In the distance, the congealed salad's enraged cries tore through the swamp, amplified by the high walls of the hole. Jerome pressed on, following the trail of the gum that lay along the path. It wound left and right around smaller puddles of pudding, and he wondered if that meant he was near the outer edge of the swamp.

Once again, he thought of Cleetus and felt the threat of panic rising in him. He had to find the bear. If he lost both Kupcake and Cleetus, he would just give up. He may as well turn around and walk back to the hole and let the congealed salad absorb him, to spend the rest of his life being slowly dissolved in its gelatin next to the strange cookie.

The gum rope came to an end, and Jerome saw that it was tied to the base of a thick candy stick tree. He stared at it, unbelieving. How? Who had tied it? Around him, the swamp was silent. As he looked back at the knotted gum, he heard a soft sigh. Fear pierced him and he stepped backward, ready to run at the first sign of a pink tentacle.

But the sigh came again, followed by soft grunts. Jerome's heart leapt as recognition cut through his panic. "Cleetus?" Several yards away, the gummy bear sat at the base of another tree, its snout resting lazily on one paw. Jerome rushed forward and hugged the bear, who looked up and blinked sleepily at him.

Jerome stepped back. "You were sleeping? Seriously? While I was fighting off that thing? I was nearly eaten!" He swept an arm behind him. Cleetus blinked. "Of course, you were sleeping. How am I surprised?" He looked back at the gum rope. "Who did this? I'm assuming it wasn't you, since I've never known you to do anything in your sleep other than drool and fart."

Cleetus blinked again, but then he turned his head and looked off to one side. Jerome followed the bear's gaze, but saw only scrub brush and dirt. "I don't understand. Did the cake who tied this leave that way?" Cleetus didn't answer - naturally – and only continued to stare at the brush.

Jerome opened his mouth to say something else, but stopped when the brush began to rustle, the small branches shaking as something pushed through. "Dammit, not again," he mumbled. He took a wide stance and held up his fists. Whatever came through there might leave with his corpse, but it was going to take a few bruises with it. Maybe a split lip or a black eye. At the least, a dislocated thumb or a really nasty hangnail.

With a final shake, the branches parted and a small, yellow shape emerged. The creature hopped forward and stopped, its beady black eyes staring at him expectantly from above its small beak. The yellow marshmallow peep hopped forward again, in a tiny movement, and then blinked. "You did this?" Jerome asked, pointing at the gum rope. The marshmallow bird shifted to see the gum rope, and then looked back to Jerome. It shuffled slightly in place – a gesture that Jerome somehow knew meant: "Yeah, man. Who else would have saved your ass? That big green lazy bitch over there?"

Jerome blinked. "Got a bit of a mouth on you, don't you?"

The peep blinked back.

"Okay, then," Jerome said. He walked over and slapped Cleetus on the rump. "Get up. We gotta go. We still have to get that Bag of Never-Ending Powdered Sugar." He looked at the peep. "What's your name?"

The yellow marshmallow blinked, giving the impression of: "Stephen."

"Alright," Jerome said, and he snapped his fingers at Cleetus.

Cleetus sleepily pulled himself up to his feet. Stephen shuffled, the gesture seeming to say, sarcastically, "You're welcome."

Jerome stopped and regarded the peep. "I'm sorry, you're right.

Thank you for saving me. I genuinely appreciate it. But I'm in a bit of a hurry. I have to get—"

"The bag of powdered sugar, yeah, I heard you." Stephen wriggled. "Look, where I come from, if someone saves your ass, you owe them. So, I'll be coming with you until you repay me."

"Repay you?" Jerome nearly shouted. "Look at me! I'm dirty, I'm alone, I lost a boot and my sword, and you think I have the money to repay you?"

The peep only blinked and regarded Jerome. Jerome stared, incredulous, and then shook his head and waved at the peep to follow. "Fine. Come on."

12

They continued through the pudding swamp carefully, Jerome atop Cleetus and leading the way with Stephen the peep following close behind. Jerome looked back occasionally to make sure they weren't pulling too far ahead of the small marshmallow that had saved his life. Every time he looked, Stephen was still there, his body wriggling forward quickly and keeping a good pace with the lumbering bear.

As they wove between noxious pools of pudding, Jerome found himself watching for any hint of the congealed salad monster. He had heard the dull echo of a roar filtering through the trees, but the sound had been faint and very far away. Even so, it had made his heart hammer in his sponge, and it had taken everything he had to keep Cleetus from bolting in sheer panic.

They arrived at the mouth of the cave they'd sought out a few hours later. Jerome stared at the opening, a gaping thing that split the earth in a jagged line. Even from several yards away, he could feel the cold seeping from it. Around them, the tortured candy trees stood still, as if waiting to see what he would do. The landscape was silent – no sign of the congealed salad horror, no other small gummy creatures flitting about.

With a sigh, Jerome slid from Cleetus' back and stretched. As he pulled a few supplies from the packs strapped to the bear, including a torch, he gauged the entrance to the cave and then looked at the gummy bear. "You're going to stay here," he said. The bear instantly shuffled off and found a large Red Vine tree to curl up against. Within seconds, the large bear was sleeping, soft snores sliding from his jaws. He turned and looked down at Stephen. "You coming with me?"

The peep blinked, looked at the cave, and then looked back at Jerome. It wiggled, the gesture conveying: "You'll probably die if I don't."

Jerome glanced at Cleetus, sleeping soundly at the base of the tree. "Why don't you stay here with him? I'll feel better if someone responsible is keeping an eye on things out here till I get back."

Stephen blinked at Jerome.

"Seriously. I'll be fine. Be back in a second."

Stephen turned and shuffled towards the bear, with the movement suggesting: "Moron. When you're dead in there, trapped in a jello mold or worse, I'm eating this damned bear."

Jerome watched the peep cross the space and settle against Cleetus' green stomach. Stephen blinked back at him indignantly. "Go on, then," the gesture said. Jerome shook his head and entered the cave.

Just inside, Jerome stopped and lit the torch, holding it well in front of him. The flame hissed as moisture from the ceiling dripped onto it.

The passage led gradually downward, and after a few minutes of walking, the ceiling and the passageway opened up, the ceiling extending above and beyond the reach of Jerome's torchlight. He poked the flames in different directions, hoping to find anything that could clue him in to where the bag would be.

Twisting to his left, he thrust the flaming stick again. *Nothing.* The orange glow lit a patch of stone a few yards across, but Jerome's searching and tired eyes saw no other passageway or indication that he was on the right path. As he pulled the torch back, though, something did catch his eye. He paused and waved the torch up and down, then from side to side. His eyes caught the barest hint of a glint – far off in the distance. Jerome let out a breath and started in the general direction of whatever it was he'd seen, his feet scraping and stumbling over the uneven floor.

As he walked, the flash of his firelight reflecting off of something far in the distance continued, guiding him on like a cinnamon siren. Jerome pressed on, his breath coming in short gasps as he rushed forward. This could be it, he thought, the passageway or door that would lead him farther into the cave to find the bag. He wondered how much farther down he would have to travel. Surely, there would be traps or even guards down deeper, and he would have to figure out a way to—

He stumbled to a halt and stared, disbelieving.

In the orange glow of the firelight, just a few feet before him, stood the object that had caused the reflections. A wide table coated in edible gold-leaf spanned several feet to either side of Jerome and seemed almost equally as deep. Ornately carved legs curved down to the uneven rocky floor of the cave. The table seemed so out of place in the middle of a cavern, but there it was.

Sitting in the middle of the table, just at the edge of Jerome's torchlight, was a burlap sack bulging beneath a twine tie. The bag was small, slightly larger than Jerome's fist. It sat alone on the table, as if someone had placed it there before attending to other business. Jerome approached cautiously, his eyes flitting over the table and then to the stone walls around him, searching desperately for a trap or some hidden creature who might be guarding the bag.

Despite the shadows that danced from the torchlight, the cavern remained still and silent. Jerome pressed against the table and stretched forward, just able to snag the top edge of the bag with one fingertip. He pulled the heavy sack forward and undid the tie.

"Seriously?" he whispered as he stared at the white powdered sugar filling the pouch. Again, he looked around, and once more he saw nothing rushing towards him to defend the prize. Jerome shrugged and re-tied the string, then tucked the pouch into his shirt.

"That," he said as he started back across the cavern floor, "was stupidly simple."

He stopped as his torch revealed movement ahead and to either side of him. Shadows bulged and shifted as things pressed forward from the darkness. As the first of the fat, smooth bodies crept into the light, Jerome's attention was also pulled higher up towards the ceiling, where misshapen forms seemed to be detaching themselves from the walls to begin rolling down towards him with a dry clicking.

His enjoyment of having so easily obtained the Bag of Never-Ending Powdered Sugar evaporated as he looked at the dozens of hot tamale gummy candies and nerds slowly closing in on him.

13

Kupcake growled in frustration as the drawer handle slipped from her numb fingers and clattered to the floor. The growl morphed seamlessly into a long, quavering belch that seemed to shake her entire body. The princess grimaced, tasting the memory of the last batch of cookies which the guard had brought for her. *The least they could do is spring for something better than vanilla wafers*, she thought. Another small bubble of a burp rose up quickly, and she exhaled long and hard. With a wistful smile, she thought about how Jerome would occasionally tease her about her decidedly unladylike burps.

Focus on the now, she scolded herself.

She stared down at the handle, sighed, and bent to retrieve it while monitoring her guts for another wave of gas. As her fingers closed around the curved metal, she felt the sudden urge to fling it through the bars of the single window of the room. Her arm tensed, readying for the action. *No*, she commanded herself, and dropped her arm to her side. *I worked too hard to get it free from the dresser to throw it away now*. Never mind that it had been hanging by a single screw that was rather flimsy and seemed older than the Ladyfinger Crusades.

Thinking back to a time when her mother had locked Kupcake in her chambers, insisting that the daughter heir could not leave the room until she'd mastered the art of needlepoint, Kupcake lamented her current lack of sewing implements. Surely, if she'd had a thinner needle, she could have picked the lock by now, just as she'd done that time to escape her room and sneak to the kitchen – where she'd prepared a meal for the staff. When she'd been found by the queen, Kupcake had asked what good needlepoint was when compared to feeding those who normally cared for you? Naturally, her mother's answer had had to do with how, once upon a time, a well-executed needlepoint fabric had quelled an uprising by a tribe of cinnamon rolls.

Taking a step forward to the window now, Kupcake examined her work of the past two hours. Once she'd freed the handle, she'd begun using its flat edge to chisel away at the licorice holding the iron bars firm. Turned out, in addition to being one of the single nastiest candies in the land of All That's Good (But Never Goes to Your Hips or Butt), black licorice was also, when coated in a thick layer of hardened caramel as these bars were, one of the hardest. Two hours of intense labor behind her, and she'd only made a few paltry scratches in the shiny black surface.

If I could only get one loosened, that would give me the encouragement to continue, she thought. But once she could remove them, then what? From her vantage point, she couldn't see much beyond the window other than blue sky and wisps of clouds. She wondered how high she was. Unfortunately, she couldn't see enough out her window to do the math. *A princess locked away in a tower,* she mused darkly. *And with not enough bedsheets to fashion a good rope to climb out with, either. But, one thing at a time,* she reminded herself. *Focus on what you have, what you can do right now.* And right now, that was to chisel away at these bars, no matter how long that took.

Of course, that goal was predicated on her being in the room for a significant period of time. Truth was, she had no idea how long Devil's Food Cake planned on keeping her here. At least until he got what he wanted, her father kneeling before him in subjugation. The thought of her father, stately and kind, bending his knee to a confection as despicable as Devil's Food Cake, turned her own cake sour.

How long before her father sent the Fudge Army? Or even the rock candy guards? Surely, he and every candy and confection at his command were racing across the land, aprons waving in the wind, rolling pins and toothpick swords and cake skewer lances gleaming and eager to stab, to cut, to....

Where were these violent thoughts coming from? She stepped back from the window, placed the drawer handle atop the dresser, and turned away, one hand drifting to her mouth. She'd never had such thoughts before. She'd always seen the good in confections, the best in candies. Even the sours and the flaming hot candies had their good qualities. No, it was this place affecting her. She looked around the room. It was being locked in here, having been forcefully taken from her home and thrown in here, in this....

Cell. This is a prison cell.

To alleviate the fluttering panic starting to rise in her, she paced throughout the room. She knew the dimensions by heart at this point. Fifteen steps from window to door. Eleven steps from the wall to the bed. *If you could call it that,* she thought. It was nothing more than a silicone baker's mat resting on four posts. Other than the bed and the broken dresser, the room had no furniture. There was no mirror, no washbasin, nothing to afford its occupant even the smallest level of comfort. The floor was dirty, uneven stone, the walls made of the same. And in the corner to the right of the window, the stone walls seemed to ooze moisture.

"My father is going to destroy him for this," she mumbled. "He's going to rip Devil's Food Cake apart, layer by layer. He'll melt his frosting and—"

She stopped, once again surprised by the venom in her words and thoughts. She'd never wished such harm on anyone, and hearing herself do so now filled her with shame.

"Don't stop now," a voice said from behind her. "I do wish to know what will become of myself and my frosting."

Kupcake spun and saw Devil's Food Cake staring at her through a small window in the door. His eyes regarded her with cold interest, as if she were a curious gummy bug speared on a slab for his study.

The lock rapped open and the door swung into the room. Devil's Food Cake stepped forward. He moved to one side, and she watched with growing fear as German Chocolate Cake stepped around from behind his master. The cake who had stolen her from her ride, with more slaps and kicks than she felt had been necessary, moved quickly towards her. A look of pure irritation and fury on his face told her all she needed to know. She never saw his hand move, but felt the open-palmed slap all the same.

"How dare you talk like that about your host?" he growled, standing over her where she lay on the floor with one hand to her reddening cheek. Her other cheek exploded with pain as he bent and slapped her again, and she had to fight to bite back a cry.

Behind German Chocolate, Devil's Food Cake spoke. "Go on. Please, tell me what else your... *father*—" he said the word sourly, as if the very term was despicable, "will do to me and this castle." He gestured to the walls around him. "That is, of course, if he has the sprinkles to even come here."

Kupcake looked past her assailant and her captor at the open door. Instinctively, she felt her body tense, ready to spring past him and out of the room. But the thick body of a sour straw guard angled around the doorframe, and all of her hopes of sprinting to freedom drained away from her.

"Try it, bitch," German Chocolate snarled.

Devil's Food Cake saw her movements and chuckled. "Really? You know you wouldn't make it more than a step or two past the doorway before you were apprehended. And, trust me, my guards won't be gentle. They take great pride in their captives remaining as such."

"What, then?" she demanded as she pulled herself up and onto the silicone mat bed. "What are you doing here? Did you come just to mock me and my father? To make me dislike you more than I already do? Believe me, too, that's a pretty big feat. I tend to love everyone." She shifted her eyes to the confection that had struck her. "And why hit me? Surely, you don't hate everyone and everything. Surely, there's some compassion within you?"

German Chocolate sneered and raised a hand again, but a snap of the fingers from Devil's Food Cake stayed the blow. Devil's Food Cake remained quiet for a long moment, regarding her. His features were impassive, and once again Kupcake felt no more significant to him than a small crumb left on his plate.

"Your cowardly father has yet to respond to my demands that he present himself here and kneel before me. He has sent no word, no messenger, nothing."

"My father doesn't negotiate with stale pastries like you." *I hope I'm wrong, though*, she thought.

Devil's Food Cake chuckled silently, only the gentle movement of his shoulders betraying his amusement. "I have considered all things regarding this matter. It seems that your father is too afraid to actually come. Which, given his history, makes complete sense. He's so quick to accept praise for the doings of others, and even more quick to shift blame for wrongs away from himself.

"I even considered, briefly, that his silence is because perhaps, deep down in his cake, he doesn't love you. The fool only loves himself, really. Ah, I can tell by your eyes that you think I'm making things up just to sound nasty. No, girl, believe it or not, I actually know your father quite well, as pathetic as he is. We have a bit of a history together, he and I, although I'm sure he's never spoken of it. Too afraid to admit his transgressions. Which is why I know now that it is his own deep cowardice that keeps him locked away in his castle, too scared to do anything to rescue his own daughter."

Kupcake felt rage flush through her again, and she opened her mouth to hurl insults at him, to voice her suspicion that he enjoyed intimate acts with rice puddings and week-old peach cobblers. Yet, something inside her stopped the words before they formed. *He wants something*, she thought. *He needs to do something to spur Father to come here.*

Her eyes narrowed. "What do you want?"

There was the soft scuffle of feet on stone in the doorway, and Devil's Food Cake stepped to one side.

A large, chocolate-covered coconut candy dressed in baker's whites, with a hairnet mask covering its face, entered the room. Kupcake's stomach churned at the mere sight of the candy. *Coconut. Why did it have to be coconut?* She shuddered at the thought of the gross flakes touching her. But what it held in its dark, clawed hand made her butter run cold, and she barely felt German Chocolate Cake's hands clamp down tightly on her wrists.

Kupcake struggled against German Chocolate's hold, wriggling her body back along the silicone mat bed until she hit the wall. The foul cake growled and pulled her back towards the edge of the mat, where he held her fast. "Stay still," he breathed heavily in her ear. His breath was hot and moist against her cake, and she could hear the trembling excitement in his voice.

The chocolate coconut candy stepped towards her and raised its offset spatula. Bringing it forward, the candy lightly scraped away some of her frosting, the motion producing only a small discomfort on her head. With a deft flick of its wrist, the candy then deposited the scrapings into a container. The process was quick and not entirely unpleasant, and Kupcake found herself slightly confused by the theatrics of her captors.

"Not like that, you damned gumdrop!" German Chocolate Cake growled at the coconut candy. For its part, the candy stiffened and looked in wide-eyed confusion at the cake who had shouted. "Give me that Baker-damned thing." Before the candy could look to Devil's Food Cake for approval, German Chocolate leaned forward and snatched the spatula free.

"Get over here and hold her," he demanded, switching places with the coconut candy. Then, with an almost maniacal glee mirrored in his eyes, German Chocolate Cake brought the spatula down and across her frosting and cake.

This time, the pain was immediate and intense. A searing pain flared across her head as she felt frosting and sponge come free under the harsh assault.

Kupcake's screams mixed with German Chocolate Cake's laughter, bouncing off the thick walls and along the hallway beyond.

14

Jerome whistled in appreciation and more than a little fear at the sight of all of the chewy red bodies, his torchlight reflecting off their smooth, gelatinous surfaces. Interspersed between them, and climbing atop one another to form small but formidable piles, were the misshapen lumps of hard candy. He turned from side to side, taking in the wide swaths of the encroaching enemy.

"All of you little buggers?" he asked with wonder. The words had barely floated past his lips when a group of tamales leapt for him. Instinctively, he twisted, bringing his torch up defensively. The lead tamale struck the flame and began melting, its cry sounding shrill in the echo chamber of the cavern. The others brushed against him as they passed, and Jerome gasped as their cinnamon bodies left burns across his cake.

Without giving him time to pause, the nerds rushed forward, their shells crackling against the stone as they moved. Jerome kicked at one pile and sent the small candies flying. He saw them briefly silhouetted by the torchlight before they were lost to the darkness.

Burning raked across him again as more tamales pressed forward. Jerome kicked wildly and swung the torch in wide arcs. More red bodies melted, and those who didn't shrank away from the guttering flames.

Jerome grunted with the effort of each swing as he fought to gain ground and move away from the gold-leaf table. More flashes of searing pain from cinnamon burns screamed across him as he staggered in what he hoped was the direction of the entrance. Twice, he stumbled and fell to his knees. Each time, though, he managed to scramble back to his feet just as the nerds reached him. He swiped at them with a backhanded swing and sent them scattering. The tamales burned; he didn't want to find out what the nerds did if they got close enough.

A faint suggestion of light ahead, muddy in the gloom, caught his attention. Hope surged through him and he cried out in triumph as he shoved the torch directly into a tamale, grinning as it dissolved into a bubbling pool. "Eat it!" he growled as the tamale died. Jerome lurched ahead, kicking wildly and just missing some nerds who were regrouping. His eyes fought to determine how much farther he had to go before the entrance tunnel.

His foot caught on a rough patch of stone, and Jerome slammed into the hard ground, pain enveloping his mind and bright spots flaring in his vision. The torch clattered out of his hand and spun away, its fire sputtering and then dying. The darkness was sudden and in the moment the gentle light of the entrance tunnel was lost to him. A cold and tickling panic flooded his cake as the tamales and nerds shuffled closer. His hand grasped spasmodically for the torch, fingers groping in vain against the darkness. Finding nothing but hearing his attackers closing in, Jerome crawled to his feet and began staggering away at a rushed pace. From behind came the whispered slithering of pursuit.

Slowly his eyes adjusted, aided by the increasingly bluish glow of the entrance tunnel, he felt the first tickles of nerds reaching his legs. Their movements were light as they skittered across him, and the feeling sent a shudder of revulsion through him. Jerome leapt to his feet and shook his legs in a parody of the Lava Cake Dance he'd once seen his father do. The soft tickling of nerds on his body fell away.

Jerome took a breath and sprinted forward, aiming directly for the tunnel. His feet pounded on the stone, the slithering of tamale bodies in close pursuit all around him. All of the places where they'd touched him burned fiercely as he moved. Almost blind with panic and the need to escape, Jerome ran, waving his arms in defensive swipes in case any nerd or tamale launched itself at him.

He plunged into the gently sloping tunnel, the opening - beyond which he could see Red Vine trees - seemed so small and so far away. Knowing the tamales and nerds weren't the type of candies that required cold darkness and that they very well would pursue him out of the cave, Jerome raced towards the exit.

He flinched, jerking his head lower as he heard a short, soft whisper then felt a quick fluttering of wind over the top of his head. Jerome slowed as a rattling thump sounded to his right. Embedded in the wall were three white- and red-striped peppermint sticks, still vibrating slightly from their impact. Curiously, he pulled one free. It came, but not without some effort on his part. He held it up and marveled at the razor-sharp point to which the stick had been honed. He saw grooves almost halfway down the length of the shaft, too, indicating how deeply the stick had been embedded in the wall.

"You have to be shitting me," he groaned. "Peppermint stick darts?" Behind him, he heard the chittering of nerds and tamales shifting against stone in eager anticipation of his impending skewer. They were clumped in a loose mass at the edge of the light, content to let the darts do the work for them. Movement at the cave's opening caught his attention as Stephen shifted into view. The peep twisted its head, the gesture seeming to scream: "You'd better run, muffin boy!"

Jerome ran. The air around him exploded with the whispery exhalations of peppermint projectiles, the wall beside him reverberating with the impacts as the missiles buried themselves deep in the stone. Three times, he felt scalding pain as one of the arrows scraped across his body: once in his upper back, and twice across his already damaged legs. He howled in pain at each one, but continued on, refusing to slow even in the slightest.

He broke into the open air like a marathon runner crossing the finish line, his head and shoulders leading the way and his legs propelling him. As soon as his feet touched grass, though, he felt all of the strength going out of his legs and he fell forward.

When Jerome came to a stop, he struggled to roll onto his back, and then lay there panting and staring upward through the twisted branches of the Red Vine trees. Soon, Stephen shuffled into his view and blinked down at him as if to say, "You know there's a side entrance that's not guarded, right?"

15

Jerome guided Cleetus to a stop at the edge of a wide field which sloped down into a rocky landscape. Dead, yellowing grass swept ahead of him like a vast ocean broken only by the numerous chocolate-covered marshmallow boulders to be seen jutting out of the ground.

"The Land of the Danish Wedding Cookies," he said, as if announcing their location to a tour group. Cleetus stared at the terrain contemplatively, but Stephen just blinked at him and turned away, directing his attention elsewhere. "We'll camp here for a little while," Jerome decided. He turned to the saddlebags and retrieved both his canteen and the pastry patch kit.

Jerome applied the icing salve to his numerous scrapes, burns, cuts, and various ouchies, breathing a deep sigh of relief as the medicine seeped into his cake. He sat back and reveled in the diminishment of the pain. "You look like an amateur baker dropped you on the way to the judging table, kicked you for calling their mother a raisin, and then decided to let a blind chocolate squirrel try to patch you up," blinked Stephen before he went shuffling off into the underbrush.

Jerome set the pastry patch kit aside and picked up the Bag of

Powdered Sugar. He felt the give of the sugar inside against the pressure of his fingers, and the heft of the bag in the palm of his hand. The bag was supposed to always be full, no matter how much you pulled out. It was one of the forgotten and fabled artifacts lost during the Eleven-Day Pretzel War.

He placed the bag on the ground and studied it. Jerome remembered learning about the war - just one of many fought in the Land of All That's Good (But Never Goes to Your Hips or Butt), but easily one of the most depraved. For ten days and a full night (the 'eleven' in the title was a point argued by historians, some wanting to give credit to the first night where the pretzels had engaged in a rather vicious game of Stiff Peaks), Dark Chocolate, White Chocolate, and Milk Chocolate forces – all claiming the birthright to pretzels – had slaughtered each other on the Graham Cracker Fields.

It hadn't been until one particularly crafty semi-sweet milk chocolate soldier stumbled across the bag while raiding a nearby caramel farm for supplies that the tide of the war turned. The chocolate, thinking it had found a great food source, started to leave with the bag, but was attacked by the farmer's wife. In the scuffle, the bag was upended and the vast majority of the contents spilled onto the floor. The wife was also coated in the white sugar. When the chocolate looked, however, he saw that despite most of the sugar having fallen out of the bag, the container remained full. And, to his astonishment, the person who'd attacked him suddenly looked like his commanding officer, who he knew to have been ground to crumbs earlier that day.

The chocolate grabbed the bag and ran. Realizing what they had and not wanting to look a gift baker too closely in the mouth (gift bakers, being part-time seasonal help, had horrible dental hygiene as a rule), the Milk Chocolate forces used the bag to coat themselves. With the sugar coating, they were able to present themselves as allies to the White Chocolate forces. The White Chocolates, confused by the sudden influx of forces to their side - but assuming them to be simple reinforcements - were quickly overtaken. The trick worked so well that it was repeated against the Dark Chocolate forces. That would have worked, too, but for a rainstorm that poured down like cascading glaze over donuts. Their powdered sugar disguises ruined, the Milk Chocolates had no choice but to negotiate terms with their darker, more bitter brethren.

The Bag of Never-Ending Powdered Sugar had vanished after that, falling into myth and mystery. Since then, hundreds had sought it. This small, unassuming bag.

Jerome prodded it with a toe. The legends said that the bag could also provide boundless energy and strength, and could - supposedly - heal wounds, even if a muffin was an inch from death.

He pulled the bag back into his lap and opened it, looking again at the thick white powder kept within. He paused, wondering if it would be wise to test the bag's energizing powers. What if it was something he got a taste for and couldn't stop using? It was bad enough that he was going to have to use several handfuls of it for his disguise... did he really want to be addicted to the confectioner's sugar also? With a never-ending supply, the threat was both real and terrifying.

Jerome firmly re-tied the pouch and placed it back in the saddle-bag. He would not give in. He would use the powdered sugar for his disguise, get into the Land of the Danish Wedding Cookies, find the Piping Bag of Ganache, and make straight for the Black Licorice Castle. Once his mission to rescue Kupcake was complete and she was safely back with her father, King Red Velvet, he would turn the bag over to the king. And if the king didn't want it, Jerome would give it to the Moon Pie Wizard for safekeeping. The group ate a quick meal, Jerome sharing the few provisions he had with the peep.

As he ate Jerome watched the evening shadows lengthen, growing from the landscape as if they were nocturnal creatures waiting for the slow banishment of the sun before creeping out of their crevices. He thought about the next day and the challenges it would bring. Was the Moon Pie Wizard right? Would the Bag of Never-Ending Powdered Sugar really disguise him as a Danish Wedding Cookie? *It had better*, he thought. *Otherwise, those crazy bastards will make short work of me. Cleetus, too.* Stephen, he thought, would probably be just fine. The peep seemed indestructible. But if those cookies saw through his disguise, if they looked at him and saw only a fat blueberry muffin covered in powdered sugar, then there was no telling how bad it would get. He hadn't been exaggerating when he'd told the Moon Pie Wizard that no cookie, pastry, or even candy had gone into those lands and returned whole, assuming they'd returned at all. He'd even read about the crumbs of some luckless adventurers being spread across the grounds just outside the border to the Danish Cookies' land as a warning to anyone who would enter.

No, those cookies were definitely not moist, if Jerome was being fully honest. But even if he got in there, he had no idea of where to go to find the Piping Bag of Ganache. He had no map of the lands. He combed his memory of stories about the realm, and could still find nothing regarding artifacts or caves.

Why are you doing this?

The question appeared in his mind suddenly, and he froze. Why was he committed to doing this at all, when the king would surely have sent the Fudge Army and rescued Kupcake by now? The possibility of his true love sitting safely back home in the Lemon Icebox Castle, her feet propped up on a stool and a nice fire roaring nearby while he was out here risking his life needlessly, seemed very real.

It was true, he admitted to himself, that there was no real way for him to know if his journey was all for nothing. He had no way to send or receive a message from the king, and even if he had, nobody would have answered him. Members of the royal court didn't correspond with muffins.

So, he thought, the question remained. Why was he doing this? Did he really believe that King Red Velvet wouldn't move to rescue his daughter? No, of course he would. But the mere thought of sitting at home, doing nothing and waiting, counting on others to rescue the princess, sent his stomach into knots. Regardless of whether or not Jerome got to the Black Licorice Castle and found that Kupcake had already been rescued, or was in the process of being rescued, Jerome knew with every grain of his flour that he had to do everything he could to help her. Besides, he reminded himself, nobody would expect a rescue attempt by a single muffin. There was a better-than-even chance that he'd get to the castle and be able to sneak in while Red Velvet's forces held a position outside the walls.

Jerome sighed and pushed the thoughts away as best he could, readying himself and Cleetus for sleep. He got confirmation that Stephen would be up for a while, so the peep would take the first watch and allow the muffin to get some badly needed rest.

The sounds of Cleetus snoring followed him down into unconsciousness.

16

"Hurry up and get that shit on you."

Jerome paused, his sugar-coated fingers nearly touching his nose as he looked at the peep.

Stephen blinked impatiently. "Make sure you get all of your berries." The small yellow marshmallow cocked its head appraisingly. "You ever consider getting those things frosted? I've heard that getting the berries frosted opens all kinds of ladyfingers, if you know what I mean."

"I do know what you mean, and I have no interest in other ladyfingers. And, be patient. I'm working on it. This isn't as easy as it looks, you know!" Jerome snapped as he smeared more of the sugar across his face. He closed his eyes and rubbed more of it onto his cake. He could hear Stephen shifting impatiently.

After what felt like hours, the job was done. Or at least in the general neighborhood of doneness. Jerome held his arms out and turned in a circle. "Well, how do I look? Did I get it everywhere?"

Stephen just blinked at him. "You look like an asshole." Cleetus sniffed at his sugar-coated friend, then grew suddenly more interested in a small chocolate ant crawling across the ground. Jerome dropped his hands to his side. "You know you could just use this stuff to sneak into the Black Licorice Castle and rescue your woman your-self." Stephen shifted. "Wouldn't need to go traipsing off into the land of the batshit-crazy cookies."

"That's part of my master plan." Jerome pointed towards the border of the Danish Wedding Cookies. "But if I can find the Piping Bag of Ganache in there and take it with me, then I think my chances will be pretty good when it comes to getting to her and getting us out alive."

"Where do I put money on that?" Stephen blinked.

Jerome smiled. "I knew I could count on you to bet on me. You're not as bad as you make yourself out to be."

"Um, yeah, sure. Betting on you." Stephen blinked before rolling his eyes.

Cleetus chuffed a laugh. Ignoring his companions, Jerome took a breath to calm himself and watched the sun rise. Stephen had let him sleep much longer than he'd expected, and as a result, Jerome felt very well-rested and ready to continue with his quest. He took a moment to consider just how far he'd come to reach this moment. Not to take anything away from their abilities, but the threats he'd faced so far had been of a relatively easy sort. From here on, though, the dough would get tougher.

They walked for hours, the brown grass giving way to barren dirt with scattered pebbles and the occasional chocolate-covered marsh-mallow boulder. The sky was overcast, which Jerome was thankful for. He didn't know how the powdered sugar would react if he began sweating profusely.

As they navigated around a large marshmallow rock formation, Jerome saw what looked to be an old, dried-up riverbed carved into the dusty ground. It snaked its way from far in the distance, winding and doubling back on itself before passing to his right.

Jerome pulled his canteen out from his pack and, after taking a long drink, looked down at Stephen. "I don't suppose you have any thoughts on which way to go?"

The peep shifted gently in the dirt. "Do I look like a tour guide?"

Jerome rolled his eyes and, tugging the reins of a reluctant Cleetus, led the group towards the riverbed. As they neared, his eyes caught movement. Something small and furtive shifted among the rocks, flashes of dried yellow visible as the thing moved. Panic surged through him, and he let one hand drift towards his waist – where the toothpick sword had once hung. His fingers grasped nothing, and he felt his heart lurch at the memory of losing the sword to the congealed salad.

Snatching a rock from the ground, Jerome raised his hand, ready. He heard Stephen moving, and glanced that way and saw the peep signal: "Wait a minute before you go decapitating everything we see."

They approached, and after several yards, Jerome could hear soft grunts and mumbled curses. His ears picked up on only one voice, though, and he allowed himself a breath of relief. Still, his feet slowed their approach towards the edge of the riverbed.

The source of the noise was a single Danish Wedding Cookie. A large portion of the cookie was missing, having crumbled away long ago... or it had been bitten away, Jerome thought. It walked in circles, kicking at rocks and mumbling to itself while gesturing wildly with both hands. Nearby, Jerome saw a small pouch that looked like a half-deflated balloon.

"...without me? Who's going to raise them? Stan? That waste of butter? Or that dolt Mary who has margarine between her ears? Ha! They'll fail, and then they'll realize what they've done! Be too late by then – isn't that right, Roger?" The cookie didn't even hesitate for a potential response from the invisible Roger. "Damn straight! I'll be nothing but dried-out crumbs by then, and then they'll be sorry! We'll see their sugar coating streaked with tears! 'Oh, Balthus, why did you have to die?' Why? because you assholes—" The cookie paused, its feet scuffing and kicking loose rocks across the hard ground. His face turned towards Jerome, and his eyes - already squinting in the light - closed even further. "Eh? Who's there? Dammit, Roger, why didn't you warn me someone was coming? I could have put out food or made tea. That you, Stan, come to watch your handiwork? Come to see the fruits of your labors? I won't give you the satisfaction, you dried-up, raisin-filled discount cookie!"

"I'm sorry?" Jerome answered.

The Danish Wedding Cookie paused in his tirade and staggered closer. "Who are you?"

"Jerome."

The cookie snorted. "You're a fat bastard of a Danish Wedding Cookie, aren't you? You got any food you can spare? Or did you eat it all before you even got a mile away from the house?"

Jerome's heart beat quicker. *He really thinks I'm one of them.* A thrill raced through his stomach. *The powdered sugar is working!* "That's not very nice, you know. Do you talk to everyone you meet that way? You're out here talking to yourself, so I'm not really sure you're in the best position to be insulting the first confection you see." Jerome turned to go. "Have fun drying out and crumbling away."

"Wait! Wait, wait, wait. I'm sorry!" the cookie called, his voice clear over the lip of the riverbed. "I've been out here for a couple of days now and—" he gestured at the limp bag, "my food is all gone."

"You ate everything already?"

"I was hungry, tubby. Surely, you get that. Besides," the cookie quickly added as Jerome turned once again to leave, "it's not like they gave me much. The whole point was to leave me out here to die."

"Why would they do that? Did you hurt someone?"

"Graham crackers and the Great Mother Baker, no! Nothing like that. I just got to the point where, well...." He gestured at the missing portion of his body.

"You started to dry out and crumble?" Jerome supplied.

The Danish Wedding Cookie sighed and nodded. "I'm sure you understand. It's our way. Eventually, we all come to this. You may take longer than normal, though," he said, squinting up at Jerome. "Holy Rolling Pin, you're a big one, ain't ya?"

Time to step it up, Jerome thought. *Make it look good.* "We don't treat our elders that way in my clan," he said.

"Clan? The hell do you mean, *clan*?"

"Crap," Jerome whispered.

"You done fucked up now," Stephen blinked.

"What I mean is that we never treat fellow cookies that way,"

Jerome hurried to say. "Everyone deserves respect." The old cookie's face was screwed up in confusion. *I'm losing him*, Jerome realized. "Here! Let me get you some of my food." He reached into the saddle-bag. The old cookie looked at what was offered, let out a disappointed breath, and then crammed the food into his mouth. He chewed vigorously while continuing to squint at Jerome.

"The hell is that?" he asked, nodding towards Cleetus.

"Oh, that's Cleetus. He's my trusty steed. And that—" he pointed towards the peep, "is Stephen. He saved my life recently, from a congealed salad mon..." the words died on his lips as he saw Stephen's warning wiggle. Jerome looked back at the cookie and saw that he was being watched even more suspiciously.

"We don't have Congealed Salads here, son," the cookie said slowly as he swallowed his bite. "Only the confections in the Outlands have unholy things like that. Are you sure you're from here?"

"Yes!" Jerome blurted. "I am. I just go exploring outside the borders, out in the... Outlands. My father gave me permission to go looking for anything that could be useful around the house, or new areas we could expand into."

"Who's your father?"

Jerome felt his stomach drop. His mind scrambled for a name. "Rickard. You may not know him, as we live—"

"Out past the old Birthing Kitchen, yeah, I know Rickard! How's that old dried-up confection doing? He owes me money, you know."

"What's your name again?" Jerome asked, relief flooding in at having guessed a name that resonated.

"Balthus, boy, don't you remember me?"

Jerome gave a nervous chuckle. "Of course, I do. It's just been a while and, well, it's rather hot out and I've been traveling for a few days. Plus, I'm still not over the whole congealed salad monster thing."

Balthus nodded. "I understand. I went out into the Outlands once myself when I was a younger, fresher cookie. Found myself a really nice set of wax lips one night. Boy, I tell you, we had us some fun!" He laughed and turned to sit on a nearby marshmallow boulder. "So, what were you doing out there again? Looking for something useful?"

Jerome retrieved his canteen to kill some time and to think about his next move. From the corner of his eye, he saw Stephen watching the entire scene play out. "Jump in anytime," Jerome whispered.

"You're doing just fine, Robert Brownie Junior," Stephen wiggled.

"Well," Jerome improvised for Balthus, "I had read about one particular artifact, an old magic that it's said could bring greatness to those who possessed it."

"I know exactly what you're talking about," Balthus cut in.

Jerome turned and blinked. "You do? Really?"

"Of course! And it's not out there!" He gestured towards the border of the lands. "It's here, in the castle. Damned fools don't know what they have in it."

"Are you... what? Seriously? It's here, in the castle?"

"Did all the cakes that you ate clog your ears, tubby? Yes, it's here, in the castle. I found it that one time after I finished with Audrey, the wax lips. Brought it to Lord Flanta, but the idiot didn't realize exactly what it was. That, or he didn't believe me. So, he threw it in a storage room down in the castle, and there it sits. I can take you straight to it."

"Hang on," Jerome said, holding up a hand. "Where did you find it after you spent time with Audrey?"

"In a barn. It was just lying there in the straw. I went in looking for a chocolate bunny or animal cracker to ride out of that town, and there it was. Of course, I realized what it was immediately."

Jerome looked at Stephen, who only shrugged. He next looked at Cleetus, who gave a slow, lazy blink. Finally, he turned back to Balthus. "Let's go, then!"

"Ah, hang on there, tons of fun, I'm not just going to take you to it and then come back out here to die. You gotta do something for me in return."

"Absolutely. Anything."

"You have to convince Lord Flanta to let me live out my days in the castle in comfort. No more of this leaving-me-out-in-the-waste-lands bullshit. I want a room, a good baker's mat bed, and plenty of simple syrup. And I want someone to track down Audrey, too. I could use a good... waxing."

Jerome swallowed hard. Could he really do all that? Passing the eye test with one sun-baked, old and dying cookie was one thing, but convincing the king of the Danish Wedding Cookies that he was one of them was something completely different. Jerome snuck a glance at his sugar-coated arm. He'd need another dousing before getting to the castle, that was for sure.

Stephen blinked and wiggled into view, the gesture clearly stating: "Don't do it."

He looked back at Balthus. *I have to,* he thought. He conjured an image of Kupcake in his mind, with her beautiful cake, her perfect frosting, and her one eye slightly higher than the other. He shook his head and thought, no, that was just in his picture back home. He was pretty sure her eyes were symmetrical. Mostly.

I have to do this. I can do this. For her. Anything for her, to get her home safe. It doesn't matter what happens to me, or what I have to go through, as long as I can get her back safely.

The old cookie stood rocking back and forth on his feet, waiting for Jerome to make a move. Finally, Jerome nodded. "Let's go. I'd be happy to speak to Lord Flanta on your behalf." That didn't seem to satisfy Balthus, so he added, "I will even go to my father and guarantee that he pays you what he owes you. It's the least I can do."

Balthus' face split into a wide grin, showing crumbling teeth lined with his own powdered sugar. "Alright, chunk, we got a deal. Come on."

Behind him, Jerome could hear the wiggling facepalm of Stephen, accompanied by: "You dumb muffin bastard."

17

Stuart eyed the package warily, an electric tingle running through him. Something wasn't right about it. The box was soft pink, its hard shell bound with simple brown twine. It wasn't big at all – only a few inches square. Just big enough to hold a couple of cookies or very small pastries.

The box now sat on a small table which was innocuous in its smallness. However, considering the method of its arrival - in the hands of another gummy pickle, who had personally handed it over to Stuart with a slimy smile – it caused fear to grip the king's personal aide. Now, Stuart had the most unpleasant task of delivering it to his lord and master. Taking a deep breath, he picked the box up, still feeling surprised by its weight, and entered the Cake Stand Room.

King Red Velvet sat atop his ornate cake stand, speaking in a low voice with his Minister of Finance. Stuart wondered if the monarch was considering paying Devil's Food Cake a hefty ransom to return Princess Kupcake. He felt anger and frustration swirl within him at the prospect of rolling over and paying that disgusting, foul-hearted cake anything. But what other options did they have? The king would never go there personally, and yet that seemed to be the only option Devil's Food Cake would consider. The other option seemed to be war. But would King Red Velvet really consider calling in the aprons and bringing all those loyal to him up against the sour forces within the Black Licorice Castle? King Red Velvet abhorred the idea of fighting, but surely the possibility was being considered.

Yet, Stuart had to admit that there had been a sense of trepidation on the part of the king. It was almost as if he felt too nervous to do what most everyone felt needed to be done in order to have Kupcake returned safely.

Put those doubts out of your head, he admonished himself. *The king will do what's right and Kupcake will be returned soon.*

Slowly, Stuart crossed the expanse of the Cake Stand Room's floor, his feet echoing softly against the stone. As he approached, the king and the minister noticed his presence. They whispered something more to one another before the minister nodded and stepped away. The oatmeal cookie didn't acknowledge Stuart as he approached. Stuart didn't mind the rebuff, as it was commonplace for those higher in the hierarchy to ignore assistants or anyone lower than them. Plus, the Minister of Finance was about as pleasant as yogu—

Stuart's mind shut off the word as a shudder coursed through him. He whispered a quick prayer to the Great Baker Herself that he be forgiven for even thinking of such a vile, evil thing, and then focused his attention back on the king.

"What's this?" King Red Velvet asked, his voice thin and weary with stress and emotion.

Hearing the pain in his lord's voice and seeing the wetness barely contained within the confection's eyes, Stuart swallowed a large lump. He had no idea what was in the box, but considering its source, he was certain it wouldn't be anything good. He fought against his duty to respond to the question and presented the box.

"You've a delivery, my lord," Stuart managed, holding the box up.

King Red Velvet's eyes settled on the object. Stuart saw something dark shift behind the king's gaze, and felt his heart crumble a little more at the cake's ordeal.

"Where did it come from?"

"A... gummy pickle delivered it just now, sire."

"Where is it now? The pickle? Was it that same smarmy one from earlier?"

"No, sire, a different pickle this time. It's in an antechamber just off the main gate. Guarded by four of our best."

The king nodded and took the box. Slowly, he undid the twine and, after a moment's pause, opened the box's lid. King Red Velvet's face was stone for a long moment as he beheld what was within the box. Then, he took in a loud, shuddering breath and let the box slip from his fingers. It bounced gently and landed at the base of the Royal Cake Stand.

Stuart moved to pick the box up. He lifted it, this time feeling white hot terror coursing through his cookie and peanut butter frame. "Holy Rolling Pin," he croaked.

The box was filled with a wide, thick, ragged piece of torn chocolate cake topped with frosting. The best, lightest, most perfect peanut-butter buttercream frosting.

18

The castle of Lord Flanta, King of the Danish Wedding Cookies, looked to Jerome like what a castle would be if designed by a young chocolate chip... if said chip had been dropped on its point a few times and then given parchment paper and pencil. The multi-colored structure was made from a combination of candy stones and marshmallow boulders. However, it slanted in areas where it shouldn't, and its towers rose crookedly. As Jerome and his companions approached, he even noticed that one tower - if it could be called that - jutted out from the side of a wall and was suspended (how, he had no idea) parallel to the ground. Windows looked out at all angles from around the horizontal... well, it was a tube, he supposed. The tower ended in a cone-shaped point, the flag mounted atop it hanging down as if held up by a stiff breeze. "You've a good eye, my boy," Balthus said. "That's the Super Tall and Straight Tower from Where You Can See Everywhere. It was designed by Rick."

"Who's Rick?"

Balthus shrugged. "He's Rick."

A moat of thick sludge circled the castle, and Jerome eyed it with more than a little disgust and rolling of the stomach as they crossed the narrow drawbridge.

Balthus saw Jerome studying the viscous liquid and said, "King Flanta tends to take the bodies of his enemies or any of those who have disappointed him and crumble them into the moat. That's what gives it the thickness. It also serves as a warning to all of those out there—" he waved an arm in the direction from which they'd come, "who may be foolish enough to consider attacking."

Or those inside who are considered anything that could irritate the king, Jerome thought, and he once more risked a glance at his powder-coated body.

They were stopped at the castle gates by a pair of guards holding plastic toothpick swords that looked like they'd been left in a baker's oven too long, their blades drooped and curved comically. Neither guard seemed to mind, and they raised the bent weapons menacingly.

"What business do you have here?" one demanded, shaking his sagging sword at the new arrivals.

Balthus cleared his throat and stepped forward. "Stand aside, you ridiculous crumb. I'm here to see Lord Flanta. Don't you know who I am?"

The second guard squinted and looked Balthus up and down, then shifted his gaze to Jerome. Jerome felt his cake recoil in fear over the effectiveness of his disguise. "Yeah, I think I know you," the second guard said. "Ain't you the one who the king sent to dry out and crumble?"

Balthus flapped a hand dismissively. "I have someone to present to Lord Flanta. Jerome here is one of our fellow citizens who has spent a lot of time in the Outlands and who wishes to bring news of his journeys to the king."

The guards turned their full attention to Jerome, who stood stock still and gave what he hoped was a reassuring smile. Slowly, incrementally, the first guard's eyes widened. His powdered-sugar coating seemed to pale even beyond its natural color and he gasped, "Oh, my great Rolling Pin, it's you!"

Jerome's cake guts twisted. He took a slow step backwards, reaching behind him for Cleetus' reins in case they had to make a run for it.

The guard moved forward and placed one hand on Jerome's chest. The hand was hot and moist, and Jerome pulled away in fear that the touch would rub off some of his disguise. Plus, it felt really icky, like the guard had been handling moist fondant.

"Who is it, then?" the second guard asked.

The first guard, his eyes locked on Jerome's face, said, "Him! It's him! He's the one who... we have to get him to Lord Flanta immediately!" He backed away and gestured for Jerome to follow. "Come with me. The king is right this way." Without waiting, the Danish Wedding Cookie guard moved down the hallway.

As they followed, stepping carefully over the warped and twisted floors, and ducking in places where the ceiling dipped low, Jerome looked at Balthus – who ignored his companions. The guard led them on for what felt like miles through broken, twisted, and rolling corridors that most confections would have described as having been designed by the completely insane, and with the express purpose of rendering any who passed along them as mad as a sun-bleached brownie.

Occasionally, they would pass rooms in which Jerome could see broken or rotting furniture, along with the random Danish Wedding Cookie who was often mumbling to itself or arguing violently with another of its kind. These cookies would sometimes see the group and, spying Jerome, exclaim something unintelligible before rushing out into the hallway to start following the group. By the time they'd reached what was supposed to be an arched doorway – but in reality looked like it had been designed by a cross-eyed gummy monkey – they had a following of close to thirty cookies, all of them talking and arguing excitedly. Over the bent and weirdly angled arch were large letters proclaiming that, beyond it, there lay the Great For Company But Still Perfectly Fine For Everyday Use Cookie Platter Room.

The cookie platter room was just as warped as the rest of the castle, with buckling floors and ceilings. In more than one spot,

Jerome saw windows, with their glass made of spun sugar, embedded in the floors. Some gave a vista into the room or corridor below while others bisected a wall. Most were simply dark on the other side.

Scattered around the room, along the walls and on the raised steps to the dais, stood a multitude of Danish Wedding Cookies. They'd all ceased talking when Jerome crossed the room's threshold, their wild eyes following his movements across the floor.

Panic tugged at the edges of Jerome's mind. At no time had the guard leading them stopped or even slowed down enough to pay attention to the muffin's repeated requests for a brief stop in a restroom. Jerome desperately wanted to re-apply more powdered sugar. It would only be a matter of time before his muffinness showed through, and then it would be all over. Kupcake would never be rescued.

He let the memory of her, with the sound of her laughter, fill his thoughts, and he felt the immediate calming effects. His chest swelled with love and affection for her.

I got this. Totally have this, he repeated to himself.

Jerome focused on that feeling as the guard led them to the base of the dais and looked up at Lord Flanta, who sat on a wide, grey cookie platter. The King of the Danish Wedding Cookies was a large cookie whose crust was completely hidden beneath a thick coating of powdered sugar. Held loosely in one of his hands was a green French rolling pin scepter.

The guard and Balthus dropped to one knee, their heads bowing. Jerome hesitated only for a second, during which Stephen gestured at him, "Get down, jackass," and lowered himself to one knee, as well.

As they knelt, Jerome heard soft whisperings from the contingent behind them, and then heard the voices spread to those around the room. *Kupcake, give me strength*, he thought. *Please don't let them see through this disguise.*

"Stand," came the command from the king. The group rose, and Flanta asked, "What is all this?"

Balthus shifted uncomfortably, and Jerome could see the cookie's fear. The guard spoke first. "Sire, your highness, he of the most dense and strong cookie and thickest sugar, I have brought you... the savior."

As he'd said that, he'd pointed at Jerome and backed away quickly.

Gasps thundered through the chamber and more than a few cookies shouted unintelligible thoughts, but Flanta held up a hand and the room slowly fell to silence.

"The... savior?" he repeated, stretching out the last word incredulously.

"Yes, sire, he is the one who has come from near the Outlands border, come to save us from the impending invasion."

King Flanta jerked at the proclamation as the room once again erupted into screams.

"...save us from the lemon squares..."

"...has to be a lemon square spy..."

"...we should sacrifice him to appease the lemon squares – it's our only hope!"

"...I prefer brownies, and I'm not ashamed to admit it anymore!"

Jerome looked down at Stephen, who only blinked, and then turned his attention to the cookies surrounding them. Many seemed as warped as the castle itself, their powdered sugar barely coating their bodies. Several cookies, he saw, were arguing vehemently with the floor or the wall, one even gesturing wildly as it screamed at a tinfoil-wrapper suit of armor.

"They're all mad," Jerome mumbled to himself.

Stephen shuffled: "You see a drinking fountain we can throw through a window to get out of here?"

The exclamations continued, with the audience seemingly torn between deciding if he were some savior, a spy, or a sacrifice.

"State your purpose here!" the king said loudly, his voice slicing through the din. The king leaned forward, and the other cookies lowered their voices to a low rumble rather than pitched shouting.

Jerome shuffled from foot to foot, his mind racing. "They are right. I am the savior! I, too, have heard about the armies of the lemon squares massing in the hills beyond our borders," he said before he'd even realized he was speaking.

"Dude... what the fuck?" Stephen blinked.

"Even on my father's farm, where we grow sugar cane to be converted to powdered sugar, we've seen evidence of their scouts. We've heard of them burning other villages just beyond our borders! They terrorize good, law-abiding cookies and pastries, and to this, I say, 'No more!' We will not sit back and take this abuse! We will not roll over like so many timid gummy bears!" He turned to Cleetus and mouthed 'Sorry.' "No! We will fight! We will guard our lands and our fellow cookies with everything we have; we will crumble rather than kneel before those disgusting lemon squares! I have come all this way, and even spent time in the Outlands, searching for a weapon, one that I have read will eliminate the lemon squares completely and allow us to live in peace for the rest of our days! It's only that... well... I learned that it's actually here, in the castle somewhere."

The entire chamber went silent, every cookie staring open-mouthed at Jerome. Even Stephen seemed to be agape. Slowly, the peep blinked: "What. The. Fuck."

The king cleared his throat and shifted on his stand. "We will address this 'weapon' soon enough. But tell me again about your origins and this farm of yours."

As the king spoke, Jerome felt the air in the room shift, but to what he wasn't exactly certain. "Yes," he said, stalling for time, "it's a modest farm far to the north, only a mile or two from the border. My father and I run the farm, my dear mother having dried and crumbled years ago when I was but a small morsel. We grow, as I said only a few moments ago, if you'll recall, sugar. We harvest the sugar and, um, do stuff to it to convert it to powdered sugar which we, uh, then sell to...." His voice trailed off as his brain caught up to the fact that he was talking completely out of his muffin wrapper.

"You sell it to whom?" the king asked, his voice deep with suspicion now.

Jerome's mouth worked, and he felt a bit like a Swedish Fish.

"He's a small cookie, a local vendor. Name's Bernie. You probably don't know him."

King Flanta studied Jerome for a long moment. The cookie's eyes bored into Jerome's cake, and it seemed as if the temperature in the room increased. Finally, Flanta spoke again: "Who are you really?"

"I... I told you, I'm Jerome from a farm up north where we—"

"We don't have farms here. Especially not farms that produce sugar. Every cookie knows that our powdered sugar comes from a magic bowl situated on the fifth floor of this very castle. So, no, you aren't a simple sugar farmer from up north. Granted, you must be immensely brave to have tamed a gummy bear, but no self-respecting Danish Wedding Cookie consorts with... those... things!" He'd spat the last word, and pointed accusingly at Stephen. To the peep's credit, he kept all vocal motions to himself.

Jerome opened his mouth, his muscles now firmly under his control even if most of the feeling in his body had exited via his feet with a slow, draining sensation. Before he could say anything to attempt to reverse what was happening, Flanta cut him off.

"No, you're certainly no farmer. And you sure as oven aren't the savior. I don't know how you did it, entering our realm as one of us, but I can only assume that you're either acting on your own - which is in itself no good - or you are indeed a spy or emissary of the lemon squares who, even now, threaten our very way of life, not to mention our existence!"

At the king's words, the hall erupted in cries once again. Jerome's ears picked up the same arguments – that he was a savior, he was a spy, and he was just one of them who had certainly gone mad. He even heard a few cookies arguing that he was a new baker sent to help the females of the realm create more Danish Wedding Cookies. Faintly, he heard one cookie ranting loudly about how his love for brownies could no longer be contained and he didn't care what Mike said about it.

"Take them all to the dungeon!" Flanta commanded.

19

Jerome leaned back against the grimy wall, feeling its rough edges digging into his cake. Most of his powdered sugar disguise had long since rubbed off, and as he sat in the dingy darkness, he found it difficult to care. Balthus, upon seeing Jerome's true self exposed, had simply grunted and nodded as if it was nothing more than what he'd expected. The old cookie had given Jerome a good look before he'd moved off into the darkness while mumbling something about a muffin coming to save them all from lemon squares.

Jerome wondered, not for the first time, where Stephen and Cleetus had been taken. When they'd departed the cookie platter room, the guards had split them up, leading them down separate warped corridors with signs reading "Sticky Buns Suites" and "Absolutely Not the Dungeon" while his hall had a sign reading "Icky Sticky Dungeons This Way". He swallowed a painful lump at the thought of Cleetus being alone and scared in a cell, not understanding why he was alone or where Jerome was or why they'd been separated. Tears swelled in Jerome's eyes, and he rubbed the syrup drops away with the back of one hand.

A soft scraping sound reached him from the darkness beyond his immediate vision. Although he'd not explored much after being tossed in through the main gate, Jerome got the sense that the dungeon was massive. As he'd sat there lamenting the latest developments in his journey, he had heard the occasional moan or sound of movement far off in the darkness. There was light in the large chamber, too, but it was soft, muted, and didn't provide enough illumination to allow one's eyes to ever fully focus on anything until it was very close.

He'd seen a few of the unfortunates trapped down here with him, most of them being haggard and chipped cookies - more than a few Danish Wedding Cookies, most mumbling to someone named Ikehorn as they shuffled through the darkness - and the occasional odd pastry. The fact that Jerome had rarely seen them spoke to the sheer expanse of the dungeon.

A fresh round of shuffling steps came out of the gloom, and Jerome tensed, readying himself to spring up if the large, dried-up twinkie was coming back. Jerome had learned the spongy creature had been stuck in the cells for weeks, and as a result, its mind had twisted worse than the floors and walls of the castle itself. Not that twinkies had ever been known for their ability to do higher math or even remember simple shopping lists, but still. Soon after the guards had closed the door behind Jerome, the twinkie had found him, its mouth slack and with small rivulets of cream oozing over its gums and falling on the floor with soft, wet splats. It had approached in jerking motions, its fingers working greedily. "Eat you," the twinkie had hissed. Each time, Jerome had managed to find a small rock or other item to throw at it, the object denting the sponge and driving the demented snack cake back into the shadows.

Now, the scraping sounds grew louder, the vague shape of Balthus materializing and growing clear. Jerome gritted his teeth. What did the old crumb want now?

"You never spoke to the king on my behalf," Balthus' voice floated ahead of him. "We had an agreement."

Jerome stood up, his rage boiling within him like the hot center of a lava cake. "An agreement? You're coming to me now with this shit?

The agreement was that you'd take me to the weapon, and then I would speak to the king. Instead, you led me straight into a room full of cookies as insane as..." his mind searched for the right phrase, "as... Danish Wedding Cookies! All of whom seemed to be confused as to whether I was a savior or a spy of a—" he made air quotes with his fingers, "lemon square army threatening to invade the land! Like that's even a thing!"

Balthus stopped a few feet away. "First of all, there actually is an army of lemon squares. They tend to keep to themselves in the Sugar Plum Mountains. We Danish Wedding Cookies are at constant war with them, and the squares send raiding parties close to and sometimes just inside our borders. And, third, you are close to the weapon. I never said in which order we would do things. But since I brought you to the king first, why didn't you get him to agree to let me live here in the castle rather than out in the wastelands?"

Jerome started forward, ready to pound the idiot cookie into crumbs, and then crush those crumbs into dust and then scoop up the dust and pour it down the nearest drain... when something the cookie had said stopped to him.

"We're near the weapon?"

"Why didn't you convince the king?" Balthus shot back indignantly.

Jerome swallowed his fury. Continuing down this path would be like beating his head against the baker's counter and would never achieve anything. "I did," he said. "Don't you remember?"

"What?"

"I did convince him to let you live here in the castle. See?" He held his hands out, indicating their current surroundings. "We're in the castle, and I'm pretty sure King Flanta is going to let you stay here for the rest of your days. So, no more drying out in the sun. No more searching for simple syrup. No more worrying about where you're going to sleep. You're here in the castle, in the lap of luxury."

Balthus considered this, the fingertips of one of his hands resting on his lower lip. He turned and surveyed the room. His face lit up as he turned back to Jerome. "You're right! This is pretty great! You did it! I had complete faith in you, my boy. Never once doubted you. Wonderful!"

Jerome breathed a silent sigh of relief. "So, you'll take me to the weapon?"

"Oh, Holy Rolling Pin, yes. Absolutely! Come on, it's this way."

Keeping close on the cookie's heels, Jerome followed Balthus through the dark wetness of the dungeon. As they progressed, he heard rather than saw a few other guests of King Flanta: ragged breathing, the soft patter of cookies crumbling to the stone floor, and even pastries being asked if they wanted to renew their home warranty.

Again, Jerome marveled at how large and open the dungeon was. From what he understood, King Red Velvet had a dungeon that boasted individual cells into which offenders were thrown. But Flanta just had one large open area closed off by the occasional gate. Again he wondered why Stephen and Cleetus hadn't been brought to the same chamber as him. They arrived at one such gate and, without pausing, Balthus pushed it open and stepped through. Jerome stopped short. "How... what?"

Balthus stopped and turned back. "What? This gate is always open. It doesn't lead out of the dungeon – only into the storage areas. Come on."

Shaking his head, Jerome followed. They stumbled over the uneven floor and past doorways through which Jerome could see only inky blackness, but from which emanated the soft and sour aroma of mildew.

They continued deeper into the darkness, and Jerome began to wonder if his guide, like most every other Danish Wedding Cookie he'd met, was just insane and had forgotten where they were going. He half-expected Balthus to turn at any moment and seem surprised that Jerome was even there, while asking if the muffin knew where they were heading.

Jerome was about to speak up when Balthus came to a quick stop, forcing Jerome to dance to one side and bump against the wet, grimy wall in order to avoid knocking them both down.

"Something wrong?" he asked the cookie, who looked to be peering off to one side.

"We're here. Can't you feel its power?" Balthus' voice seemed to scrape against the very air.

Jerome waited, controlling his breathing and focusing on feeling. He felt nothing but cold and more than a little wetness from where he'd bumped against the wall. His stomach growled. One of his ears itched.

Balthus stepped out of the main corridor and entered an open doorway. A soft click and a scrape came, and then light flared in the blackness as Balthus lit a large candle. He held it up and faced Jerome, clearly waiting for the muffin to enter the room with him.

Jerome gaped. "There are candles down here?"

"Of course. Why wouldn't there be?"

"Are they in the main dungeon cell, too?"

"Well, yes, there's one about every ten feet on the walls."

"Why...?" Jerome's voice was shrill, and his throat constricted on the word. "Why aren't they lit? Why don't the confections stuck in there light the damned things and at least have something to see by?"

Balthus looked confused, as if he were talking to a gumdrop that had been created to be missing most of its sugar coating. "Because they're prisoners. Having light like that rather defeats the purpose of sitting in the dungeon, don't you think?"

"What...?" Jerome managed, and then he shook his head. "You know what? It doesn't matter. I don't have the time or the energy. What is this?"

Balthus looked around. "This is Storage Room 217." He held the candle higher, and Jerome could see in the soft illumination that there were dozens and dozens of wooden crates of various sizes all stacked haphazardly atop one another in a massive pile. Some were open, their lids laying askew next to them, whereas others remained sealed tight. Interspersed throughout the room were occasional crates whose wood had begun to rot and collapse.

"It's here?" he asked. He swallowed thickly against a dry throat.

"The last time I saw it, yes. Flanta had no idea what he possessed, so he had it brought down here."

"You don't happen to remember what crate it was in, do you?"

Balthus scoffed. "Do you think I'm as loony as those cracked cookies up there? Of course, I remember." He gestured towards the ceiling. "It was a brown one, I think." His face screwed up as he fought to remember more. "I want to say that it had the image of an animal cracker yak on it."

"A yak."

Balthus held an arm up to his face, letting his hand dangle down. He swung it from side to side, imitating a long nose or trunk. "A yak."

"That's an animal cracker elephant, you twit."

"Agree to disagree. Either way, no sense in debating it. Get to looking. I'll start over here."

Jerome bit his lip and stepped towards the closest box. The lid was slightly off-center, and he pushed it off. Inside, he saw mutely colored plastic straw. Nestled within the straw was a warped purple picture frame surrounding a badly painted image of King Flanta standing atop the highest peak of the Sugar Plum Mountains, with scores of dead lemon squares at his feet.

This is going to take forever, Jerome thought as he looked to the next box. It contained some old and cracked plates. Jerome let out a groan. He heard the thumps and rattles of Balthus sifting through boxes on the other end of the room.

Jerome buried himself in the work, moving methodically from box to box. The inventory found in each ranged from dinnerware to art to candles and other room decor to - oddly - lots of muffin and cupcake wrappers. He even found, in one large box, several cake toppers that featured the impression of King Flanta holding hands with a myriad of confections (both male and female) as well as more than a few animal crackers. It seemed that the coordinators of any potential wedding wanted to be prepared for any eventuality.

Time passed, marked only by the bumping and scraping of boxes and lids, along with soft grunts and gasps that came from Jerome and Balthus as they worked their way through the large storage room.

Jerome was pulling away yet another half-rotted lid when he heard Balthus gasp. He turned, but the Danish Wedding Cookie was lost to sight because of the piles of boxes between them.

"What is it?" Jerome called.

There was a scrambling noise, and the sound of boxes being disturbed and clattering together before falling to the ground. Then, Balthus appeared, breathing as if he'd just run a marathon. "I found it!" he cried as he waded, stumbling, through opened and overturned crates. Jerome's heart leapt into his throat as he looked at the object the cookie held up reverently.

But his words caught in his throat and he furrowed his brow as he looked at the object. "Um, Balthus?"

"It's glorious, isn't it?"

"It's a rusted whisk." To Jerome, the old crank-handle whisk looked like it had already settled in for a good decaying somewhere when it had been stuffed into a box. He could almost hear its desperate wishes for a quick slip into oblivion.

"Well, sure, it needs a little polishing, but this is it! The greatest weapon ever created! With this in your hands, you'll be able to defeat those lemon squares handily. It's pitiful that King Flanta had it put down here; he clearly had no idea of its importa—"

"Balthus."

"—nce. Yes, we'll clean it up and get it—"

"Balthus!"

"—out to the Sugar Plum Mountains, and you'll see. What? Why are you staring at me like that?"

"That's not the weapon."

Balthus blinked, and then he looked down at the whisk in his hands. "What do you mean? Of course, it is."

Jerome sighed. "I'm looking for the Piping Bag of Ganache. I was told it's here."

Balthus' face wrinkled in disgust and confusion. "That old thing? Why the oven would you want that?"

Jerome felt hope surge within him again. He gripped the cookie's arm, pulling Balthus close. "You know where it is?"

Balthus shrugged as best he could with one arm gripped by the muffin disguised as a cookie. "Yeah. I saw it like four boxes ago. But trust me, you don't want that thing." He hefted the whisk again. It rattled pitifully in his grasp, the rotting remnants of the wood grip on the handle slipping off with a weak thump. "This! This is what you want! Reduce your enemies to batter with this thing!"

Jerome barely heard the cookie as he scrambled away as fast as he could, pushing through and past boxes, sending them and their contents tumbling away in a furious landslide. "Where?" he screamed.

Balthus groaned, but then he called out, "Yellowish box over there on the left somewhere. Picture of a yak on it."

Jerome pushed and threw boxes away from him until his eyes finally rested on a box that was half-buried under several lids. The image of a gummy frog was burned into one side. The wood was old and yellowing, and the slats were several inches apart, almost giving him an unfettered view into the container. He saw more plastic straw inside as he threw the lid off, hurling it away like a frisbee.

There it lay, nestled in the straw like what it was, the holiest of artifacts. Jerome stared at it breathlessly. The Piping Bag of Ganache was about as long as a toothpick sword, with a wide canvas body laid flat like a deflated balloon. The bag's body tapered down to a single silver tip which ended in triangular spikes.

He picked it up, the bag heavy and limp in his hands. Studying it closely, he still saw nothing remarkable about it.

"How do you even use it?" he whispered. He looked through the remainder of the straw and found nothing that looked like frosting or icing to load into it.

"Useless," Balthus said from behind him. Jerome didn't respond, only continuing to look at the item in his hands. Surely, there was some trick to using it, but he couldn't think of what it would be. Without ammunition, the piping bag seemed to be exactly what Balthus had called it. Useless. How was Jerome supposed to use this to storm the Black Licorice Castle and rescue Kupcake?

Jerome let out a long, slow breath and turned to leave.

"How do we get out of here?" he asked as he carried the piping bag out of the storage room. Balthus followed, lugging along the rusted whisk.

"Well, now that we have this..." he rattled the whisk for emphasis, and the handle made a noise as if it were begging for the sweet release of a trash compactor. "We can overpower the guards. No, wait, that won't work; they're really good guys, despite having locked us in here. I'm sure they have families. We'll just have to explain to them that we need another audience with Flanta, and convince him to let us go forth on his behalf and do battle with the lemon squares."

"I thought you were going to stay here?"

Balthus screwed up his face in a look that suggested Jerome had tried to sell him time-share. "What?"

"I convinced Flanta to let you stay here, remember?"

The Danish Wedding Cookie seemed to consider that then brightened. "Right. But you agreed to help me lead an attack on the Lemon Squares if you recall."

"I never said that at all," Jerome interjected but Balthus ignored him, lost in his own monologue.

"So once we show Lord Flanta that we have the whisk, he'll immediately authorize the mission."

"I have to rescue Kupcake first."

"Who? Oh. Still holding onto that fantasy, eh? Okay. We'll pop down there, get her out and then you'll come with me to help drive out the Lemon Squares."

Jerome was getting tired of sighing, but he felt another one escape his lips. "Fine. Let's go back to the main room and see if we can get the guards' attention."

He followed Balthus along the corridor, on through the unlocked gate and into the main cell of the dungeon. The gloom pressed in, despite the candle that Balthus carried. Jerome heard Balthus move ahead quickly, angling for the gate with guards. Another sound reached his ears as something approached from the left, however. He turned, bringing the piping bag up instinctively.

Bent and misshapen, the aging twinkie emerged from the dark.

Its spongy cake was matted with grime and beaten smooth from weeks of bumping into the various walls. It opened its mouth, ragged spongy teeth jutting outward. Beyond the broken crags of teeth, Jerome could see some of the creature's cream filling. It stared at him balefully with bloodshot eyes, one of which was drooping as the cake surrounding it decayed.

"C'mere," it rasped, reaching forward with its hands bent into claws. "I'm sick of seeing you. You and your perfect muffin cake. I'm going to eat you, boy. I'm going to eat you aaallll up."

Jerome stepped back, voicing a sharp warning, but the twinkie either didn't hear him or ignored him. One pitiful claw swiped the air, and Jerome felt the wind of its passage across his face. This twinkie was getting too close, he thought. He retreated again, but hit an uneven stone and went tumbling onto his ass.

The twinkie uttered a sound somewhere between an irritated snarl and a hungry screech as it darted forward. Time seemed to slow, and Jerome watched the creature scrabbling towards him, its eyes gleaming.

Beneath his arm, the piping bag seemed to grow, the canvass of the bag bulging and pressing into his side. Without thinking, Jerome squeezed it, aiming the nozzle at the twinkie.

A jet of brilliant frosting erupted from the spiked tip, hitting the twinkie directly in the face and knocking it backwards. The blast only lasted a moment, but when it stopped, the twinkie was more than half-covered. The deranged, spongy cake screamed in agony as the oozing sugary paste ate into his body, dissolving cake and filling all at once. The twinkie thrashed about until the glaze reached its arms and the skeletal appendages began disintegrating.

Seconds later, it was over. The twinkie was gone, only small pools of yellowish goo remaining behind to account for its existence. The piping bag deflated to its original state, its tip clean as if it'd never been used.

Jerome stood up with his heart pounding against the cake of his chest. Had that really just happened? Before he could give the matter any further thought, a thundering explosion rocked the castle. He staggered, fighting to stay on his feet. Through the rumbling and patter of dirt and small stones falling from the ceiling, he heard Balthus screaming after the guards who had, it seemed, abandoned their charges and begun heading towards the commotion. Jerome had started in that direction when three other deep booms reverberated throughout the dungeon.

"What's happening?" he yelled.

Balthus stood gripping the bars of the gate and staring into the now empty hallway. "Those cowards left. Something is happening."

"Obviously."

"And they just took off like spineless taffies! When I get my hands on them, I'll crumble them into the Sweetwater River, I swear to the Great Rolling Pin and the Holy Baker Herself. I'll make them sor—"

A scream followed by a series of loud crunches ripped through the din. "What was that?" Jerome asked, his voice trembling.

"Someone just died badly," Balthus answered as he stared into the suffused light of the hall. Slowly, a figure approached from around the corner, crumbs coating its entirety. As it approached, the crumbs sloughed off with a soft patter. The figure passed under a small candle that hadn't been disturbed in the explosions, and Jerome's breath caught.

"Stephen?"

The peep shook off the rest of the crumbs and blinked. "Who else did you think it would be? The Mother Baker?"

"Can you get us out of here?"

The peep shuffled as if to ask, "How much do you love me?"

"What?"

"Come on. You know you want to admit it. You think I have a sweet ass." The peep bent its head to take in the yellow billowiness of its hind quarters. With effort, it gave the section a little shake. "Admit it."

Jerome stared, mouth agape. "I...."

Stephen moved forward. "I knew it. I've seen you staring at my ass since I saved you from that damned congealed salad." The gate was unlocked, and Jerome and Balthus stepped free. Wordlessly, they followed the peep back down the hall and around the corner. Jerome stopped there, his feet refusing to move forward. He felt cake rising to the back of his throat.

"Holy Rolling Pin, Stephen, what did you do?"

The peep regarded the shattered and scattered remains of both Danish Wedding Cookie guards. "You don't want to know. They died hard."

Jerome bent and plucked up a discarded sword from amidst the wreckage. Stepping carefully, he and his companions picked their way through the remains of the guards and continued down the hall.

"The explosions stopped," Balthus acknowledged.

Stephen wriggled. "Yeah, I couldn't keep them up and rescue you guys at the same time."

Jerome, not breaking stride, asked, "What did you do?"

"I made them think the lemon squares were attacking."

"How?"

"Dude, do you really want to know the intimate details of how I rescued you, or do you just want to accept that you're free and we can get the hell out of this raisin bin?"

"We have to get Cleetus first."

"Who?" Balthus asked.

"My gummy bear. I'm not leaving without him."

"Yeah, I know where that tubby bitch is." Stephen gestured. "It's not far."

Jerome followed, all of his focus on Cleetus. Once again, his cake guts twisted at the thought of the poor bear having been left alone, separated from him by their captors. The Great Mother Baker Herself only knew what had been done to the pitiful creature.

Stephen led them through a series of corridors. Around them, they could hear the screams of Danish Wedding Cookies, with calls to arms and shouted confusion as to exactly which side of the castle was being attacked. Twice, they paused as a group of cookies rushed past, weapons clattering as they ran towards the presumed battle.

Finally, they stopped before a large, rounded door. "In there," he nodded. Jerome hesitated, steeling himself for the onslaught of horrible feelings that would accompany the confirmation of all of his fears. In an instant, dozens of appalling images flashed through his mind: Cleetus chained to a wall, with no food or water to be had; Cleetus being beaten repeatedly by cruel guards who laughed at his pained moans; Cleetus strapped to a table and being forced to endure endless poking, prodding, and cutting by malicious torturers. Jerome set his jaw and forced the door open – stepping through quickly, ready to bring the piping bag up for vengeance on anyone mistreating his friend and, if needed, swift release for the gummy bear.

Cleetus sat sprawled among dozens of thick marshmallow pillows. Around him lay multiple trays of simple syrup. Overhead were twisted, wide-bladed fans made of taffy. Jerome was several steps into the room before his mind registered what he was seeing, and before he realized that there was actual music flowing into the room from hidden speakers.

The gummy bear looked up from where he had been sleeping and blinked lazily at the intruders.

"Cleetus?" Jerome asked. The bear yawned in response.

"I told you this fat fucker was fine," Stephen wriggled.

"You said nothing like that," Jerome said. Stephen just shrugged.

It took Jerome a good ten minutes to convince Cleetus to leave the room. In the end, he had to agree to bring three of the pails of syrup and several of the bear's new favorite pillows. He drew the line at agreeing to Stephen's suggestion that Jerome sing to the bear.

Together, the group hurried along corridors towards the exit.

20

Kupcake shifted on the silicone baker's mat bed and stared at the ceiling. Pain from where the offset spatula had been employed rolled across her sponge in occasional waves. As of yet, she'd not mustered the courage to look at the damage in the mirror. Her frosting, something she'd always taken a great deal of pride in, was not the same... and it would never be the same. She knew that. And she was lucky to still have a lot of it left.

But to have it taken forcefully like that. To be held down by German Chocolate Cake and have that tool scraped across her.... *Nope*, she told herself. *Not doing this.* She promptly kicked the memory in the crotch and, while it was bent over cupping its family berries, she threw it out and firmly slammed the door behind it. That it had happened was bad enough; she didn't need to dwell on it, living through the moment over and over again. That would accomplish nothing and wouldn't get her any closer to escaping.

Escaping. In her mind, the word felt like a cruel joke. There was no escaping her confines. Since German Chocolate's scraping, she'd not been able to muster the energy to pick up the dresser drawer handle and continue her assault on the bars of the window. That avenue of attack was pointless anyway, she knew. Black licorice was one of the hardest substances known to confections. She could chisel away at it every day for the rest of her life and barely make a dent in it.

So, what else can you do? The question cut through the wave of self-pity that the memory hurled against the walls of her mind. *Think, cake, think. What else do you have that you can use to get out of here?*

She sat up, swung her legs over the edge of the mat, and considered the room. There was the thin blanket she'd been given. What could she do with that? It would serve no purpose as a means of climbing out the window, considering she'd have to be on a ground floor for it to be long enough, even cut up and tied together. And while she didn't know much, she was certain she wasn't on the ground floor.

She could fake a need for the guard outside. Perhaps when he opened the door, she could yell that there was a ghost in her room. She'd heard that this guard had been terrified of ghosts ever since he'd played with a spirit recipe and been visited by the irritated ghost of his mother, who'd berated him for leaving his underwear all over her house. Then, Kupcake could throw the blanket over the guard's face and yell: "She's come back for you! She found your dirty socks this time!" And while he wrestled with the thin sheet, she could dart past it and out into the corridor, locking the door behind her.

But where would she go? She had no idea of the layout of the castle, and no clue where the main gate - or any gate, for that matter - lay. There were sour straws and jawbreakers everywhere. It would only be a matter of time before one of them caught her.

Frustrated, she stood and marched to the window, gripping the bars tightly. She pulled on them, feeling their solidity. If only she'd had some caustic soda. That ingredient along with a couple of other, rather easily obtainable materials would get her a mixture she'd come up with before. She'd come across it completely by accident. She'd been intending to make a new kind of pretzel, one that would provide enough food to feed entire townships for weeks without going stale. She'd misread some of her own notes - her handwriting was atrocious, she hated to admit - and added the wrong component at the wrong time. Before she'd known it, the bowl, table, and floor beneath her had been eaten through, the substance oozing towards the lower floors.

Luckily, nobody had been in the lower rooms and the substance had halted as soon as it had hit the bottom of her father's castle. To explain it away, she'd blamed the series of holes on chocolate ants. Her father had had the entire castle fumigated after that.

Kupcake looked out to the grey, leaden sky beyond her window and smiled at the memory.

Reality crept back in as she realized that, even if she could get those other substances brought to her - they were very common in almost every kitchen - she still had no caustic soda. That would be more difficult to procure.

She sighed and pushed away from the bars, returning to the silicone mat bed. It was no use. Devil's Food Cake was going to keep her here until he had reduced her father to crumbs and claimed the cakedom for himself. She was pretty sure he wouldn't let her go even then. No, he'd keep her around for quite some time. If not forcing her to be his bride, then at the very least keeping her as something to be gawked at, to be laughed at, to punish for her very existence.

Why hadn't her father sent for her yet? Why hadn't he brought an army and stormed the Black Licorice Castle yet? Surely, he had the numbers, with the rock candy guards. He had enough men and equipment to lay siege to this horrible castle and force Devil's Food Cake to release her. Or to invade the castle walls and take her back.

And what had Devil's Food Cake meant about his history with her father? Not once had she ever seen Devil's Food Cake in the castle. In fact, every time the dark confection's name was mentioned, it was with disgust and a look of—

The thought broke off as another rushed in like a neighbor trying to sell the latest in Mary Cake frostings and sprinkles (guaranteed to make you the envy of all the ladies, they always boasted, but you usually ended up looking like someone who'd been driven out of Trifle Town). Had that been a look of sorrow and shame that had brushed over her father's cake like a glaze at the mention of the Dark One? She closed her eyes and tried to conjure a clearer picture within the memories, but all of the images stayed just beneath the shimmering surface of the past. There was something there, though, she knew it. Some connection between her father and her captor.

It didn't matter, she told herself. Whatever past they had - if they even did have one - while it might have been a contributing factor in her imprisonment, meant nothing now. Now, she just wanted her father to rescue her. Surely, he was on his way. Her eyes drifted to the heavy wooden door that kept her confined to the small room, part of her expecting to see it fly open under the force of a well-placed boot and for her father stride in, a wide smile on his face.

And then there was Jerome to think of. Jerome, with his easy smile, quick wit, and humble charm. And Cleetus. The corners of her mouth twitched in a smile at the thought of the bear; she loved that slow gummy bear. But Jerome must be devastated. What was he possibly going through right now, with nobody to talk to or commensurate with? With no news of what plans may be coming together to speed along her rescue? Her poor muffin was all alone, helpless. The thought of Jerome sitting in his house or caring for Cleetus, all the while worrying about what had befallen the princess, threatened to break her heart like peanut brittle.

Out of the blue, a fantasy flitted across her mind – that of Jerome riding Cleetus across the lands, toothpick sword held high as he charged the Black Licorice Castle in a one-man assault. Jerome hacking away at the black licorice walls in an attempt to carve his way inside.

She smiled. He was the greatest confection she'd ever known, but bravery and adventure had never really been his strongest suits. Oh, he was brave, certainly, but more in the way of ordering a meal without waffling over a choice. Unless there were three kinds of pie to choose from, and then he could get bogged down in indecision. But still, he was brave.

Okay, maybe not so much when it came to gummy spiders, though. She thought back to the time when she'd rescued Jerome from a gummy spider that had crawled a little too close as Jerome had waited for her to arrive. Jerome had been backed up against a

Red Vine tree and attempting to bargain with the gummy spider, offering to do its taxes in exchange for clemency. The spider, for its sake, had been more interested in the small red gummy insects that scurried through the grass than in the larger muffin nearby who for some reason kept asking if it had any 1099 forms or if it had made any donations to charity that could be itemized. Kupcake had arrived and gently repositioned the spider to a locale better suited to its needs – one far away from Jerome.

Kupcake moved her gaze away from the solid door and back to the window. Through it, she could see darkening skies as rain clouds slowly moved in. Back home, she loved sitting out on her covered patio, a tall glass of simple syrup resting nearby as she watched storms come in. There was something about them... the pressure and charge in the air that was pushed in advance of the actual clouds, wind, and rain.

A syrup tear slipped from the corner of one of her eyes and rolled down her cake. She was never going to enjoy another storm again. She was never going to walk through the fields near her home again.

She was never going to see Jerome again.

A wave of sadness crashed over her, leaving in its wake a hollow guilt. Deep in her mind, she heard the memory she'd tried to banish give a faint victory shout. She'd not done enough to convince her father to change the laws. She never should have kept her relationship with Jerome a secret. The laws were wrong, and yet she'd still snuck about and hidden their time together. Her tears came freely now, and she let them roll along her cake, down her wrapper, and soak into the thin sheet on the silicone mat.

After some time, the crying spell passed, and Kupcake returned to the window. She was gazing out at the cloudy sky as the afternoon storm rained down when she heard her door being unlocked. Reluctantly, fearful of another round of abuse - *Not this time, not without my permission. If they want more from me, they're going to leave with bruised cakes and flattened berries!* - she turned and watched as a small sour straw guard entered and placed a tray of cookies on the silicone mat. The guard never once looked in her direction.

Kupcake waited until the door shut behind the guard before she unclenched her fists. She shuffled over, picked up a cookie, and nibbled. After two bites, her stomach cramped as she once again saw Jerome's face swimming in her mind. Anger flashed and, in one smooth movement, Kupcake slipped her hand under the tray and flipped it up and off her bed. The tray spun in the air then crashed to the floor out of sight, by the foot of her bed. The rattling of it mixed with the shattering of the cookies against the stone. Kupcake slumped on the bed, one thought ringing in her mind.

If her father hadn't come for her by now, he wasn't coming at all.

Despite the fantasy that she'd held, she knew Jerome wouldn't be coming, either. He wasn't a fighter. He'd never been in a fight in his life, and only a few times had he ever strayed beyond the safety of the town. No, she realized, nobody was coming.

"Enough," she growled. She was not going to stay in this room being fed cookies twice a day and occasionally enduring the cruelties of German Chocolate and Devil's Food Cake whenever they felt so inclined to torture her. She would do what she needed to do. If her father was coming with soldiers, so be it, but there was no way she'd sit around and wait to find out.

She studied the room around her, her mind touching on each object and turning it over and over again, looking for all of the possibilities. What could she do with the drawers of the dresser? Once, she'd used her own dresser drawers as a makeshift ladder to reach a toy her father had perched up high. What could she do with the bedsheet? She'd already dismissed it as too short, and if she tore it into strips, she'd be dealing with a weight-ratio issue rather than a length one.

Speaking of the bed, could she disassemble the frame and use it in some way? Her mind poured over the possibilities like a mirror glaze over a cake. As she did, Kupcake's eyes glassed over and she stood staring. She didn't move; her eyes didn't blink. Every ounce of her focus was kept on solving the puzzle of how to get out of her room. This singular focus was one of the things that Jerome had once told her he loved most about her. He'd said that he loved that she took on problems with every pat of butter of her being, pouring all of her energy into solving it.

Of course, he'd also said that he loved the fact that during these moments she was so enraptured by the problem-solving process that she remained oblivious to other things, such as Jerome placing small twigs or gummy insects on her body. Once, he'd told her he'd been able to construct most of a small twig cabin on one of her shoulders, and been considering seeing if he could move in an entire family of gummy beetles while she sat by the Oreo Bridge contemplating how to fix the issue of poor ventilation in the kitchens of less fortunate confections.

A soft scratching noise interrupted her thoughts, pulling her from her focus and bringing her back into the moment with a start. Was someone coming? Again, she felt panic flare in her chest, but then she realized the sound wasn't coming from the door or even the hallway beyond it. No, the sound came from the floor at the end of the bed.

Kupcake paused – afraid to get closer, but unsure as to what exactly she was afraid of. Slowly, she shuffled forward and angled herself so that she could see over the edge of the mat without getting too near. The sounds had stopped as she'd moved, but now that she remained still, they started back up, timid at first and then building.

The tray that had held the cookies lay amidst a sprawling mass of crumbled cookies. Movement near the wall caught her eyes and she peered closer. When she found the source of the motion, she gasped. The activity and sounds ceased once more.

Small gummy mice stood hunched over the cookie crumbs, a couple of them with larger pieces clutched in their green or red paws. They stood as still as statues, their smooth eyes watching her in case she attacked them or tried to sell them a timeshare.

Kupcake breathed out with a smile. "Go on, sweeties, I'm not going to hurt you." The mice hesitated only a moment longer, and then, as if they'd understood and believed her words, continued about their business. They scooped up the larger pieces and carried them behind the silicone mat bed, only to return moments later with empty paws in order to snatch more pieces.

When all that was left was a single, mostly whole cookie, one red mouse crept back out and sniffed at the morsel before it looked up at Kupcake. It stood on its hind legs and, reaching out with one forepaw, pushed the cookie closer towards her, and then stepped back and reared up again, watching her.

Kupcake smiled, grateful. The mouse wanted her to eat the cookie. It was giving her the biggest piece of what remained so that she wouldn't starve.

Ignoring the thought, Kupcake nodded encouragingly and bent to pick up the cookie. The mouse watched as she bit one corner off and chewed. Then, satisfied, the mouse turned and disappeared behind the bed.

Kupcake sat on the edge of the bed and chewed her cookie, thinking about what had just happened. It was encouraging that there was still kindness even in this hard, cruel place. The realization filled her with a bittersweet happiness. She took another bite of the cookie, ruminating on the mice. Maybe she could train them and they could be her friends here, and—

"Son of a bitch," she mumbled, crumbs and half-chewed cookie spilling out of her mouth. She jumped up, kicked the tray out of the way and pulled the bed away from the wall. There, where the wall met the floor, was a rough hole in the stone big enough for her to put at least one hand into.

Kupcake stared at it, disbelieving, and then quickly got up and retrieved the drawer handle.

She had to start widening the hole.

Hold on, Jerome. I'm coming.

21

"They're all dead?" King Red Velvet rasped. A worn and dog-eared copy of a romance novel titled *All Who Wear a Saddle* tumbled to the floor in a whispery flutter of pages. "All of them?"

Stuart grimaced as he nodded. "Yes, sire. We received word not an hour ago."

The king slumped back in his chair, his hands dangling limply over the arms. How could this be? He'd sent the best of the best. Nobody had ever defeated his most elite team of rock candy guards. Granted, he'd not had occasion to send them out very often, but the two other times, they'd triumphed. Okay, sure, one of those times had been with the purpose of quelling an uprising of cookie dough balls. But the other time had absolutely been a difficult mission. *What was it?* He tried to remember the details, but couldn't.

A tickling fear grew from a small ember to a larger flame within him. He'd been certain they would have succeeded. How could they have let him down like this? With the rescue mission a failure, that would mean.... Red Velvet squeezed his eyes shut against the thought. When he opened them, his gaze fell on the discarded novel. A longing to pick it back up, to vanish from the immediate reality, pulled at him. He felt his fingers twitch towards the spread pages and the solace they offered.

No. The word slammed into his mind and brought him up to a stiff-backed sitting position on the Cake Stand Throne. This wasn't the time. His daughter was still gone, held captive. It was now up to him to do something about that since Talton and the Baker's Dozen had failed.

What could have gone wrong with the mission, though? That unit was the best of the best. How could they have failed and gotten themselves all reduced to crumbs? He looked back at Stuart, the stalwart peanut butter cookie standing the perfect distance away – close enough to speak in low tones and be heard, yet far enough away so as not to crowd the king or come within easy grasp, should the monarch decide in a sudden fit of rage or despair to take a swing at him.

"Do you..." he started, and Stuart's eyes flicked up attentively, "think we have a spy on the grounds? Someone who would have sent word ahead to Devil's Food Cake?"

Stuart's face softened as the cookie seemed to be considering this. Slowly, he shook his head. "I don't believe so, sire. We intentionally kept word of this mission a great secret. The only ones who knew of the mission were yourself and me, the team members themselves, the Minister of Defense, the minister's personal aide, two cooks who prepared the team's meal before they departed, those in the armory who supplied them, and the gate guards and stable masters. Oh, and Ralph."

"Ralph?"

"Yes, sire, Ralph, the editor of *The Baking Sheet*. He was standing near the gate when I saw the team off on their mission." Stuart paused, but then hurriedly continued. "But all of those are loyal confections and would never betray you! No, sir, Devil's Food Cake surely had some emissary along the road between here and there who spied the team. Or they were seen on approach to the castle itself and were thus captured."

"What happened to them?"

"We don't exactly know, sire. We only know that they were discovered and," he paused, "eliminated."

The king sat back again and looked to the ceiling. *So, that's it*, he thought. *The only other recourse is war.* He could call the aprons and send for other forces from around the cakedom. There hadn't been a war of this scale in the land for generations... not since the Ladyfinger Crusades. The Cookie Wars before that, and before them, the last major conflict had been the Third Pastry War.

The Cookie Wars. Red Velvet's heart thudded at the memories. Fig bars were the worst things the Mother Baker had ever conceived. The things they'd done.... But it wasn't Red Velvet's fault, not really.

That's not how Devil's Food Cake sees it, he thought. *Of course not.* When he'd learned about Reggie, the cake had been inconsolable. Screaming that Red Velvet was to blame. *Preposterous*, the king thought. *I had nothing to do with that whole business. I was simply following—*

War would mean more of the same, though. He thought back to all of the confections lost during the conflict. When he'd put the whole affair of the last Cookie War behind him, once he'd found his way back to safety and then convinced his father to recall him from service, he'd sworn to himself that he wouldn't allow open war to happen ever again. Not if he could help it.

But what other options were there? Devil's Food Cake was surely planning on having him killed. His need for revenge was that great. Again, Red Velvet reminded himself that it wasn't his fault. But the mere consideration of travelling across the land, only to sacrifice himself for his daughter, and the thought of being humiliated and then dunked in milk... it all threatened to turn his cake into meringue.

She's your daughter. Get a hold of yourself. Think about this. Why is this even a question?

Admittedly, he had done his best to stay out of harm's way for most of his life. His service in the Fudge Army when he'd been younger had been mostly ceremonial. He'd had no way of knowing that the final Cookie War would break out only a few months after his enlistment. And, of course, his father the king had insisted - looking down on his generally weak-willed cakeling son - that Red Velvet go to the front lines. "It will give you some fortitude and show the troops that the royal family is willing to fight in the same manner as the troops they dispatch," his father had told him.

He had to do this. He had to.

And after the contents of the box that the gummy pickle had brought... the king shuddered. He couldn't allow anything else to happen to his daughter. What else would that loathsome creature do to her if Red Velvet did call the aprons and march an army across the land to the very gates of the Black Licorice Castle? What else would be delivered to him in a box?

King Red Velvet felt his throat constricting even as his guts swam with nausea and horror. It felt as if someone had plunged a mixer blade into his center and flipped the switch. The only thing left to him was to do as Devil's Food Cake had demanded. He would make the journey to the Black Licorice Castle and kneel before the offending confection. It would mean his death, sure. It would mean years of darkness for the land, absolutely. It would also mean him facing the truth of that mission and everything horrible that had followed.

Maybe years of darkness wouldn't be so bad after all? That would certainly help cool the land, which could only be good for the environment, right? Darkness equaled less sun, which equaled less cake burns. That had to be a good thing. Sure, every confection in the land would be a pitiful, screaming slave to Devil's Food Cake's evil whims... but at least they wouldn't get sun-stale.

Red Velvet stood up and gritted his teeth, banishing the thought. *No more of that. No more of that way of thinking.* He would go. Kupcake would still be alive. That must account for something. She would still live to see another day, another sunrise. To find love and marry, have mini-cupcakes who would one day hopefully vanquish the disagreeable confections that would cover the land with their bitter disgustingness. She would still get to ride her animal cracker, to be among the people and give them hope in a world gone dark with the rule of the vile Devil's Food Cake. A cruel world, though it was – one filled with sours and oozing desserts and reverse mortgages.

"It would be worse than that," a voice chimed in from across the room. King Red Velvet flinched, and Stuart let out a mousy squeak and ducked as he turned towards the voice.

The Moon Pie Wizard pushed off from where he'd been leaning on the doorframe and moved slowly into the room, his staff clicking on the stone floor.

"How did..?" Stuart managed.

"He's the Moon Pie Wizard, son," King Red Velvet said. "He can come and go anywhere, anytime." He turned his eyes back to the wizard. "Moon Pie," he said, and then paused. "Um, do you have another name? Calling you just 'Moon Pie' makes me feel like I'm talking to my wife."

The wizard shook his head. "No, sire. This is the name the Great Baker Herself gave me."

The king shrugged, ignoring Stuart who stood to one side, his mouth agape in shock at the sudden and unannounced appearance of the old wizard.

"Close your mouth, boy," the wizard instructed Stuart as he passed him. "You'll catch fruit flies that way, and trust me, you don't want them. Harder to get rid of than the yeasty meringue you can get down in Trifle Town." The wizard stopped next to the king. "Things are pretty screwed up, wouldn't you say?"

The king nodded curtly. "They are. I sent my best—"

"You sent fools and soldiers no better than crumbs to infiltrate the Black Licorice Castle and steal your daughter back. Devil's Food Cake saw them coming a mile away."

"Someone told him?"

The Moon Pie Wizard blinked. "No, he literally saw them a mile away. He has the land cleared for a mile in every direction around the castle. There was no way for them to sneak up."

"How do you know this?"

A shrug. "It's my job to know things. It's part of my mystique."

The king's shoulders slumped. It was hopeless, he thought.

"It's not entirely hopeless," the Moon Pie Wizard said with a small smile.

"How did-" King Red Velvet started, and then he shook his head. "Mystique, right?" The wizard winked. "Then tell me, wizard, how is it not entirely hopeless? I can't bargain with that fruitcake. I sent my best team to bring her back; they failed. Just short of mobilizing the armies - the thought of which makes my dairy curdle, to be frank - I have no options other than to do what he wants."

"I assume that what he wants is to kill you."

King Red Velvet nodded. "I know. And, knowing him, it won't be quick. I swear he has cold, rancid butter running through his cake."

"Sire, we should send the army!" Stuart said enthusiastically. "Lay siege to the castle. We can starve them out or force them to let her go. Or we can just crash down their walls and take them by force."

"Boy, did you ever read your history lessons?" the Moon Pie Wizard asked before the king could ask the same question. "Many, many armies have tried the same thing. All failed. That castle is impervious to siege, and it would take an army three times the size of your king's to tear it down. That's provided you could even whip the Fudge Army back into shape after so long."

Stuart lowered his head in resignation. Just as the king and the wizard began speaking gain, however, he looked up, his eyes wide with surprise. "Excuse me, will you, sire?"

The king dismissed him with a quick flick of the wrist. He watched the aide scurry out of the room and vanish down the hallway beyond. Red Velvet then looked back to the Moon Pie Wizard. "What are my options?"

The wizard sat down on a chair that had materialized out of thin air. He grunted in satisfaction as he settled into the plush fabric. "He's given you no timeline, has he? No deadline?"

King Red Velvet huffed a chuckle. "I'm surprised you didn't know that. He gave me a week from the first notice. That week ended two days ago. Then, he sent...." The King's throat constricted, and he choked on the words he'd been meaning to speak.

"Yes," the Moon Pie Wizard replied, his voice low. "I know what he sent. What I don't know is if there was a deadline along with that."

The king shook his head. "It can only be assumed he meant *immediately*."

The Moon Pie Wizard leaned forward conspiratorially and asked, "Do you think you could stall him for at least a few more days?"

"What do you mean?" When the wizard didn't answer, the king continued, "I suppose I could send word that I agree to meet, but need time to put my affairs in order."

The wizard smiled. "Good. Do that. Stall as long as you can, but I wouldn't think you'd need to push any more than four days from now."

"What are you about?" the king asked. "You have a plan? Something that will save my daughter? It had better be good, as I don't like that you're suggesting she remain there for an even longer period of time. Is this plan of yours worth it?"

"It is. You're not going to like it, though."

The king stiffened. "What is it?"

"What do you know about your daughter's personal life?"

"I don't like where this is going, wizard," King Red Velvet growled, feeling his cake redden even more deeply.

"Calm yourself. You're facing death. Not only for yourself, but for millions of your subjects who are completely blameless in this. And reverse mortgages, or worse, for the rest of them. Not to mention what would happen to Kupcake if that disgusting confection were allowed to rule this land. So, answering a few questions about your daughter has to be pretty mild in comparison. Now, what do you know of her personal life? Does she have any suitors?"

The king took a deep breath and forced himself to calm down. The wizard was right. "None that I know of. She's beloved by everyone, but she has no one courting her. My wife once mentioned something about a lemon meringue from Bundt Cake Beach, but I don't think she was serious. And if someone were truly interested, I would know."

"That is where you would be wrong. As wrong as the farmer is about his daughter and the stable boy in that installment you're reading," the wizard said, pointing to the book on the floor.

"That's... I... it's just—"

"Relax. I don't care what trash you read. Trust me, I've read worse. Although, you're about to read some really... depraved bits in that very volume."

"Really?" the king replied, interest and hope mingled with excitement breaking through in his voice. Once more, he felt the lure of the escape offered by the novel. And, once more, he forced it down. "I mean, really, this can't be relevant."

"Your daughter has a love. A true love, if I may be so bold as to say so. She doesn't want you or anyone else to know, so they meet in secret. Have been doing so for some weeks now. Before you do something rash, know that nothing more than talking and some light hand-holding has happened. Nothing more. But there is love there, and it is deep and unmovable."

The king was taken aback. How could this be? How could his daughter have a love interest and he not know of it?

"Because," the wizard said, once again reading his thoughts, "you won't approve of the young man in question."

"How could that be? If Kupcake sees him and feels love, if he truly cares for her and takes care of her-"

"He's a muffin."

The king exploded off the chair. "Impossible!" he roared. "That is forbidden! Don't you remember what those confections did? I could have you dissolved in milk for suggesting such a thing! Who is it? I'll have him banished from the lands! I'll send him to the Land of the Danish Wedding Cookies for this slight against my family and the laws of decorum!"

"Actually, your highness, he's been in the Land of the Danish Wedding Cookies. Went there voluntarily. Well, I pushed him in that direction, but unless they ate him, he should be beyond their borders by now."

"What?"

The Moon Pie Wizard took a breath. "His name is Jerome. He is deeply in love with Kupcake, as she is with him. He would go to the very ends of the earth for her. Which is, in fact, what he's doing at this very moment."

The wizard next related his encounter with Jerome and the path he'd set him on. When he was done, he said, "I don't have a clear vision of him, as my oatmeal has gone a bit stale of late, but he should be past the Danish cookies and have the piping bag by now. He should be heading straight for the Black Licorice Castle."

King Red Velvet felt a hollow sinking in his cake. "Are you serious? A... a... muffin thinks he can not only make it into the Black Licorice Castle – something that my most highly trained soldiers couldn't do – but get past all the vile things that live there, and find Kupcake and rescue her? And vanquish both German Chocolate and Devil's Food Cake? It's preposterous."

The Moon Pie Wizard spun his staff between two fingers, tapping it on the floor sporadically as he did. He met the king's eyes and, in a very even tone, said, "The boy has already defeated many vile things on his way. He escaped a congealed salad, braved the Red Vines Forest, and made it into and out of possibly the most dangerous cave deep in the Pudding Swamp. He also, I remind you, went into the Land of the Danish Wedding Cookies and then made his way out with what is arguably the most potent weapon since the Enchanted Kitchen Timer that was used to such incredible ends in the first Ladyfingers Crusades. All of this, he's done, and yet he's untrained. He's not a soldier. He's never served. The muffin does light construction work, for Great Baker's sake. He's accomplishing this for one reason and one reason alone. His love for your daughter. For Kupcake." The wizard stopped spinning the staff and leaned forward. "King Red Velvet, I urge you, postpone any plans you have to give in to Devil's Food Cake. Just for a few days. Give Jerome a chance. He may surprise you."

A few more days. A few more days to hold onto what I have, to- Red Velvet almost grunted with the effort to squash those thoughts. He would not allow the old cowardice to overwhelm him again. Eying the wizard, he said, "He may get himself and Kupcake killed. But I'll consider your counsel. If you'll excuse me."

Both stood and said their goodbyes, and then the king turned and exited the room via a door hidden behind a tapestry.

King Red Velvet moved along the narrow hallway, lost in thought. A muffin? A Baker-damned muffin? The wizard had asked him to pin all of his hopes of Kupcake's safe return on a single blueberry muffin? And one who foolishly felt love for the princess? How dare he? The king's fists clenched at the thought of a low muffin even being near his daughter, let alone touching her... daring to hold her hand.

He entered his private bedroom and stood there for several seconds, uncertain of what to do first. It was ridiculous to consider that an untrained muffin could achieve what the Moon Pie Wizard claimed. If anything, the damned fool was going to hasten his daughter's demise.

No, King Red Velvet thought, *I must not let that happen. This Jerome will fail – that much is obvious to anyone with common sense. The wizard must have some personal affection for the muffin and is thus being overly hopeful. I do not have that luxury. I am above that. I am the king, and I am her father. I have but one option left to me.*

King Red Velvet moved to a nearby table, pulled out a piece of parchment paper and a quill, and began to write.

22

"Seriously? That's why that law exists?" Stephen shuffled. "Because two hundred years ago a muffin got Queen Battenberg Cake all battered up with—" the peep paused, blinking in confusion, "what would that even be? Muffincake? Cupmuffin? That's just gross. Either way, it's a stupid law."

"The royal family was so devastated that they put the law into effect that night. I heard they had the, uh, whatever it was, sent far beyond the Crepe Islands." Jerome sighed. "Cakes have always thought they're above everyone else. They founded this land and have ruled it ever since."

They walked in silence for a while, until Stephen blinked, "I had an encounter with a twinkie once."

"Did it want to eat you?" Jerome asked.

"Not in the same way," Stephen shuffled with a wink of one of his black eyes.

Balthus walked several yards ahead of the party, the rusty whisk strapped to his back. Occasionally, Jerome would hear the old cookie talking loudly as if arguing a point. Balthus would gesture wildly as he raved, shake his head, and he even once stopped dead in his tracks, pointed a finger at the empty air beside him, and exclaimed,

"Do I need to turn around and go back? I will! Just say the word. You keep this up and...." Then, just as suddenly, he'd started walking again, grumbling to himself.

Jerome wasn't sure if the old cookie knew exactly where he was going, but they seemed to be heading in a generally northwestern direction. As long as it was away from the Land of the Danish Wedding Cookies, Jerome was content to let Balthus continue leading the way.

The flight from the dungeon and through the castle had been a stop-and-go affair. Multiple times, they'd had to stop or take a detour as large patrols of cookie soldiers had run past screaming about how the lemon squares were breaching certain points along the outer walls.

Once they'd gotten free of the castle itself, Balthus had led them to a shallow, dry riverbed that stretched away into the lands. Twice, they'd been forced to hide behind rocks or scrub brush while large groups of Danish Wedding Cookies had gone riding by on the backs of animal crackers, screaming and waving bent and twisted toothpick swords as they charged past in heading towards some unseen enemy.

At the border, Balthus had paused, staring at the tree line that marked the end of his homeland and the beginning of the Outlands. Jerome had placed a hand on his shoulder. "I'll understand if you can't go," he'd told the cookie. "You've been brave and amazing so far, and I can't ask you to come with us. But if you want-"

Balthus looked pained. "I was just debating whether or not I need to go back and get clean underwear."

Jerome looked down at the cookie. "But you're not...."

Balthus chuckled and patted Jerome on the shoulder. "Come on, muffin boy. Let's get you to the Black Licorice Castle."

So, they'd followed the old, cracked cookie into what he called the Outlands. Balthus had, for the most part, continued in a fairly straight and confident direction.

They'd been walking for several hours when Jerome called for a rest. Stephen shuffled over to a pool of shade in the nook formed by the roots of a large Caramel tree. Balthus muttered something about releasing some crumbs and vanished into a thicket. Jerome led Cleetus to the tree under which the peep was resting and rubbed him down, then poured him a bucket of simple syrup. The bear stared sleepily at Jerome, ignoring the bucket of syrup.

"What?" Jerome asked. Cleetus blinked his slow, deliberate blink. Jerome stared back until understanding slipped into his mind like a cake spear sliding into a freshly baked sponge. "Are you...? Seriously?"

Blink.

Words failed Jerome, but he tore open a saddle bag, pulling out one of the pillows they'd brought from King Flanta's castle. With an exaggerated flourish, he placed the pillow on the ground and backed away, mumbling about the bear resting his posh gelatinous ass.

Cleetus sniffed the pillow, pawed at it to move it into a more desirable position, and then climbed on, his attention quickly shifting to the bucket of syrup. The bear settled in contentedly to drink.

"So, what's that thing do?" Stephen blinked in the direction of the Piping Bag of Ganache.

Jerome pulled the weapon into his lap and looked down at it. "I have no idea how it works. There's no trigger or way to load it that I've been able to find. And it's not like I found any ammunition in the crate."

"So, what did you do? Beat him to death with it, the twinkie? Because that would be pretty badass."

Jerome shook his head. "As he got closer, I was standing there, not sure what to do or how I was going to defend myself, especially with this. But then the bag just filled up. On its own. I was holding it at my side, pointing it at him, and it just suddenly got larger."

Stephen blinked a laugh. "I bet it did."

"Not like that! Get your mind out of the gutter. Anyway, when the bag filled up, I just squeezed it.... Okay, I heard it that time," Jerome said, smiling. He looked over as Stephen fell over, the peep's eyes blinking hysterically as the marshmallow laughed. Jerome joined in, the laughter overtaking him. It felt good, cleansing. With everything he'd been through and still had yet to face, it was a good thing to laugh.

Balthus returned from the thicket and sat next to them. "You should have used this on him," he said, patting the whisk. "Would have done him in faster than you can blink."

"I think the piping bag did the job pretty well," Jerome answered. He went on to explain how the twinkie had been coated - this elicited only a soft chuckle shuffle from Stephen - and subsequently dissolved, the telling of which stopped the peep's laughter.

"He melted? That's messed up," Stephen wriggled.

Balthus looked on in curious horror at the piping bag in Jerome's lap. "You're saying that bag did that to the twinkie?" Jerome nodded. "If that's true, and I'm not saying it is, then you do indeed have one oven of a weapon on your hands. It may be just what you need to get into that castle and get your girlfriend out."

Jerome thought briefly of Kupcake sitting alone in a cell. Was she hurt? Was she cold? Did she know anyone was coming to save her? "I can hope so. Although, I have no idea where in the castle she'll be, or honestly what to do once I do get there. I mean, with this—" he shook the bag, "I guess I could just blast my way in through the main gate."

"No good," Balthus said. "I've not been there myself, but any good gate guard company worth its sea salt won't just have a couple of guards on the ground who you can shoot and quickly move past. They'll have archers in towers on either side, most likely with honey stick arrows. You know what that stuff will do to your cake if it touches you? It's not pretty. Plus, they're more likely to have several guards, upwards of a couple dozen guarding the gate. Especially now that Devil's Food Cake has taken the princess hostage. They're going to beef up security against any assaults."

Jerome felt the ground shift away below him. This was hopeless. He wasn't a soldier. He wasn't a tactician. He knew nothing about fighting or how to infiltrate a castle. Oven, he couldn't even get in or out of a pantry without being noticed. He was going to go to the Black

Licorice Castle and get killed before he even got close enough to do anything useful.

"But maybe there's a way," the old Danish Wedding Cookie said thoughtfully, running a hand along his chin.

"How so?"

Balthus was quiet for a long moment, and then said, "I may know some people who can get us in. It won't be cheap, and they're a bit loony, but they may just be able to help."

"Who? Wait. Did you say 'us'?"

Balthus looked at Jerome and smiled. "Son, you didn't think we were going to come all this way with you and not actually help, did you? If nothing else, I'm going to go into that castle and lay waste to some sour straw guards and jawbreakers – bring some honor back to my people."

Jerome stared at the cookie, speechless. Finally, he was able to say, "That means so much to me, Balthus. Thank you. I'm happy and honored to have you with me. May the Great Mother Baker anoint you with flour." Balthus nodded, satisfied, and Jerome looked over to Stephen.

The peep shuffled. "Shit, I'm coming along just to see if you can actually do this. We all know that you'll fall flat on your cake if I'm not there. Plus I have a bet with Cleetus on whether or not you survive."

Jerome rolled his eyes and glanced at the gummy bear, who seemed to grin as it blinked sleepily back at him. "Okay," he said. "Who are these confections, and where do we find them?"

Balthus' eyes danced as he said, "Trifle Town."

23

K upcake stopped digging and pushed the silicone mat bed back against the wall as she heard footsteps approaching from the hallway beyond her door. The sound of keys jingling on a key ring accompanied the slow thumps of the bootsteps.

The hole from which the gummy mice had arrived had gotten much bigger in the last two days, thanks to the small metal handle she'd managed to remove from the dresser drawer. Working as quietly as she could and ignoring the lingering ache in her head where the spatula had been employed, Kupcake had managed to make the hole wide enough that she could put most of her head into it. Beyond the hole, she could see a narrow crawl space leading off into darkness as black as molasses. The space looked tight and movement wouldn't be easy, but if she could get herself in there, she was determined to attempt it.

As soon as the bed was back in place, Kupcake turned and sat on its edge. The door opened loudly, and she took a second to force her breathing to steady. At the same time, she slipped the metal handle under the single sheet, against her leg.

The large, dark form of Devil's Food Cake filled the doorway for a moment. His eyes took her in, glinting dully in the soft light from her only window.

"How are we today?" he asked, his voice deep and smooth.

Unconsciously, her hand began to rise to the wound on her head. With effort, she stopped it and forced her hand back to her lap. "Fine. I'll be better when you come to your senses and release me. I'm sure my father will be happy to forgive you your crimes as long as I'm returned unharmed."

Devil's Food Cake smiled. "Yes, I'm sure that he would just simply forgive and forget. 'No worries about that whole business with you cakenapping my only daughter and holding her for ransom. And about that whole demand that I come and bow before you before allowing you to kill me? It's cool.' Right? Something like that?" He moved into the room and took a seat near her on the bed. Kupcake's heart leapt in her chest, and she fought another impulse to look over one shoulder towards the hole she'd been digging.

"Everything alright?" he asked, his brow furrowing in what appeared to be concern. Or suspicion. Or gas.

"Fine, other than your presence so close to me," she replied, a little more harshly than she'd intended. But her tone failed to influence him.

"I only wanted to check on you, to see if there's anything you may need and let you know that your father-"

"Will be coming any day now with his army to break me out and take me home. I will ensure that I'm standing in the front row when you're dunked into the milk vat and reduced to soggy crumbs."

"Actually," Devil's Food Cake said as he stood again and took a step towards the door, "your father is coming. He sent word this morning. However, he will be without his army. In his letter, he's agreed to my terms and will be arriving in four days to kneel before me. In four days, your father will turn ownership of this land over to me." He paused, stepping deeper into the room and gazing out the single window. Kupcake shifted as quietly as she could on the mat in order to put more of herself between Devil's Food Cake and the hole she'd been digging. Without looking back at her, he added, "I have been giving things a great deal of thought lately. My original idea was for you to stand by my side as my bride and watch as your father goes to meet the Great Mother Baker."

"Was?"

He turned to face her, a soft smile playing at his lips. She noticed that it didn't quite reach his eyes. "Yes. *Was*. As I said, I've been thinking things over, and I feel that the idea to have your father dunked in milk or—" he chuckled softly to himself, "something a bit worse, is, well, to be honest, a bit too quick and permanent. You see, I need that old crumb to suffer. I need him to know that what has happened to him is because of his choices, his actions in the past. Revenge is a pastry best served cold."

"Pastries are horrible cold," Kupcake said. Devil's Food Cake waved a hand as if her opinion meant nothing. "But revenge for what? What did he do that has you so mad?"

The dark cake regarded her for a long moment before he said, "It is because of your father and his incredible cowardice that my son Reggie died at the hands of the fig bars during the last Cookie War."

Kupcake's breath caught. Her father had fought in the Cookie War? Devil's Food Cake had had a son? Wait... were pastries actually okay when eaten cold?

"You look confused," he said, a slight laugh to his voice. "Your father and I served together during the last Cookie War. He wasn't king then, but was serving as part of his obligation as a member of the royal family. In case you haven't noticed, I'm a few years older than him. My son Reggie was too young by a couple of years to formally serve. But he was a strong-willed cakeling and managed to lie his way into service. When I found out, I had him assigned to my unit."

"So, how was my father responsible for his death?"

Devil's Food Cake took several deep breaths, and seemed to be on the verge of continuing his story when he shook his head. "There will be time for that later, when your father is here and bowed low before me. What is important for you to know is that your father will not be reduced to crumbs or worse now. I will allow him to live. It's much more appealing to me to let him live with knowing that I am wed to his daughter, taking her to the silicone mat whenever I please. To let him fester for the rest of his life in knowing that I rule this cakedom and have him watch helplessly as I subvert my will upon the confections. I will have him banished to a remote land – stripped of all rights, titles, and monies. He won't have the coin to buy even the cheapest extract. Yes..." his smile widened, and now it was reflected in his eyes, "that will make for a much more fitting end for the old crumb." He held her gaze for several long seconds, and then turned and left the room.

Kupcake sank back on the bed, the breath stolen from her lungs and a hollow pit in her stomach. This couldn't be right, she thought. It had to be a trick. There was no way her father would agree to something like that. Not without laying siege to the castle first; not if there was any other possible way of rescuing her. Why not send the special forces? He had highly trained operatives among the rock candy guards. She felt the tears welling in her eyes. *Four days.* She had four days before her father arrived and sacrificed everything he was and had for her.

And how was it possible that her father had actually fought in a war? All her life, she'd never heard mention of this. And for him to be responsible for Devil's Food Cake's son's death? Impossible. It was simply impossible. And, Baker-dammit, pastries were disgusting when served cold!

Kupcake sat up, wiped her tears away, and pulled the bed back from the wall. Picking up the drawer handle, she began again chipping away at the stone wall again, ever so slowly widening the hole.

Four days.

She vowed to be done and out of her cell in two.

24

"You sure you want to order another one?" Stephen blinked.
Jerome held onto the edges of the table to prevent it from tilting in the gently swaying room. He didn't remember the room moving when they'd first entered, but now that he'd been sitting there a while and had had a few drinks, it absolutely had a sway to it. Maybe more of a sashay. The motion of someone trying out for the Buttery Swangdoodle Dance Troupe. "Ch'oo talkin' 'bout?" His voice came out thick and slow.

"Just saying, that's your fifth one, and you're not drinking some pansy-ass cooking sherry. That's some strong stuff in that cup. I've seen people—"

"Yeah, well, I sees no peoples," Jerome cut in, wildly waving one hand at the room around them. They'd been waiting in the dining room of the Mixing Bowl Hotel for three hours. "Balph, Balthz, Baldh – that cookie ain't come back yet. He's out there—" he waved his hand again, flopping it over his head, "probably gettin' all yeasty. Feasty yeasty, that one is."

At first, Jerome had thought that Trifle Town looked like neither a trifle nor a town. They'd crested a hill on the outskirts and paused, looking down through the fading sunlight upon the sprawling obscenity that had been their destination.

His eyes had taken in haphazard streets, a twisting and turning warren of maze-like avenues that doubled back on themselves and seemed to make absolutely no sense to the eye. The buildings here were, mostly, of different colors and practically stacked atop one another. That, he assumed, was where the name of the town had come from. The buildings - Jerome couldn't tell if they were houses, businesses, or a mixture – had been formed with no thought put toward organization. Small clumps of structures bunched together in spots, and then there would be large swaths of ground where only a single dwelling stood. On that first glance, he'd been able to see lights from torches or - yes, he'd confirmed it through squinting - several fires burning unchecked in the streets.

"Gentlemen," Balthus had said as he'd spread his thin arms wide, as if he were presenting the most glorious thing in the land, "I present to you, Trifle Town."

"And remind me what it is you expect us to find down there?" Jerome asked.

"Supplies, for one," the old cookie answered. "There are a lot of vendors down there who can equip us for the rest of the trip."

"We don't have any money."

Balthus waved his hand irritably, as if shooing away a fruit fly. "Minor detail. I have some favors I can call in. More than a few confections down there owe me money. We'll get by."

Jerome sighed. "Okay, aside from supplies, you said that there are some confections down there who could get us into the castle?"

"Aye, I did say that. And we'll talk with them soon enough. But first, we need to get down there, secure some rooms, and eat. We need to rest, take care of Cleetus there, and regain our senses."

"Every minute we waste," Jerome snapped, "is another minute Kupcake is stuck in that Baker-damned place! It's another minute that that underbaked cake can put his hands on her."

"Calm down, boy," Balthus quipped. "I haven't forgotten about your precious *petite fours* or whatever she is. The point is," he added, speaking over the protest Jerome was starting to voice, "the ones we need to talk to are probably completely hammered right now, and there's no way we're going to get any kind of sense out of them. We're also going to have to show some kind of cash up-front to get their interest, and it's going to take me a little time to get that together."

"I don't know how comfortable I am with you bankrolling this operation," Jerome said.

Balthus looked him up and down. "You got any cash on you? Maybe hiding in that Bag of Never-Ending Powdered Sugar you used to sneak into our land?" He shook his head. "Then, don't worry about it. You can pay me back when we get her home. You or the king. Besides, like I told you yesterday, I have a pretty big stake in this myself. So, just look at it as me paying for my own crusade and you just being along for the ride, if that makes you feel better."

It didn't. People who paid the bill usually wanted to call the shots, Jerome thought, and the last thing he wanted or needed was to have Balthus direct the group. But he decided to set those concerns aside for the moment and just go with the old cookie's plan. The prospect of a meal and the chance to sleep in an actual bed was very appealing. He'd not gotten a good night's sleep since being at the Moon Pie Wizard's house, and the thought of an actual bed with actual pastry sheets and an actual gumdrop pillow appealed to him.

Balthus led them down the hill and into the fringes of the town. As they approached, Jerome could smell the odor of burnt cookies, as well as over- and undercooked cakes. The wind shifted, bringing him the soft, semi-solid stench of flan for a grotesque moment. Jerome's stomach rolled, and he felt like he was going to be sick, but then the breeze changed directions and he found himself able to breathe once again.

The first signs of life appeared after a block, with small gumdrops skittering around corners and through gutters, other hard-coated fruit candies resting in doorways.

"Fuck you looking at?" demanded a very intoxicated bottlecap from where it leaned against an alley wall. Jerome mumbled a half-hearted apology and hurried to catch up with the rest of the group.

Stephen gave him a reproachful look, and then shook his head and moved on.

After a few more blocks, many of which required Jerome to leap over puddles of what looked like congealed glaze, Balthus turned to face the group. "Okay, we've been through some pretty nice areas so far, but keep close for the next four blocks. We're entering the slums, and trust me, you don't want to be alone out here." Jerome opened his mouth to protest the notion that any of the dwellings thus far had been *nice*, but the Danish Wedding Cookie moved quickly away – forcing the rest of them to rush to catch up. Beside Jerome, Cleetus chuffed a concerned noise.

"I know, bud," Jerome said, patting the gummy bear on the shoulder. "We'll be through this soon and will get you something to eat."

The stone street slowly disintegrated until they were walking on bare earth, their feet squishing in the thick muck. Jerome refused to look down, afraid to see what he was treading through. After several more steps, Stephen climbed on top of Cleetus to avoid getting bogged down in the mire.

The buildings around them were 'buildings' only in the sense that they had had perhaps once considered having four walls. In most cases, they now only had two or three. All were made out of black, molding Red Vine tree limbs or waterlogged baker's boxes, their material limp and swollen. Half-chewed candies and pastries, their coatings or cakes dented and torn to expose softer insides, lay about. Each appeared to lack the strength to fully sit up. They peered with vacant stares and slack mouths at the group that passed by.

"Now, that's what I'm talking about," Stephen shuffled after they'd traveled several blocks. Jerome followed his gaze and saw several small, scantily clad Sugar Babies milling about on a corner, two of whom were talking to a white powdered doughnut. The doughnut threw nervous glances over its shoulder before turning back to the Sugar Babies and pointing eagerly to its doughnut hole. "Dude's gonna get him a double-pack," the peep wriggled. Behind the babies, standing on a Red Vine log, was a Sugar Daddy dressed in purple robes. The daddy held a thin candy thermometer as a staff and watched his charges with narrow eyes.

"You're gonna want to stay away from the working girls," Balthus called to them. "Unless you fancy a case of yeasty meringue. Hard to get rid of, that. I had a buddy catch it years ago. They had to fill him full of custard for three weeks just to combat it. Trust me, you don't want it." Jerome watched Stephen eye the working girls longingly, and then they were moving past and continuing down the block.

"What about Reject Jelly Beans?" Jerome asked. Balthus stopped so suddenly that the muffin nearly collided with the old cookie. Balthus turned and grabbed Jerome's arm tightly. His eyes shifted from side to side.

"Shut up!" he hissed. "You don't want to mention them too loudly. Holy Rolling Pin, I hope nobody heard you. If they find us, you just run, hear me? Don't look, don't question, just run. And pray!"

Stunned into silence, Jerome only nodded.

The Mixing Bowl was small and narrow, but deep. They huddled in the entrance while Balthus approached a mallowmar that eyed them suspiciously. *Everyone looks at us like we're going to rob them,* Jerome thought. He flinched as Balthus erupted into a loud argument with the mallowmar, his hands gesturing wildly. From the snatches of conversation he could discern, Jerome learned that Balthus had used to frequent Trifle Town more than he'd initially let on, and so he knew several people. The mallowmar grumbled something back, then thrust a couple of keys at the old cookie. Balthus asked another question, got another grumble in response, and finally returned to the group.

Passing the keys to Jerome, he said, "You guys are upstairs at the end of the hall. There's a dining room down there." He pointed past the front desk and into the gloom. From the darkness, Jerome could hear the soft scrape of utensils against plates and low conversation. "Go get Cleetus settled. There's a reputable stable half-a-block away. Tell the guy I sent you and he'll hook you up."

"Is this...?" Jerome started.

"It's fine, muffin boy. They may rob you blind in the streets, give you all sorts of infections, and sell you on a pyramid scheme, but the one thing people here do take pride in is their ability to care for our mounts. Cleetus will be treated just as well as, if not better than, he was with Lord Flanta. Now, I have to go track down a few people and get the money owed me, and then I'll be back to meet you guys for dinner."

"When do we meet the confections you mentioned?"

"Patience. You'll pop one of your unfrosted blueberries if you don't calm down. The leader is one of the people I'm going to be tracking down. If I can find her, I'll bring her with me tonight. Worst case, we'll find her in the morning before she completely sobers up."

So, now they sat at the table, Jerome's mood worsening with every passing minute as he ordered vanilla extract after extract. The thought that they were wasting time while Kupcake sat alone, enduring untold horrors, pressed down on him like the heel of the Great Mother Baker's hand working up gluten.

"I'm telling you, when that cracked cookie shows up, I'm going to flay the powdered sugar off of him," Jerome slurred.

"You'll do no such thing," Balthus said loudly as he entered the room. "Get your muffin wrapper out of its twist. I'm here. I wasn't gone that long."

"Where the hell have you been?" Jerome demanded. "Every minute we're—"

"Oh Holy Rolling Pin, you're not starting that shit again, are you? She's going to be just fine. Besides, I told you where I was going. I got plenty of supplies. Sent the new stuff to your room. Plus," Balthus said, "I found her." He stepped aside and gestured with one hand so that Jerome could see...nothing.

Jerome blinked. "I know I've been drinking, but there's nobody there, you old crack-"

"I'm down here, you stodgy shit," came a pinched voice. Jerome shifted his gaze downward and blinked again as he focused on a light pink macaron.

"I'm a... what did you call me?"

"What, you think you can make a crack about how short I am, and

I can't point out the fact that you look like you're all sorts of backed-up and haven't been laid since the Great Baker Herself first folded in the cream?"

"The little bitch has a point," Stephen shuffled.

Balthus cleared his throat to break the sudden tension. "Jerome, Stephen, this is Maddie. She's the leader of Tempting Tarts, the band I was telling you about."

"What instrument does she play?" Stephen blinked.

Maddie moved closer and climbed up into a chair, at which point she reached across the table and, with nimble fingers, plucked Jerome's newly delivered vanilla extract from his hand. In one swift motion, she downed the entire thing before slamming the cup down on the table and fixing him with a haughty, pink-eyed stare. "Balthus tells me you have something in mind for me and my crew."

Jerome's mouth worked like a Swedish Fish for a moment, the only sound he was able to muster being a soft croak of disbelief. He looked over at Balthus, who was beaming at Maddie.

Maddie waved at the bartender for another drink and then looked back at Jerome. "You'd better either start using that hole to talk with or one of those nasty, diseased confections out there will come along and put something in it that you don't want. And, you—" she said, turning and pointing at Stephen, "call me a 'little bitch' again, and I'll melt you down and use what's left to clean my toilet."

Stephen shuffled a laugh. "I like this chick. You sure you don't have a little peep in you somewhere?"

"No. And before you ask, I don't want some in me, either. Holy Rolling Pin, you're like a shuffling cliche."

Jerome felt a laugh bubble out of his throat before he realized it, and immediately regretted it when he saw Stephen's embarrassed expression. "Sorry," he mumbled. Stephen only glared at him.

"Now," Maddie said, "let's get down to it. What is this job you have for us?"

Jerome hesitated for only a moment. He glanced over at Balthus, who nodded encouragingly, at which point he took a breath and related the current situation to Maddie. He explained the cakenapping (she already knew), his connection to Kupcake (Maddie laughed at this for twenty minutes, during which Jerome felt no bigger than a chocolate chip), and his journey so far. He left out the part about the Piping Bag of Ganache, worried that a mercenary like Maddie may demand that as her payment or, worse, steal it from him.

When he was finished, he took a sip of the new vanilla extract cup that had been placed on the table, snatching it up before Maddie could react or object. She narrowed her eyes at him, giving him an appraising look. "You did all of this on your own?" she asked finally.

Jerome nodded. "Well, I did all of it with my bear, Cleetus, but we also picked up Stephen—" the peep blinked a scowl at the macaron, "...and Balthus along the way. So, no, I've not done it all on my own. I wouldn't have gotten half this far without these guys. And we need you and your gang... er, band... er, *crew* to get us the rest of the way."

Then, Maddie asked the question that Jerome had been dreading. "What's in it for us?"

All eyes swiveled towards him. Jerome took a fortifying swig of his extract and met Maddie's stare. "I don't have much money." Immediately, he felt the room deflate. Maddie looked at him for a moment longer, and then stood up.

"So long, then." She turned to leave, and Jerome leapt up, knocking his chair over.

"Wait, I said I don't have much money, but King Red Velvet does! If we rescue his daughter, if you get us in and back out again, alive - that part is really important - then I'm certain he'll pay you anything you want. Just name your price. Balthus said he'd pay your initial retainer." The old cookie nodded and patted one pocket.

Maddie stopped and turned back to the table. "You think you can speak for the king? What makes you so sure he'd even hold up a deal made by someone else in his stead? Besides, there's the simple fact of..." she looked him up and down. "You know, who you are and who she is. What makes you think that he'd honor a deal?"

Jerome's mind swirled. How should he answer? How *could* he answer? What could he possibly say – he, a simple muffin who had never been this far from home in his life? Even if he sold everything he'd ever owned, it wouldn't be enough to pay Maddie and her band to help them. And she was right. King Red Velvet wouldn't give him the time of day just because he was a muffin, never mind agree to pay these macarons what they wanted for rescuing Kupcake.

"Please," he said, "I love her." Then, at the unchanged expression on the macaron's face, he added, "I'm going to try with or without you."

"Then, you'll die." She turned to Balthus. "Good seeing you again." Without looking back, Maddie left the dining room. Jerome stood staring into the shadows of the hallway, hoping she'd come back while knowing better. Finally, he sank down into a nearby chair.

"Fuck her," Stephen wriggled. "I got you guys out of Flanta's castle; I can get you into and out of the Black Licorice Castle. It will just take a few days of prep and planning. Anyone know where I can get a custard-filled chocolate sheep?"

"We don't have a few days," Jerome mumbled. He pushed away from the table and stood up again. "I need to go clear my head. I'll be back later. Don't wait up."

Jerome staggered away from the small group and down the hall. He passed through the front door of the inn and into the cool night air. His senses cleared slightly, the ground beneath him ceasing its dance routine. He chose a direction at random and moved down the street.

He didn't notice the tall, thin form detaching itself from the shadows of the inn's doorway to follow him.

25

The ankle-deep muck squished a rhythmic tune beneath his boots as Jerome wove around mudpuddles and piles of discarded trash. He ignored the catcalls of various candies to one another and to him, the muffled sounds of arguments from behind the cardboard walls of dwellings or shops, and the occasional sound of breaking sugar-glass.

But as bad as the sights and sounds were, the smell was worse. Parts of Trifle Town smelled like week-old cake left out in the hot sun and then mixed with yog— He paused and whispered a quick prayer to the Holy Rolling Pin and the Great Baker Herself for even having thought of the repugnant stuff. He pushed on through air thick with sickly sweet, sugary smells, not certain of his destination and only wanting to get further away from the inn, as well as the memory of Maddie leaving as she'd matter-of-factly informed him of his upcoming demise.

Of course, he was going to die mounting the rescue attempt, he thought. He'd never really had any illusions that his scheme would work, especially when he'd started the journey. Piping Bag of Ganache or no, it was foolish to think he'd make it to the Black Licorice Castle, let alone penetrate the walls. And what would he do if he managed to slip inside? He had no training, and nor did he have a clue as to where Kupcake would be. Then, to get her out of the castle before Devil's Food Cake was aware and sent his henchman German Chocolate Cake after them? He shook his head. It would be as impossible as saying no to timeshare salesmen.

So, he thought, since he would certainly be dead in another couple of days, he may as well enjoy his time while he could. He looked up from the dirty street and found another bar amidst the cacophony of buildings around him. On weary and less than reliable legs, he stepped into the Sugar Sifter.

The bar was barely populated, and Jerome – not wanting to be bothered – chose a booth in a dark corner and settled happily into the shadows. He just wanted to drink more extract and forget the horrible situation he was in for a little while.

Jerome barely registered the sound of the door swinging open a few moments after he sat down. His eyes didn't flick upwards to observe the new arrival pause, survey the room, and stiffen slightly when Jerome was spotted.

The newcomer moved smoothly to the bar, spoke to the barkeep in low tones, flashed a smile, and retrieved two glasses and a bottle of peppermint extract. It wasn't until the visitor walked straight across the floor, ignoring the few other patrons hunched over their own cups to stop at Jerome's table, that the muffin even bothered to look up.

"Yeah?" Jerome asked, his voice thick and heavy with stress and exhaustion.

"You look like you could use a drink or six," the soft, velvety voice slid through the air. The bottle was placed gently on the table, and then the two glasses. "May I?"

"I'm not much in the mood for company, sorry."

The visitor slid into the bench seat across from Jerome and poured extract into both cups. Sliding one across to Jerome, she said, "But you're going to get company. I can't let someone like you just sit here and sulk. Who knows what could happen to you? I heard there were drunk Mary Cake representatives on the prowl, looking to give a makeover to anyone who looked at them sideways. The last thing you need is to look like a one-muffin bachelorette party."

Jerome blinked down at the drink, felt his fingers curl around the cup, and then looked up at the confection across from him. She was tall, thin, and shapely. Her light brown cake formed in a multi-pointed star was highlighted by brown and white crystals.

"You're a churro," he said. "I've never met a churro." He considered that, and scoffed slightly. "Never met a lot of things before I left home. Can't say that anymore. But I don't even know anyone who's ever actually met a churro. Old Man Nougat once told a story about running away with a churro when he first got his peanuts, but I never really believed it."

She smiled, the gesture seeming to light up the dim booth. The smile filled Jerome with a sense of lightness and happiness, but only for a brief flash, there and gone. In its wake, a stirring coldness seemed to seep into his cake. The churro held up her cup and tilted it forward, inviting him to toast. As he did, she said, "To lost loves, to new loves, and to no regrets."

They drank. Jerome winced as he swallowed, the extract burning as it slid down to his stomach.

"What's your name?" Jerome asked.

She filled the glasses again. "Cinnamon. And you're Jerome."

"How...?"

Cinnamon shrugged. "You hear things. I hear things. When I see something I'm interested in, I make a point to know everything about it." She took another swig of extract. Licking her lips slowly and seductively, she next said, "In this case, that's you." Jerome couldn't help but notice the way her eyes had danced as she'd said that. The look was seductive on the surface, but he saw the flash of something predatory beneath it. Was this beautiful pastry really interested in him? He shook his head in a weak attempt at clearing the sucrose fog that seemed to have found its way in.

"I don't follow," he said.

"I was in the Mixing Bowl. I heard you talking."

Jerome felt his heart lurch at her words. "You heard—?"

She chuckled, the sound like windchimes and dead leaves. "Of course, I did. You didn't see me in the corner. That's okay. Most people don't notice others in that place."

"I don't see how anyone could not notice you," he said, and blinked, the words sounding as if they were coming from someone else's pie hole.

Cinnamon smiled broadly. "Thank you," she said. "So, you're Kupcake's boy, eh?"

Jerome felt his cheeks brighten. "Yeah, I mean, I guess. Well, I mean, we've spent some time together."

Cinnamon eyed him appraisingly. "Not bad. Certainly baking above your weight class there, considering you're who you are."

Jerome ignored the old, familiar jab and took a sip of the peppermint extract. It went down smooth and then blossomed into a ball of heat in his stomach. "So, what do you want?"

She wants to cook you and eat you. She wants to swallow you while you lay here screaming. The thought slithered across his mind like a gummy slug, and he blinked in surprise.

The churro smiled again, and the horrible images scattered like shards of broken candies. "You seemed sad. I thought I could help you out... take your mind off of things." She reached a slender hand across the table and touched his arm, her touch as hot as the drink in his belly. "I could make you forget about all the horrible things you've seen so far. I could make you forget about everything. For a while."

Each word seemed to stab into Jerome's mind, evaporating his thoughts. He took a breath and leaned back, pulling his cup towards himself and holding it protectively against his chest.

"I'm not going to give up what I have with Kupcake just for a night." Again, his voice seemed to be coming from far away, through layers of phyllo dough.

"I'm not talking about just a night, sweetie."

Jerome looked at her, his brow furrowed. "What are you saying?"

"I can take you away from all of this!" She waved a hand absentmindedly. "I have a nice place at the base of Marmalade Lake. Let me take you away."

Again, thoughts squirmed into his mind unbidden. *Your crumbs on her lips, your butter running thickly down her chin. Her teeth lunging forward to rip more of you away while you scream, scream, scream....*

One of Cinnamon's fingers touched the back of his hand, and once more the horrible thoughts melted away. Jerome shook his head. Those last few words had been in the churro's voice. How was that possible? *Mother Baker, I've had too much extract,* he thought.

"You'd make a good companion. I've always liked muffins. Besides," she lowered her voice and leaned close. Jerome could smell the spices in her breath. They were almost as intoxicating as the drink. "I can do things that she can't. Or won't. You'd never have to ask. Just do. Anytime. Anywhere. I can make you very, very happy for a long, long time."

"Why would I do that?" he asked, but even as the words slipped out of his mouth, he felt a soft pull... an urge to go with this beautiful churro. He was a muffin, after all; he had urges. And she was so beautiful. What was so wrong with a confection this attractive wanting him? Why wouldn't he just go? It would be the easiest thing in the world.

Cinnamon pressed her appeal, "You know that, because of who you are and who she is, it can never work out. Her father won't allow it. The laws won't allow it. And that's only in the event that you actually survive what you're planning. But I could give you all of what you and every other confection wants. I saw you and knew you were perfect. Then, I heard you talk – the way you spoke about love and devotion. I want that. I want that with you."

Going to kill you, kill you, kill, kill, eat you–

Jerome shuddered at the intense feelings of need and hunger that accompanied the thoughts he'd just had. All delivered into his mind with the sweet, dripping tones of the churro.

Cinnamon pulled one of his hands close and ran one of his fingers along her bottom lip, once more sending the strange thoughts to the ether. Again, Jerome felt that almost irresistible pull towards the churro. It would be nice, he thought. Living out the rest of his days at the shores of Marmalade Lake, he and Cinnamon entwined in each other's arms.

You're going to scream for the rest of your life-

He felt a stirring deep inside and allowed visions of their trysts to float through his mind. It would be wonderful, he thought. But beneath that, swimming far below the images of all the things she would do to him and would let him do to her, there was something colder, something screaming for attention. Something he couldn't quite focus on clearly.

"You're thinking how great it would be, aren't you?" she asked as she poured them another round. Her voice droned, drilling into him with a strange cadence. He reached out a hand that felt like it had been filled with the lightest marshmallow fluff and grabbed the bottle of extract. It lifted easily, and he saw it was just over half-empty, although Jerome didn't recall drinking that much. He took another long drink, and the thing further down beneath the happy thoughts fell even more quiet. "It could be nice," he admitted. The admission muted the deep-down something all the more, even as a tiny part of his mind fought to focus on the faint something. What the oven was it?

Her eyes lit up with hunger as she gripped his hand tightly.

"It will be more than nice," she purred. "Come on. We can leave tonight. Nobody will ever need to know, and we can be in my home this time tomorrow. Together. Who knows?" she asked, pulling him to a standing position and moving to push her body against his. "I may not even be able to wait that long. I may just have to have you here and now." Her breath was hot, sensual on his cake.

Going to tear your throat out in an alley, going to leave you dying in the mud while she chews and chews and-

Jerome felt his willpower crumbling, and felt his thoughts and memories of Kupcake, of Cleetus and Stephen, of everything slipping away like excess flour being brushed from the counter. It felt good, to let go and have no worries, to focus only on Cinnamon and what she would be able to provide him. He nodded dumbly. Yes, he could see a life with her. Suddenly, he felt agitated that they weren't on the road to her home already.

"Let's go," he said, his voice coming to his ears from miles away. Cinnamon smiled brightly and led him towards the door.

They wove through the tables with Cinnamon looking back only once, her smile not reaching her hungry and eager eyes. Jerome, his head swimming, staggered along behind her. A small tartlet carrying a tray of cups drifted close by on her way to another table and Jerome lurched to avoid a collision. His hip connected with another table, and he bent forward as the table slipped along the floor, the sugar glasses atop it falling off the chipped and splintered edge with a high-pitched crash.

The noise cut through the fog in his mind like a rolling pin slamming into a mound of softened butter. Jerome remained as he was, bent over the table and feeling the scarred Red Vine wood. He blinked rapidly. With each passing of his eyelids, the fog dissipated and reality, hard and loud, crashed back in.

What the oven am I doing?

He looked towards Cinnamon and saw not the lithe, beautiful churro, but a bent and twisted creature whose cake was dark and shiny from having baked too long. All along her form were furry, spongy patches of black and green mold. Cinnamon glared at him with only one good eye, the other having gone the color of white chocolate. She opened her mouth, and he saw gaps of glistening gums where teeth were missing. The few that remained were jagged, splintered things. Her hands, skeletal claws, groped for him.

"No," he said, but the force of his word wasn't enough. He shook his head. "What... what did you do to me? I...." He swallowed thickly. "I want nothing to do with you."

"Come back, baby. I'll make you feel so good," Cinnamon said. This time, her voice was dry and brittle, the sound of stale pretzel sticks breaking.

"I belong to Kupcake," he said, firmly this time. Jerome pushed back from the table and stumbled away from the hideously overbaked good as it screeched and reached for him. Her clawed hand swiped through the air, the tips of her talons whistling as they moved inches in front of him.

Vaguely, he was aware of the other patrons crying out in surprise and fear, their own chairs toppling as they stood and rushed to get clear of the scene unfolding in the center of the tavern. Jerome's hands flailed, occasionally finding a glass or plate and gripping it before hurling it at the advancing, blackened churro. The objects connected, cracking against her rough body or bouncing away unbroken when they hit one of the patches of mold.

As he backed through the tables, Jerome saw a yellow shape in the center of half-a-dozen smaller dark ones. "What the hell are you doing here? Who's that?" Stephen shuffled. Jerome, unable to look away from the hideous monstrosity that advanced on him, ignored the questions. But as he passed the peep, Stephen pushed forward and bumped the muffin with his head. "Oi, prick! I'm talking to you!"

Jerome risked a glance at Stephen. The peep stood with three Sugar Babies on either side of him, their profession clearly marked by their state of near non-dress and heavy applications of Mary Cake free samples.

He heard Stephen swear, and then the peep rushed forward and rammed the demon churro, sending her sprawling towards the door. She fell with a screech, her clawed hands pulling chairs over with a crash.

"For fuck's sake, she's a Baker-damned siren, man!" Stephen blinked. "Holy Rolling Pin, where did you find her?"

"I...she...."

Stephen looked at the Sugar Babies, longing and frustration mingling in his eyes. "Better shove off, girls. I need to stay with my friend, lest he get his ass eaten." The peep wriggled, and several chocolate coins fell to the floor. "For your troubles," he blinked. The Sugar Babies picked the coins up and, with sidelong glances at Jerome, filed out of the bar.

Cinnamon lay on the floor, her burnt and twisted form writhing as she struggled to get up. Jerome saw her truly, an evil creature that lived only to feed on the unsuspecting few who were unlucky enough to come into contact with her.

If I hadn't seen clearly when I did, she would have killed me. Great Mother Baker, he realized, *I was going to go with her.* Panic swept over him. *How could I even have considered that?*

Cinnamon clawed her way up and stood, glaring hatefully at her two opponents. "Last chance!" she hissed. "You know you don't have a future with that *cupcake*!" she spat. "Come with me, and I'll make-"

The words were cut off as a chair slammed into her, knocking her back across the floor.

"Bitch talks too much," Stephen wriggled. He only had time to suggest that much before a glass bounced off of his fluff, knocking him to his side. Jerome looked up and saw Cinnamon kneeling opposite a table, a look of triumph on her withered face.

"Bitch talks too much!" she mocked in a high-pitched voice, and then threw another glass. Jerome ducked, but felt the wind of it passing overhead. He flipped a table on its side, the legs snapping off as he did so, and he dragged the dazed peep behind it.

"Stay here," he said curtly, and hurried off.

"The fuck was I going to go?" Stephen blinked after him.

Jerome moved quickly through the room, ducking as glasses and plates and the occasional chair or stool flew through the air, only to crash against the floor or walls and pepper him with fragments. Other patrons ran about, scrambling desperately for safety, throwing themselves behind overturned tables. *Great Mother Baker, what I wouldn't give for the Bag of Ganache right now*, he thought as he snatched a half-empty bottle of extract off the floor and slid under one of the few remaining unbroken tables. He cursed himself for leaving the bag hidden beneath the floorboards of his room at the Mixing Bowl.

As soon as he settled under the table, Cinnamon screamed and redoubled her assault. As he worked at shoving a napkin into the bottle he'd picked up, he thought she had to be tearing down the very walls and throwing the bricks at him, such was the fury of her assault. *There's no way there's that much stuff left in this place.* Her artillery bombardment crashed down over him, and he flinched with each impact.

When the rag was ready, he looked desperately around until he found what he needed. Around the corner to a short hallway that led to the bathrooms, there stood a single candle holder, its one candle standing bravely against the pressing darkness of the corridor. Jerome gathered himself and darted forward. Before he could reach the candle holder, though, a custard pie screamed and landed with a thud only feet away. The pie's eyes were wide with shock as it slid across the floor and came to rest against the wall, the wet contents of its body spilling out from a wide, jagged wound.

Cinnamon screeched in rage as Jerome ducked around the corner. New sounds of furniture being hurled marked the churro's progress across the room. *Gotta hurry*, he thought. *Stephen is a sitting peep out there.* Plucking the candle out of the holder, he touched it to the makeshift wick he'd created and watched it consider – think about it, ruminate, debate on the pros and cons of things – and then finally decide and catch. The fire, happy with its decision, eagerly climbed the rag towards the syrupy contents in the bottle.

In one smooth motion, Jerome spun around the corner and let the bottle fly. His face split in a grin of triumph as he felt the bottle leave his fingers, but it shifted into a look of surprise and then one of 'oh shit' as he saw Cinnamon there within only three paces of him... and the bottle flying end over happily burning end, on over her head towards the long bar at the other end of the room.

The bottle erupted at the same time that Cinnamon slapped him, the blow sounding like a thunderclap against his cake. He heard a roar and wasn't sure if it was the pain in his head or the fire. Blindly, he lashed out, his fist connecting with the soft ickiness that was a patch of mold on her upper chest. The punch didn't hurt the churro, but was so sudden that it stunned her into standing still and looking down at the dark spot which still held a faint impression of Jerome's knuckles.

"You punched me?" she gasped, and for a moment, he heard the velvety smoothness of the voice she'd used to ensnare him.

He'd opened his mouth to speak when a shadow moved behind her, and Cinnamon crumbled into a heap at his feet under the chair that Stephen slammed down on top of her. The peep stood there with his sides pumping furiously like a bellows, and stared down at the unconscious confection.

"Eat that, bitch!" Stephen blinked. Then, with a glance over his shoulder, the peep shuffled, "We gotta get the fuck out of here, muffin boy. They're going to be looking for us."

"What about-?" Jerome gestured at the unconscious churro.

"Motherfucker, you set this place on fire and this bitch was going to eat you. You hear me? *Eat you.* And trust me, churros don't use forks. But, more importantly—" the peep seemed to take a breath, and then shuffled, its small body shaking with emotion: "YOU SET THIS FUCKING PLACE ON FIRE!"

Jerome leapt over the prone body of his would-be devourer and rushed out of the tavern, staying close to the peep as they hurried down the street with the night closing around them, the smoke and sound of flames fading in the distance.

26

The next morning, Jerome woke with what felt like an entire army of sour straw guards marching through his head and the sharp acrid tang of smoke in his nostrils. He lay back on the small, thin mattress and stared at the ceiling, thinking about the previous evening. *Cinnamon. The churro.* He thought back to her sliding into his booth in the bar, plying him with peppermint extract - at the thought of the drink, the pounding in his head renewed itself with gusto and his stomach rolled - and trying to convince him to run away with her. And for a sickening moment, he'd almost been ready to, so powerful had been the siren's powers. Did that mean that his love for the princess was not strong enough? Did that mean that he wasn't as committed to her as he'd believed?

No. He refused to accept that. He would never stray from Kupcake. She was the only confection he ever wanted to be with. He wouldn't have gotten up from that table with the churro if he hadn't been magicked and entranced by her powers.

I did, though. I was halfway across the room before I came to my senses. What would have happened if I hadn't? Would I even still be alive now? He thought back to the fight, and the screams of anger and rage that the churro had bellowed as they'd struggled in the bar.

A soft scraping drew his attention, and he looked over to see Stephen shuffle into the room. "I was starting to wonder if you were dead," the peep blinked.

"I didn't thank you for last night," Jerome said. Stephen regarded Jerome coolly, and then wriggled, "You mean for stopping you from almost fucking a churro?"

Jerome's body ran cold at the words. "I-"

Stephen bumped him. "You can't be held responsible, man. Those things hypnotize their victims; make them think they're seeing the hottest piece of dough around. Kupcake herself would have been swayed if she'd come into contact with that thing. Don't feel bad. Come on, let's get out of here. Unless you've forgotten, you set fire to a building last night. People are going to be looking for you. We gotta get the fuck out of here, and fast."

Jerome held a hand to his aching head. "You said *almost*," Jerome said, neither as a question nor a statement, but somewhere in between.

The peep shuffled closer, reaching the edge of the bed and blinking, "Yeah. When I came in, you were more than halfway to pound-town. I have no idea why because she was uglier than Cleetus' droppings. But, luckily, I was there to save your ass. Again."

"She seemed beautiful to me, at the time."

"Yeah. Peppermint extract and a siren will do that. You're lucky I came in when I did. Otherwise, she would have fucked you dry and then left you to crumble in an alley somewhere. Or worse. I've heard of those things eating muffins like you. Eating them alive."

"So, sometimes they don't have their way with their victims?"

"In those instances," the peep shuffled, "the sex comes after."

Jerome forced himself to sit up. He blinked away the wave of dizziness that flooded his mind then stood up. "We have to get on the road. That's the only way we're going to get to the Black Licorice Castle."

"You suck at motivational speeches," Stephen wriggled as he followed Jerome out the door. "More importantly, we gotta get out of here before the owners of that bar come looking for you."

"You keep reminding me, yeah. What about Cinnamon? You think she could be out there looking for me, too?"

"That was her name? Holly Rolling Pin, how hard up are you? Cinnamon? Let me guess, her daddy was a tres leches and he abandoned her when she was but a wee spot of cinnamon and sugar?"

"Shut up," Jerome mumbled.

"You like 'em trashy, don't you?" the peep blinked. "I hear ya. I was going to get my freak-peep on with those Sugar Babies last night until I stepped into the leading role of 'Save Jerome's Muffin Ass Part Two'. Yeah, there's a chance she'll come after you. All the more reason to get Balthus and that big green bear, and get the hell out of here." They went downstairs, moving carefully around a pair of chocolate covered peanut clusters passed out in the hall, the stench of stale extract wafting from both candies.

They found Balthus sitting at a table in the dining room, a cup of hot maple syrup in one hand and with his own eyes looking bloodshot. He grunted a greeting and waved for more mugs of syrup to be brought to the table. "We need to get out of here," Jerome said as he grabbed his mug. "Stephen and I, we, uh, got into a bit of trouble last night."

Balthus stared at him across the table and then raised a bony finger. "I told you two not to mess with those working girls. Great Mother Baker help you if you have the yeasty meringue, I swear."

"It's nothing like that," Stephen wriggled. "Jerome may have set a building on fire, that's all."

Balthus looked at the peep for a long moment before he swung his head slowly to stare at the muffin. "You. Set. A. Building. On. Fire."

"Had to be done," Stephen blinked. He looked at Jerome. "I didn't see that you had any other choice."

"I mean—" Jerome started, but Balthus held up a hand.

"I don't want to hear it." He sat back and let out a long breath, swirled the last of his syrup, and then downed it in a single gulp. "We're going to have to get out of town quickly. Let's order breakfast first, though."

"I thought you said *quickly*," Jerome said.

"Of course, I did!" Balthus snapped. "As soon as I've finished my breakfast, packed my things, and ordered lunch to go." He winced. "You may want to do a little cleaning up of yourself also. Then, we'll be quick about leaving. The owner of that building is most likely going to come looking for you."

"Any word from Maddie?"

"Not a peep," Balthus said, and then looked at Stephen. "No offense."

"Dust yourself," Stephen shuffled.

Jerome sat back while Balthus called the waiter over and ordered food. Guilt over jeopardizing the mission weighed heavily on him. So what if the macaron had refused to help? He'd made it this far without her. Made it through the Red Vines Forest, through the Pudding Swamp and that horrific congealed salad monster, and it had all been fine. All without help. He stole a glance at Stephen, who was looking at a Sugar Baby sleeping in a pool of syrup at a corner table, her sequined dress hanging almost completely off her curved body.

Okay, maybe he'd had a little help there. But still. He'd made it this far, and he would make it the rest of the way. Even if Balthus and Stephen went their own directions - after last night, the way the peep was staring doughnut-holes through the unconscious and snoring Sugar Baby and the way Balthus continued to grumble to himself, that was a very real possibility - Jerome would forge on anyway. He was certain he'd most likely die trying to save Kupcake, but that was alright. If that was what was required of him to save her, then he would happily do it. It would suck, of course. He was sure there would be pain and gasping and probably more than a little scream-ing, and a few tears thrown in for good measure, but they would be all offered happily.

He swallowed the last of his syrup and put the mug down. Looking at the others, he asked, "Are we ready?" Their silence answered his question. "Balthus, I want to reiterate again that you don't have to come along. Nor do you, Stephen. This was my quest to begin with and, the Great Baker Herself willing, I will finish it."

"You go into that castle alone and you'll be finished, all right," Stephen blinked.

"The fluffy yellow bastard is right," Balthus croaked, his voice thick and rough around a mouthful of deep-fried butter. "I already told you, I'm going with you. I have a personal interest in this whole thing, showing the world that us Danish Wedding Cookies aren't completely crumbled." He chuckled – a rasping sound that produced flecks of fried batter from his lips. "Besides, I want to see you get that saucy little lava cake out of there."

"She's a cupcake."

Balthus waved dismissively. "I'm coming with you. I plan on personally putting my foot up German Chocolate Cake's pie hole, if you know what I mean."

"Nobody knows what you mean, you crazy bastard!" a voice called out from the darkness of the hallway. Their whole group turned as Maddie slowly emerged, cloak billowing gently behind her and one hand resting on the shiny pommel of a plastic toothpick sword.

Jerome stared at the macaron. "What are you doing here?"

Maddie placed a gloved hand on his shoulder. "I thought a lot about what you said last night. Well, not a lot, as I spent a good bit of the night in the company of a couple of Jolly Ranchers until someone set fire to the tavern next door to us. But your sincerity really stuck with me." She searched his eyes. "You love this Kupcake?"

"With everything that I am, ever have been, and ever will be."

"Yeah, that's what I thought." She sighed. "The Tempting Tarts are at your service. We'll go with you and do what we can to help you rescue Kupcake."

Jerome felt his chest swell, his throat begin to close up, and tears well in his eyes. "That's—" was all he got out before a slap rocked his head back.

"Don't start that shit, son!" Maddie said, her hand still poised in the air from the first blow. "Else, I'll give you another. Me and mine aren't coming on this trek if you're going to be all weepy the whole time."

Rubbing his jaw, Jerome nodded. "Fair enough."

27

The Tempting Tarts consisted of nine macarons, most different in color and filling. More than a few had cracks or gouges in their cookie – evidence of hard-fought battles. Two had eye patches, and their exposed eyes passed over Jerome and his companions with bored disinterest. Most kept their distance from the muffin and his group, speaking softly amongst themselves but falling silent and brooding anytime Jerome wandered near.

However, there were two, twins with identical lime green cookies and light pink filling, who seemed to always be in a happy, bouncing mood. They were introduced as Mopsy and Richard, and despite disapproving scowls from their party members, they openly engaged Jerome with mindless prattle and endless questions about his journey thus far.

"Is it true that you killed a whole congealed salad by yourself?" Mopsy asked, barely able to contain the excitement in her voice.

Jerome opened his mouth to answer, but Richard piped in, "How'd you do it? Did you eat it afterwards? I hear they're good to eat."

"Yuck!" Mopsy spat. "Who would want to eat that?"

"Some people do," Richard said defensively.

"You wouldn't know what to do with a congealed salad if it sat on your face and wiggled," Mopsy teased. She then proceeded to dance around her brother, wiggling her rump and singing, "Wiggle, wiggle, wiggle. Wiggling on Richard's stupid face."

Richard endured the teasing for a few moments before he snarled and dove at his sister, knocking her to the ground. They rolled through the thick grass, grunting and cursing each other as they fought.

"The fuck's with them?" wriggled Stephen. "Wait, you didn't tell them you single-handedly defeated that congealed salad, did you? You know that was me, right?"

Jerome pulled his attention away from the fighting macarons and gaped at the peep. "You? You did nothing! I led that thing into that ravine. I was the one who lost my sword to it. What did you do?"

"I lowered that bubblegum tape to you so you could get out."

"Exactly! How is that defeating a congealed salad?"

"By getting you out of there, I left that thing trapped in the ravine."

"You left it... what?"

Stephen blinked slowly, as if addressing a child. "Because I removed you from the ravine, I left the monster trapped down there. It had no way of getting out, and therefore it certainly died sooner or later."

"I was the one who led it down there in the first place!"

"Maybe, but only by pure accident. You were just flailing about and fell into that hole. It's not like you devised a strategy to lure it down there."

"Bloody Great Rolling Pin, are you serious? You think that was all you just because it was stuck down there after you pulled me out - which, by the way, I did. All you did was lower the gum. I did all the work! You think that gives you the credit for killing it?"

"Of course. Like I said, eventually it most likely died down there."

Jerome snorted. "You have no way of knowing that. It could have crawled out on its own."

"Yeah, but probably not. I mean, you have legs and arms and you couldn't crawl out of there. You had to have me. And without me to help it out also, it most likely died. Thus—" Stephen wriggled in a gesture that seemed to indicate himself, "credit."

"Why do I bother even talking to you?" Jerome asked as he returned his attention to Mopsy and Richard, who had by now ended up with Mopsy sitting on Richard's shoulders, slapping at his face while he ran in circles trying to knock her off by jumping every third or fourth step.

Richard yelled things that were unintelligible, but Mopsy kept screaming, "I'm wiggling on you! Can you feel my butt?"

"What are those morons doing?" Maddie asked. Jerome jumped at the soundless appearance of the macaron.

"Yeah, your jumpy ass killed the congealed salad," Stephen wriggled in a huff.

Ignoring the peep, Jerome said, "You gotta stop sneaking up on people like that." He took deep breaths in an attempt to still his racing heart.

Maddie looked at him skeptically. "Sneaking up on people is mostly how we get paid, you know. It's kinda hard to stop doing just because you have a weak constitution."

"I don't have a weak... oh, you know what, it doesn't matter. They're—" he pointed towards the fighting siblings, "fighting or something. Strange behavior for siblings," he said.

"Maybe," Maddie conceded, "but I've seen the two of them pull the raisins out of raisin bread and eat them while the bread watched."

Jerome shuddered.

"What are they fighting about this time?"

Jerome started to answer, but realized he had no idea. "I have no idea."

Maddie snorted amusedly. "May as well let them get it out of their system now. If they don't, chances are that something will trigger one of those idiots at the wrong time and they'll start arguing right when we need everyone to be quiet." Jerome and Stephen followed Maddie as they caught back up to the rest of the tarts. "So, you really snuck into the Land of the Danish Wedding Cookies?" Maddie asked after a while.

"Yeah, but wit-"

"Fluffernutter!" Richard screamed, which set Mopsy off on a new tangent of insults and taunts – mostly things about parts of her brother being weaker than limp taffy.

"I had help," Jerome continued.

"You mean the Bag of Never-Ending Powdered Sugar?"

Jerome touched the bag where it hung on his belt. "Yeah. I still can't believe it worked."

"I'm betting it didn't," Maddie said. When she caught Jerome gaping at her, she continued, "Look, everyone knows those Danish Wedding Cookies are five ingredients shy of even half a cookie. You probably could have walked in there wearing a mallowmar suit bought off the rack at Happy's Cheap Discounted and Totally Unbelievable Costumes, and they wouldn't have batted an eye."

"I don't know... they were pretty suspicious of everything. Even each other. Wait, is that store a thing?"

Maddie cocked an eyebrow at Jerome. "Like I said, shy of half a cookie."

"Anyway," Jerome continued, "I went in there."

"What happened then?"

"They threw me in the dungeon."

"You're not very good at this whole adventuring and rescuing thing, are you?"

Jerome felt a twinge of irritation. "I never claimed to be."

"What did you do for a living before all of this?"

"I build and repair gingerbread houses. Occasionally, I'll come across a mixer that needs attention. Small things like that."

"Not bad work," Madi admitted. "Maybe when I finally retire, I'll open a shop doing something like that myself. I'm pretty good with my hands, and I've been known to be able to assemble things a time or two."

Jerome only nodded, not sure how to respond. They continued on in silence, listening to the insults and curses hurled at one another by the twins. Ahead of them, the rest of the tarts walked in pairs, followed by Balthus and Cleetus. Stephen shuffled along in the grass behind Jerome and Maddie.

"Why did you really decide to help me?" Jerome asked.

Maddie was quiet for a while, and Jerome began to worry that the question had irritated her. He braced himself for a slap. "I was in love once," she admitted. "That surprises you?" she asked, looking at him from the side of her eye. Jerome shook his head. "Liar." She smiled. "It's okay... I'm not the easiest on the eyes, and certainly not the sweetest confection to ever roll off a spatula, Great Baker anoint me. But yeah, I was in love once. We were together for a few years; spent every waking moment with each other. She was a chocolate cream cake, and was everything to me."

"How did you guys meet?"

Maddie shrugged. "You know how it is. You're completely wasted at a bar, about to make a fool of yourself by either picking a fight or going home with the ugliest gummy there—"

"You didn't know which one you were going to do?"

"There was a lot of extract involved. Plus, sometimes they're one and the same. Anyway, Rebecca swept in like melted butter. The second I saw her, I knew. You know?"

Jerome smiled, thinking about the first time he'd ever seen Kupcake. She'd been emerging from a school, having gone there to read to the cocoa nibs and then walking right out into the sunlight, her frosting gleaming. She'd looked at him and smiled – something she probably did every day to almost everyone she encountered – but it had floored him. For a full minute, he'd been unable to breathe or move. He'd just stood there gaping at her. She'd been radiant, everything he'd ever dreamed of even when he hadn't known he was dreaming. Then, she'd been past him, moving down the street, and he'd realized he'd stepped in animal cracker droppings.

"Yeah, I know," he said. "So, what happened?"

Maddie chewed on her lip for a long while, her eyes distant as she plodded along across the field. Finally, she said, "I don't want to say its name."

Coldness swept through Jerome, pooling in a heavy ball in his stomach. "You don't mean," he started. She nodded. "Where in the name of the Holy Mother Baker did she come across," he looked around, and then whispered, "*yogurt*?"

A hardness came into Maddie's eyes, and he saw her jaw clench. "You shouldn't say that name. You don't want to see what happens if you say it too often or too loudly."

"But... how?"

"I don't know. All I do know is that one of our neighbors sent word that what was left of her body had been found in the woods about a mile from our house."

"How did they know it was... you know?"

"They said that there were small amounts of it still on her," Maddie answered. Her voice was taut, each word pinched and forced out. "They had to burn it all, lest even those bits hurt or kill someone else." She took a deep, shuddering breath. "I never got to say goodbye."

"Great Rolling Pin, I'm so sorry!" Jerome reached out and placed a hand on the macaron's shoulder. Maddie shrugged it off.

"I left home that very day. Packed only what I could easily carry. I met the rest of these—" she nodded towards the tarts, "and we've spent every day since living like it could be our last. But, one day. One day, I'll get revenge. I swear it to the Great Baker Herself."

They walked for a while more, neither speaking. Eventually, Maddie said, "That's why I agreed to help you. I could see that same look in your eyes that I used to have when I looked at Rebecca."

"It means a lot to me, really. Thank you."

Maddie just nodded. She looked up into the sky. "It'll be dark in about an hour. We need to find a place to camp. Mopsy, get off your brother's head and go gather us things for a fire!" Several yards away, Mopsy groaned like a petulant teenager, but she also stood up from where she'd been squatting on Richard's face while her brother had kicked and squirmed beneath her. Free of his burden, Richard sat up gasping for air and wiping at his face.

"You're sick, Mopsy!" he yelled after her, but the tart was already skipping away through the grass in search of things to burn. Maddie led the group towards a copse of trees, and the band began making preparations for camp. Maddie pulled items for the evening meal out of a large bag and said, "We'll get an early start in the morning."

"How long till we reach the castle?" Jerome asked.

Maddie looked at him seriously. "We passed into the realm of Devil's Food Cake about three hours ago. We should be on the edge of his castle's grounds tomorrow afternoon."

28

"That's..." Jerome's mouth seemed to dry up before any other words could form. He stared, eyes wide, through the licorice tree branches and across the wide expanse that surrounded the spiky and completely evil-looking castle. Dozens of yards away, standing tall from the flat earth like spikes testing the doneness of batter, were several licorice poles. Attached to the poles by thick cords of butcher's twine were the dried and chipped remains of several rock candy guards. Jerome stared at them with horror numbing his mind. Who were they? What had happened to them?

"Yeah," Maddie said, her voice low. "That's it. And those—" she jerked her chin towards the crumbling candies mounted on the poles, "are what remains of soldiers sent by King Red Velvet. I recognize the insignia. First Batch of the Baker's Dozen Rock Candy Attachment. I had run-ins with a couple of them long ago."

"We're supposed to go into that?" Stephen shuffled. "Fuck that. Jerome, you're cool and all, except for that whole congealed salad thing, but that right there is suicide. I ain't getting strung up on a pole. This marshmallow is too delicate."

Jerome tended to agree with the peep, but couldn't bring himself to say so. "Actually, it doesn't look that bad – dead candies aside."

From the corner of his eye, he saw Maddie turn and glare at him like he'd just turned into a gummy toad. He kept his eyes focused beyond the remains of Red Velvet's special forces and on the giant, sprawling black monstrosity in the distance as he asked, "What's the plan for getting us in there?"

He could feel the heat of Maddie staring at him for several long moments before she spoke. "That—" she pointed at the expanse surrounding the castle, "is one mile of open ground. You can see that there are no trees, no rocks, no hills or dips. Nothing behind or within which we can hide. The moment we step free of these trees, we're going to be spotted, and a few minutes later, picked up-"

"Or killed," blinked Stephen.

"-by sour straw guards," Maddie finished.

They all considered their options. Finally, Stephen blinked, "Could we disguise ourselves with grass and crawl across the field? I heard about a tart who did that once back in the Ladyfinger Crusades. Made it all the way across a huge battlefield and was able to kill the opposing commander with a candy thermometer. And from what I read, that field was much bigger than this one. And it was teeming with enemy confections."

Maddie stared at the field, chewing her lower lip and considering the option. Finally, she shook her head. "Look at the grass. It's all short. Anything taller than a few inches would stand out immediately."

"So, what then?"

Jerome straightened. "The Bag of Powdered Sugar!" Maddie frowned at him, but he went on, holding the bag up for the others to see. "This is one of the items that the Moon Pie Wizard sent me after. I found it deep in a cave guarded by hundreds-"

"Twenty," Stephen shuffled.

"-of evil, vile candies. Thousands of them, probably."

"Fifty at best, and only if you were seeing double," Stephen blinked.

The other tarts seemed no closer to understanding him, so Jerome went on, opening the bag so they could peer inside. "It's filled with a never-ending supply of powdered sugar. Dates back to the Ladyfinger Crusades, probably even before that. Anyway, you coat yourself with it and it will disguise you as whatever you need it to. We could coat ourselves with it to appear as a bunch of sour straw guards. They'd let us walk right in. We could use it to get all the way to Kupcake's cell and free her. Great Baker, we could even use it to get to the Cake Stand Room here and kill Devil's Food Cake! They'd never be the wiser!" He dug out a fist-full of sugar, and was reaching for Maddie when she held up a hand and shook her head.

"No. No disguises."

Jerome's hand hung in the air, small drifts of powdered sugar wafting to the ground. "Why not?"

"We tried a disguise once, about six years ago. We were smuggling something – I won't say what, and it's not important – into a town near the Potato Canyon. Place called Silpat. Horrible place; makes Trifle Town look like a few sprinkles playing dress-up with their mother's Mary Cake samples. Anyway, we disguised ourselves and, just as we reached the place to meet the guy, Mopsy had a reaction to the costume."

"A reaction."

"She thought she was a chocolate rabbit. Then, Dale and Abbott got it in their heads that not only were they made of cream cheese, but it was their sole mission in life to hunt down and eat a chocolate rabbit. Before you knew it, half my group was chasing each other around the streets screaming about how they were going to eat each other, with the other half screaming about how they had to fulfill their life's work by sitting in pudding. It was a shitshow."

"But how could costumes do that?"

"It doesn't matter now. But, there's another reason we can't use that."

Jerome waited.

"Aside from what I said to you yesterday about not really believing it works, it's not heroic enough. There aren't any songs about how a confection disguised itself as something else and infil-trated enemy territory."

"What about the guy I just mentioned, the tart with the grass and the Ladyfinger Crusades?" Stephen wriggled. "I'm positive he had songs about him." He began shifting around to the tune of "Comin through the grass, gonna batter your ass."

Jerome sighed. "Fine, but if we can't use the disguise, then what's your plan?"

The macaron turned and faced Jerome, her dark eyes sparkling in the early morning light. "We're going to let ourselves be captured."

29

R oscoe bolted up from his chair, where he'd been starting to doze. Guarding Random Hallway Number Seventy-Three in the Black Licorice Castle was not what he'd had in mind when he'd grown up training to become a sour straw guard. Being a sour straw, he'd been born into the life and had thought of nothing but the ultimate goal of becoming one of the elite guards. He'd spent his days learning the history not only of the guards - which was rather fascinating stuff if you felt that being employed to guard random doors or tents at various locales after an army had conquered some new village or land - but of the castle, as well as military history and tactics. He'd gone to guard school, which sounded like something a pastry with no future and no other options would attend so that he or she could end up guarding a remote ware-house in the middle of the night, but was actually rather grueling and demanding.

But, upon graduating and earning his plastic toothpick sword, he'd found himself assigned to a small unit and given the duty of guarding one of the dozens of seemingly random hallways that twisted and turned throughout the guts of the dark castle. He spent his entire shift, ten hours every day, sitting or standing or walking the length of the fifty-foot hallway. The hallway itself was unremarkable. No doors, no windows. Only five torches were spread evenly along one wall. He knew the hall itself was somewhere near the rear entrance of the castle, but that was it. At either end, the passage turned and connected with another hallway that was, of course, also guarded by a solitary watchman.

So, when his sergeant and front gate commander Tibus pounded around the corner and yelled for him to suit up, that there were intruders on the grounds, Roscoe nearly deposited crystalized sugar all over himself in the process of responding. He grabbed his sword and followed the confection in charge, though, their feet thudding on the stone floor.

They reached the rear gate where other guards were milling about, hands fluttering from sword hilts to belts to cloaks to hats and back to swords as they readied themselves to intercept the intruders. Roscoe's heart beat like a gumdrop hopped up on chocolate-covered coffee beans. He looked around and saw that, in addition to himself and Tibus, three others from random hallways had been drafted. In total, there were ten sour straws prepared to make the trek across the field.

"Who is it?" he asked Tibus. Tibus glowered at him, but shook his head.

"No idea. I heard it's a group of about twelve. Seems they're just strolling, lazy as you please, across the field."

"Heading here?"

"Where the hell else would they be heading?"

"Are they dangerous?" one of the other guards from his element asked. Tibus ignored the question.

"Okay, listen up!" the gate commander called, his voice loud and crisp. "We have a group of twelve plus a gummy bear heading this way. They seem to be a disorganized lot, so it's likely that they are lost, or they're some group of idiots who think they can come here and lobby for the release of Kupcake. We're going to go round them up, bring them back here, and shove them into cells. Assume nothing about these confections. Remember your training. Let's go."

Roscoe followed Tibus and the others out of the gate and into the field, where the bright morning sun slapped him in the face. He trudged across the field and tried to think back to his training, but couldn't remember anything about intercepting a group of confections crossing a field. Advancing on an enemy position, sure. Lobbing gobs of putrefied cookie dough into an enemy encampment, check. Standing for hours and watching nothing happen in a solitary hallway for almost half a day, double- and triple-check. But nothing like this.

Within moments, he was able to see the group – all twelve of them, plus the green hulk of a gummy bear – walking towards them in a loose cluster. The gate commander ordered swords to be drawn. Roscoe had never drawn his sword in this manner, only in training exercises against fondant targets. It felt strange, holding the plastic weapon and knowing that he may be forced to use it. Suddenly, he wasn't sure if he could. Drive the pointed tip into the soft body of another candy or pastry? Watch as they writhed on the blade in pain, with him hearing their screams as they perished? The thought made his sugary insides twist with abhorrence. Maybe this whole encounter would go quickly and quietly. Chances were, with such a small group, the intruders meant no ill will.

They reached the approaching pastries moments later, and Tibus called for both parties to halt. He motioned for his squad to fan out and partially encircle the newcomers. Roscoe took his position and watched as the gate commander approached the front of the new group, which included a large muffin, a small macaron, and a-

"Holy Rolling Pin, that's a Danish Wedding Cookie!" he hissed. Tibus growled for him to shut his trap and pay attention.

Tibus held out a hand, and the approaching intruders stopped. "You know whose lands these are!" Tibus barked. It was not a question. "Why are you here?"

One macaron stepped forward. "We caught these," she said, indicating the muffin, the Danish cookie, the gummy bear, and....

Roscoe's breath caught. A marshmallow peep. *Oh Great Mother Baker, those things are evil.* His own ma had told him stories of roving bands of peeps, yellow and pink creatures who would skulk around the woods near villages and creep in through any open crack, contorting their bodies to fit until they were inside. Then, the screaming would start.

Roscoe shuddered. He'd rather face yogu... his mind snapped off the thought like scissors cutting off a thread of dough. Best not to invoke that name. Instead, he focused on what the macaron was saying.

"...plotting to sneak into the castle. We being loyalists to Devil's Food Cake—"

"You are, are you?" Tibus mused.

The macaron blinked, and then stammered, "Of course, half of us fought with German Chocolate Cake in the Raisin Skirmishes several years back. Anyway, we caught them and thought we'd bring them to you guys; let you deal with them."

Tibus eyed the macaron, his brow furrowing. "Why didn't you just reduce them to crumbs yourselves? Hoping for a reward, is that it?"

The macaron smiled and glanced at her companions. "Now that you mention it."

Roscoe held his breath as Tibus stared at the group, clearly trying to decide whether or not to bring them in or destroy the lot there and then. Finally, the old guard's face relaxed and he waved to his other guards.

"Bring them inside." He stepped aside and waited as the newcomers were marched past him. Roscoe fell into step behind the sergeant.

When they were near the gate, and the shadows of the high castle walls had settled over them like a thin, cooling blanket of foil, Tibus called a halt. "Gather their weapons!" he commanded. Roscoe thought it a bit odd that he'd waited till now to do this, but decided he didn't know the first thing about apprehending people. All he knew was how to count things out of boredom while guarding Random Hallway Number Seventy-Three.

The other sour straw guards moved closer, their hands reaching out for the captives' weapons. There was a shout, and then a sudden thrashing. Other shouts and curses leapt into the air, only to be cut short. Roscoe heard the distinct sounds of toothpick swords being put to use and then felt a heavy weight collapse on him, knocking him to the ground. He looked up only to see Tibus on top of him, his thick gummy insides gazing wetly out at the world. Tibus' eyes stared blankly at his last remaining guard. The gate commander's mouth moved in an attempt to give a final order, but no sound came out. He stilled, his body sagging.

Roscoe swallowed against the syrup that threatened at the back of his throat and scrambled away from the body of the gate commander. He heard steps coming towards him and looked up in time to see the peep shuffling closer, its black eyes staring straight through his soul.

Roscoe now knew what the confections in those houses had felt so long ago. He began to scream, but the sound died as a whimper as he fell into blackness.

30

Stephen looked down at the unconscious sour straw guard and then back at Jerome. "I think he pissed himself."

"Get him up!" Maddie commanded. Jerome stood transfixed, still shocked by the speed with which the Tempting Tarts had dispatched the guards.

"You're not going to kill him, are you?" he asked.

Maddie watched Mopsy and Richard pull the unconscious guard to his feet. Mopsy slapped him lightly in the face, and then, that having had no effect, slapped him harder. The guard gasped and blinked in shock. When his eyes focused, they drifted over his captors before settling on Stephen. The guard shrieked and promptly passed out again.

"Damned Flaked Butter," Maddie cursed, and instructed Stephen to move to the rear of the group and out of sight. For good measure, she had Cleetus stand in front of the peep, completely blocking him from the sight of the guard. Then, she motioned for Mopsy to try again. This time, the guard retained consciousness and looked on in horror at his fallen comrades.

Maddie stepped closer. "You are going to take us inside and show us where they're keeping Kupcake," she informed the guard.

"I... I have no idea where they're keeping her."

"Look. We both know you do. That's a large castle, but you're one of the guards. You know where they're keeping her. And you're going to get us in there, past your other buddies, and take us to her room."

"No, seriously. I have no idea. I just guard a hallway."

"A hallway."

The guard nodded. "Yes, Random Hallway Number Seventy-Three. It's fifty feet long. It's just inside the rear entrance of the castle." He pointed towards a door nearby.

"And it leads to other hallways and doors and stairs that will all take us to Kupcake."

"I mean, if you say so. But seriously, I went through the academy only to guard a hallway. I have no idea where she's kept or even how to get there."

Maddie considered all this, and then stepped forward. "Well, you'd better figure it out really fast, my friend. Otherwise, I'll call the peep back out here. And we both know what he'll.... Son of a bitch, he fainted again."

31

———

"I swear, sire, I have no idea where he went!" the sugar cookie aide gasped. "The last I saw of Stuart was when the Moon Pie Wizard came to visit you. He left the castle on the back of an animal cracker stallion and he's not been heard from or seen since. I am sorry, sire." The cookie bowed his head in deference to show how sorry he truly was.

Better that he run away, thought King Red Velvet, than to see this. He looked forward, over the top of his own animal cracker steed, and saw the gates of Black Licorice Castle ahead. He turned and glanced back at the large clearing he'd just crossed. The memory of learning of the fate of his commando raid came swimming back through his mind. The Moon Pie Wizard had been right. Devil's Food Cake really had seen them coming a mile away. He shook his head. Devil's Food Cake held all the recipe cards in this matter. There was no getting around it.

And, he thought for the hundredth time since making the decision to come here, *you have to atone for what was done. The time for hiding and denial is long past. Remember, you do this also to ensure that your daughter lives. What is important is that your actions prevent any further harm to your only child.* He shuddered at the memory of her cake and frosting smeared into the box that had been delivered days ago.

The rumbling of the main gate opening broke into his thoughts. Moments later, a small group of confections emerged, riding atop licorice-flavored wafers. At the head of the party rode German Chocolate Cake, his jawbreakers and sour straw guards flanking him.

"I see you came to your senses," German Chocolate Cake said as he approached. "It took you long enough."

"That burnt crumb of a master of yours didn't really give me much of a choice, did he?" Red Velvet scowled at the other confection. "Cakenapping my only daughter, threatening both me and her, sending..." his voice tightened, and he noticed a surge of excitement and pleasure in German Chocolate's eyes, "a box of... I can't even say it. Despicable. It's an affront to all of—"

"Shut up," German Chocolate Cake interrupted him, a tone of boredom creeping into his voice. "The measures taken were what was needed to get you here. And, I may add, nowhere nearly as dire as they could have been. So, just stop your inane ramblings about honor and propriety, and follow me. Devil's Food Cake is going to want to see you as soon as possible. He has... plans for you."

King Red Velvet stared, stunned at the other cake. In his entire life, nobody - not even his own father, who'd been notoriously harsh - had ever spoken to him in such a manner. *Keep calm*, he thought. *Go along with their puffery until you can see Kupcake.* He nodded in a tight, curt gesture, and then spurred his mount to follow German Chocolate Cake.

"Leave your men here," German Chocolate Cake said without a look back. "The lord of the castle only wants you."

Red Velvet stopped his mount and stared at his dark escort who, after a few steps, turned his own mount and looked back at him with the expectant gaze one would have given a cakeling who'd been told to finish all of his dinner. Red Velvet began to protest, in an automatic response, that his personal guard went wherever he did as a means of ensuring his safety. *But you're not getting out of here alive*, he reminded himself, feeling the last of his hope fall like a souffle. He let out a long breath and turned to the closest guard. "Wait here." The guard's eyes widened in surprise, but his training quickly intervened and he regained his composure. Nodding, he relayed the order to the others as King Red Velvet followed German Chocolate and the sour straw guards.

They entered the castle with more of Devil's Food Cake's guards materializing to surround them. A resounding boom jolted King Red Velvet as the gates were closed behind him, separating him from his guards. The king fought the urge to turn and bolt back towards the gate, to scream for his soldiers to pry the bars open and rescue him.

The courtyard was large, though not nearly as large as the one he had at home. Walls, walkways, and battlements rose all around him, and before them was a large, rounded opening that fed into the castle proper. German Chocolate Cake had dismounted and stood near the opening, waiting patiently. Red Velvet approached before he stepped out of his own saddle.

"You will come with me," German Chocolate Cake said. Red Velvet noticed the indifference with which the cake eyed him. In that look, Red Velvet understood that, to German Chocolate, he was but a leftover crumb, something fit for the trash bin. He was simply something in the path of this bitter confection's master's path to ultimate rule.

"Once I was respected and even feared by the forces of Dark Chocolate," Red Velvet said quietly.

"Yes," purred German Chocolate, "but now...." He shrugged. "This way, your highness," the cake sneered as he gestured through the doorway. Red Velvet stepped forward into the darkness.

32.

Kupcake paused in her digging to catch her breath. The tunnel she'd started had grown quickly and several times led her into a series of crawl spaces between walls or between floors. The way had been dirty and full of cotton-candy cobwebs. She picked absently at one that had materialized seemingly from nowhere and landed across her cheek.

She swallowed, grimacing at the dust and grit in her mouth. This was not what she'd had in mind when she'd started this endeavor. She'd long since moved beyond the gummy mice's domain, at least. Tight to either side of her were thick, concrete walls. She exhaled, fighting the rising sense of despair. What had she been thinking? Tunnelling out? There was no *out*. She was just exhausting herself. If she weren't careful, she was going to end up bringing a wall down on herself or - worse - being buried in an avalanche of dirt and small rocks, only to suffocate after hours or days of not being able to find her way out.

"Stop that!" she commanded herself. "You will not die down here. You're going to find a way out. There's always a way out. If the mice got in, then you can get out." She breathed deeply, spat out more grit, and then started digging again. Despite the weariness in her shoulders, the constant ache in her back, and the numbness in her hands, she attacked the dirt ahead of her powerfully with the dresser handle. Its edge was blunted, having been used on both dirt and rock, yet the tool was still effective.

After a few minutes of feverish digging, the tool jarred in her hands, sending a painful shockwave up her arms and into her shoulders. Kupcake winced at the pain, but then she smiled. She'd hit a wall. Carefully, she cleared the dirt away, exposing the large blocks. She'd learned that while the inner walls of the castle were made of blocks, those blocks were held together by a mortar made from salt water taffy. It was hard and held well, but more than once, she'd found areas where it was starting to soften. She did so now, probing the seams with her fingers until she felt spongy resistance. Then, she attacked that area with the handle, pulling chunks of taffy out and watching them plop quietly into the dirt at her knees.

When she'd cleared enough away, she pushed the block away from her, smiling as it grated against its neighboring stones before falling into the larger room beyond the wall. Ignoring the thud of the brick on the stone floor, Kupcake peered through the hole and saw a large chamber that was only dimly lit by torches along the walls. It was a room deep in the center of the castle, she thought. No windows. Never mind that, though; if it was a room, it would have a door leading out. She would rather take her chances in the halls of the castle than digging in the darkness.

Half an hour later, she'd managed to loosen and remove four more stones. The hole was small, but she felt that she could squeeze through with a little more effort. There might be a little damage to her cake and buttercream frosting, but that was the least of her worries. She'd have it all fixed when she got back home.

Home. The thought of it paralyzed her. She missed it so dearly. Her father, her mother, all of her friends in the castle. She missed riding her animal cracker horse; she missed taking walks down to the Oreo Bridge. She missed...

Jerome. Her heart seemed to twist and pulse within her chest.

What was he doing now? Did he know she was being held captive? How was he taking it? She hoped he hadn't tried to go to her father to offer help. Her father was a wonderful, kind, and generous man, but he had no love for muffins and stood fast by the rule that muffins and cupcakes were not to mix.

Kupcake realized she was crying now, gentle butter tears slowly trickling down her cheeks as she thought of her love, and his kindness and generosity and the horrible fact that, because of their differences and the laws of the land, the ignorance of confections refusing the truth of the past, he couldn't do anything for her. Once more, she vowed to herself that once she became free of this nightmare, she was going to force her father to change the laws of the land so that she and Jerome could be together without fear of repercussions.

"Rotted confections to the laws," she grumbled, wiping away her tears with one dirty hand and pushing herself through the hole.

The room she found herself in was extremely large and, she noted with surprise, not without a window. A heavy shutter was closed over a single large window, effectively blocking any outer light. The room itself was populated by old statues clothed in tin-foil armor, each one holding old dust- and cotton-candy-draped toothpick weapons. *Some storage room for museum-like pieces*, she thought, and moved to the window, ignoring the aching stiffness in her knees.

She pulled the shutter open, swinging it in and against the wall, and recoiled from the onslaught of sunlight that poured into the room like water through a sudden opening in a pipe. Slowly, her eyes adjusted, and she blinked until her vision was clear and she could focus. She leaned towards the window again and breathed in the cool fresh air.

Her breath caught as she realized what she was seeing. The window faced the front of the castle, and far below her, she could see the main gate and the courtyard inside it. There were several figures moving in a large group in the courtyard, coming from the gate.

Her eyes locked onto her father. She opened her mouth to scream down to him, but quickly closed it. She was too high up for him to hear her. Her eyes settled on the dark figure of German Chocolate

Cake as he led the king across the expanse and into the castle proper, both of them vanishing from Kupcake's sight.

Kupcake moved back from the window and chewed her lip, considering her next move. She had to get down to her father. She knew what Devil's Food Cake's plans were for him, and she would not allow it. Her eyes scanned the foil-clad figures around her and stopped on one statue in the corner near the door. With some effort, she wrested free from its rigid grasp a wicked, double-bladed tooth-pick sword. She gave the blade a few test swipes through the air, surprised at how light it felt in her hand while still feeling properly stabby.

Kupcake paused with one hand on the door leading out of the room and collected herself. *What's the plan?* she asked herself. Freeing her father from the guards and German Chocolate Cake was the priority. Maybe even giving German Chocolate a taste of her new, stabby friend. Her stomach knotted at the thought of harming anyone, but the soft throb of her head where the offset spatula had been employed calmed any nerves about violence. So, yes, she'd free her father and get him out of the castle and back to his men. And stabby-stab German Chocolate Cake. After that, she would turn her focus to finding Devil's Food Cake. She flexed her fingers around the sword's handle. She had a special recipe she wanted to go over with him... slowly.

A grim smile on her face, Kupcake tightened her hand on the doorknob. She'd begun to pull the door open when she caught the muffled sounds of voices. She quietly released the knob and pressed her head to the door, listening. *Guards.* From the cadence of their voices, she thought it sounded like they were changing shifts. More than once, she'd had to duck and hide in a shadowy alcove in the Lemon Icebox Castle while some of the rock candy guards had changed shifts – before she'd been able to move on to meet up with Jerome – so she knew the sounds.

Okay, not that way, then. Her eyes fell on the window and then shifted to the ragged hole from which she'd emerged. *Not going back up there*, she thought. Decided, she began rummaging through the room. The Great Mother Baker's luck was with her, as she quickly found several rugs, tapestries, curtains, and bath towels stashed in several large trunks which were themselves covered by several boxes and suits of tin-foil armor.

Using her toothpick sword, she slashed them into long ribbons and tied them from end to end. When assembled, the makeshift rope looked to her like it was at least a hundred feet long. Hoping that it would be enough to get her down to the ground, she anchored it around a massive suit of armor and dropped the length of it out the window. Before she left, she grabbed a small cake knife from one of the pieces of armor. After strapping her sword on tightly, she climbed out the window and began a slow descent downward.

After about twelve feet, her boots touched solid ground. Kupcake looked around her, surprised. She'd stopped on a balcony that was, as best she could tell, only a few yards above the ground. Glancing back up at the window, she frowned. It had certainly seemed higher from up there.

A quick glance over the balcony railing told her that climbing down to the ground wasn't an option. Almost a dozen sour straw guards were posted randomly around the a wide courtyard with nowhere for her to hide, their impassive faces staring straight ahead. For a moment, she panicked, but then she noticed the door further along the balcony. She cracked it open, glanced inside, and found that it opened to a bedchamber that had been long unused. Dust and fairy floss stretched across all of the furniture as well as the floor.

Kupcake hurried across the room and paused, listening before opening the door to the main hallway. The hall was empty, save for some wall art and the occasional bench and chair. Her own home had similar hallways, and she often wondered why anyone would leave a random chair halfway along a hall. Were guests supposed to be so feeble that they would need to stop and rest before reaching their own rooms?

Brushing aside the question, she moved down the hall. At the end, she found a stairwell that led downward. Peering over the railing, she saw that it would deposit her in the main hallway that would lead to the front courtyard and the gate - and her father's soldiers beyond that. "Yes," she breathed out in triumph. Now, to find her father.

Halfway down, she heard his deep and sonorous voice demanding to know where she was. Kupcake crouched and scuttled the remainder of the distance, one hand resting on the handle of the cake knife stuffed into her belt. When she reached the bottom of the stairs, she peeked around the corner to see two sour straw guards walking ahead of the king with a single guard behind him. Her heart leapt at the sight of her father.

Without thinking, Kupcake drew her sword and pulled the knife from her belt. She tried to steady the rapid pounding in her chest and her ragged breathing, but found them uncontrollable. She leapt from her hiding place and brought the sword up and around in a wide, clumsy arc, feeling the impact reverberate up her arm as she sliced across the chest of the closest guard. Not giving herself a chance to think about what she was doing, she next lunged forward with the cake knife - this time a bit more assuredly - and stabbed another sour straw high in the chest, close to his shoulder. Both guards collapsed with a whimper.

Before she could register the acts she'd just committed against other confections, a soft commotion drew her attention. She saw her father kicking the guard who had been positioned behind him. Searing pain along her right shoulder brought her attention back to her own predicament, however, and she saw the tip of the remaining sour straw's own sword just inside her moist cake. Kupcake looked down at it, confused, and then stepped back. The sword point came free, and she saw it had only been inside her less than a few centimeters. But the sight of her own moist cake clinging to the blade's tip sent a wave of nausea and rage through her. Before she could do anything else, the guard gave a pained grunt and crumbled to the floor.

King Red Velvet stood over the body, rubbing his fist. "They're harder than they look," he said between breaths.

Kupcake ran to her father and wrapped her arms around his cake.

When she didn't feel his own arms encircle her, she stepped back. He looked down at her with a mixture of relief and embarrassment in his eyes.

"Why did it take you so long to come?" she asked.

King Red Velvet swallowed hard with his eyes roaming around the corridor, clearly not wanting to settle on her. "It's not that simple. I sent a unit of the Baker's Dozen, but they failed. I realized I'd been putting myself above—"

Kupcake cut him off with a sharp wave of her hand. "We have to get you out of here!" Grabbing his hand, she pulled him back along the hallway towards the courtyard. "This way."

Through the arched opening, she could see the gate and, on the other side of it, her father's soldiers, most of them milling about aimlessly. Some sat on the ground and played cards while others gathered close and listened to one who still sat atop his mount, gesturing wildly with his arms. Kupcake could hear him extolling the benefits of investing in timeshares. Even the sour straws manning the gate seemed to be listening.

Turning back to her father, she said, "There's only two sour straws at the gate. We can get past them easily. Come on."

Red Velvet looked at his daughter with a mix of worry, confusion, and love swirling across his face. "How did you get out?" Glancing back at the still forms of the guards, he went on, "How did you learn to use those weapons?"

"I made it up," she said, and pulled her father out into the sunshine. She ran with her arm stretched behind her, her father a slow-moving weight. The gate seemed miles away, and the rock candy guards on the other side, a few of whom had noticed them and were approaching the gate themselves, a salvation that was still too far off for them to reach.

The two sour straw guards managed to pull their attention away from the advantages of a week near Marmalade Lake, and stepped forward and raised their own weapons. Kupcake and the king shuffled to a stop. "What do we do?" she asked. "You were a soldier – didn't they teach you strategy?"

"It's two guards, not a siege!" her father snapped. "I'll get the one on the left; you take the one on the right." He held out his hand for the sword. Kupcake handed it over. She raised her cake knife and, feeling a scream building in her chest, stepped forward to engage.

A hand as hard as frozen taffy clamped around her wrist, squeezing hard enough to make her fingers loosen from around the sword. The weapon clattered to the ground with a weak rattle. Kupcake was spun around and slapped hard. Her head rocked back from the blow and, for a moment, sprinkles danced across her vision.

Her knees buckled and she slumped to the floor, but the taffy-like grip held her tightly. Blinking in pain and confusion - already feeling the butter leaking from around her lip from the blow - she opened her eyes and stared into the grinning visage of German Chocolate Cake. More sour straw guards closed in around them. Her father's surprised and angered grunts told her they'd also restrained him.

"Going somewhere?" German Chocolate Cake sneered. "Thought you'd maybe take in the grounds? Get some fresh air?"

"Let me go," she said as she attempted to pull her arm free. The vile cake refused to relinquish his grip. Still, she struggled, pulling and twisting.

"Stop that or I'll smack you again, you little bitch." Something in the coldness of his words cut through her anger and panic. Kupcake stopped. She heard her father's gasp at the tone and language used towards his daughter, but by now, such things failed to affect her.

"Thought you were pretty clever, didn't you?" German Chocolate Cake continued. "You know that nothing goes on in this castle without my knowledge. I watched you every step of the way." He pointed, and Kupcake followed his finger to see a small chair set up off to one side, a table positioned next to it with a small mound of half-eaten cookies atop it. *Great Mother Baker, he was sitting there enjoying himself while he watched me.*

German Chocolate Cake called over his shoulder, "Bring that pastry and follow me!" He then started back into the castle, his grip more firm than ever as he pulled Kupcake along with him.

33

"This is it," Roscoe said glumly. He pointed, and then dropped his arm glumly. "It's unimpressive, and I feel horrible for that. Although I suppose I shouldn't... it's not like I designed or built it. But it's my responsibility to look after it. At least until I find my real purpose in life. My pa always said that I should aim for higher things." He shrugged. "Maybe I could get a job guarding a hallway higher up in the castle. A nicer one? Or just leave. They're not very nice to me, you know."

Ignoring the pity party, population one, Jerome stared down the length of the corridor. After he'd been revived from yet another fainting spell, Roscoe had agreed to escort them into the rear of the castle, but continued to maintain that he didn't know where Kupcake was being held and that he was only responsible for what he called Random Hallway Number Seventy-Three. Now, Jerome could see that the sour straw hadn't been lying to them.

"Do you seriously want me to feed you to the Baker-damned peep?" Maddie demanded. She slapped Roscoe on his head. "Quit screwing around and take us to where she's being held!"

"I—"

"I swear if you tell us that you don't know one more time, I'm calling Stephen up here."

Roscoe looked confused. "Who's Stephen?"

"He's the marshmallow that's going to dissolve your guts and drink them through the straw that is your head if you don't take us to the princess! I know you just picked a hallway at random to show us."

"I've been telling you, it's Random Hallway Number Seventy-Three. There's dozens of them all around. Look!" He pointed. "At the end there is the start or Random Hallway Number Twenty-Two-A. And there—" he twisted and pointed in the other direction, "begins Random Hallway Jeremy, which isn't to be confused with Random Hallway David Jeremy Junior, or Random Hallway Fredrick Jeremy Hardmeat. The numbering convention makes no sense, but it's been that way for centuries. All of them are guarded by others just like me. It's all we're responsible for. A complete waste of time and resources if you ask me, but nobody does ask."

Maddie opened her mouth to call Stephen, but Jerome stepped forward and held a hand up. "Have you ever been anywhere besides this hallway in the castle?"

Roscoe squinted and tilted his head down, seeming to think about it. "I know the dungeon is downstairs, but believe me, he wouldn't have put her down there."

"Why not?"

"It's too horrible. There's gummy rats and half-eaten jawbreakers down there. Plus other things..." Roscoe's voice trailed off as he seemed to consider these other things. "At least, that's what the other guards say. Who knows if it's true? The other guards are always picking on me, making me the butt of their jokes. Did you know that one time they told me the only working bathroom was down there?" He shook his head and sighed, "I really wish I could do more with my life."

"You're not answering the question, man," Jerome said, irritation tinting his words. "The longer you stall, the closer my friend here gets to calling the peep. So, take a breath and think. Have you been to any other areas of the castle?"

Roscoe was quiet for a long time, but then his eyes widened. "Yes! Once, when I was younger, back when I was being groomed for the Academy. That's what we call the training that we sour straw guards go through, but really it's just a week of people yelling at us and making us hit things with toothpick swords. Heck, at the end of it, they didn't even give me a certificate. Have you ever heard of that? Going through a training program – the Academy, no less – and not even getting a certificate? It's ridi-"

Maddie slapped him.

Jerome watched the sour straw guard stagger a few steps before two of the Tempting Tarts shoved him roughly back.

"Let's focus, shall we?" she suggested through a tight smile. "You were saying about how you've been somewhere else?"

Roscoe rubbed the side of his face and glanced hurtfully at Maddie, then nodded. "They were taking us on a tour of the castle one afternoon. We saw the dungeon, a selection of random hallways, and then the various rooms and quarters upstairs. They were giving us a preview of everything we might have to guard and areas where we could be assigned. I tell you, I'd rather be in one of the upstairs halls or one of the private rooms; those things are nice, and you can see out of windows in most of them."

"How many rooms are there?" Jerome demanded. Hope had surged in him, and he reached forward to grasp the sour straw in his anxiousness.

Roscoe recoiled. "Several dozen, maybe. Most of the rooms up there are display rooms or storage rooms. But there's probably twenty or so private bedrooms."

"Take us there. Now."

The guard began to voice a protest, but quelled it when Maddie raised her hand, preparing another slap. He nodded and waved them to follow.

Jerome and Maddie fell in close behind Roscoe. Maddie held her own sword unsheathed and ready in the event of trouble. Jerome turned to see Stephen and Balthus in the middle of the group, walking slowly along next to Cleetus. Jerome smiled. The large, green gummy bear seemed even more immense in the hallway. Cleetus' eyes took everything in, appearing to look for trouble, but Jerome knew the bear was really keeping an eye out for snacks. He was a cowardly bear at most times, though Jerome was very proud of him for sticking around through everything. He promised himself that he'd make sure the bear got a massive trough of simple syrup when this was all over.

They pressed on through the various hallways, occasionally cutting through large rooms. Some of the rooms were empty, others being filled with furniture or statues. Three times, they had to stop and wait for a roaming patrol to pass by. Once, Jerome watched as Maddie and three of her fellow tarts dispatched a small group of guards. There'd been no way to get around them, so the tarts had done their work efficiently.

Finally, Roscoe paused and turned back. "This is the floor they took me to. I think we're about a floor below German Chocolate's private quarters and a couple of floors beneath Devil's Food Cake's. I remember these rooms because they said that, when guests came to stay here, they would be housed here and some of us would have to guard them. The princess should be in one of them, probably in whichever one has guards outside it."

Jerome peered around the corner along the hallway. By the light of a large window at the far end of the hall, he saw several doors on either side, all closed. Unlit torches jutted out from mounts in the wall. There was something odd about the space, and it took him a long minute to figure it out.

There were no guards.

"There's no guards," he said, turning back to the group.

Roscoe's eyes took on a look of terror, and Jerome knew the straw was afraid that Maddie was going to sic Stephen on him for lying to them. "There should be!" he stammered. "I don't know why there wouldn't be any here. Honest. I swear to the Great Baker Herself."

"You think they moved her?" Maddie asked.

"Only one way to find out," Jerome said. He instructed the tarts and Balthus to check the rooms. The group spread out, weapons ready in case of an attack.

"Don't worry," Balthus said as he moved past. "I have this." He patted the rusty wire whisk at his side. "If those bastards give us any guff, I'll turn them into meringue." Jerome rolled his eyes and stepped up to a closed door. Gripping the handle, he closed his eyes, whispered a quick prayer to the Great Baker Herself, and pushed the door open.

The room was empty, save for unused furniture. Jerome's eyes took in the space, searching for signs of Kupcake. Thick mantles of dust and long, drooping cotton-candy cobwebs on most of the furniture and along the floor told him that nobody had used the room in a long time.

"Hey, muffin boy!" Maddie called. Jerome stepped back into the hallway, his heart pounding. He tightened his grip on his own sword and, with his other hand, shifted the Piping Bag of Ganache around so that he could quickly use it.

Maddie stood in the open doorway of one of the rooms further down the hall. When he reached her, she turned and pointed.

The room had been occupied. It was clean, and he could see a plate with crumbs on it sitting alone on a small wooden dresser. But he staggered when he stepped into the room.

He could smell her. The beautiful scent of Kupcake filled the room, turning it not into a small, dingy prison, but a beautiful and inviting living space.

"She was here," he breathed out, and smiled.

"Yeah, but she's long gone now."

"You think they transferred her somewhere?" he asked. Maddie shook her head and pointed towards the silicone mat bed.

"Not unless they decided to take a new route."

Jerome followed her finger and saw the hole in the wall. "It looks like your bad-ass girlfriend tunneled her way out of here." She cocked an eye. "You sure she's just a princess?"

A shout of anger and surprise ripped Jerome's attention away from the hole in the wall. He and Maddie rushed out into the hallway to find that the sounds of combat already filled the space.

While they'd been investigating the rooms, a large squad of sour straw guards and jawbreakers had moved into the far end of the hall. Jerome saw Balthus, Mopsy, and Richard all fighting the newcomers, with other members of the group rushing forward to help.

Maddie cursed and spun on her heel. "They got us," she growled, and jutted her chin behind Jerome. He turned to see more sour straw guards filling the hallway behind them, entering from a doorway they'd not yet checked. The door must have opened into a stairwell, he thought.

The lead sour straw advanced on Cleetus, who turned and attempted to retreat. The sour straw swung his sword, and Jerome watched the tip of the toothpick open a shallow cut on the gummy bear's flank. Cleetus squealed in pain and turned quickly, his front paw reaching out and slamming into the side of his attacker. The sour straw guard was hurled into the closest wall to crumple in a motionless heap. More guards moved forward, advancing on the bear who backed away from their thrusts, crying in pain when more found their marks.

Jerome looked down and saw Stephen next to him. The peep's eyes mirrored Jerome's own rage over the attacks on Cleetus.

"Fuckers," Stephen blinked.

The two confections, with Maddie close on their heels, rushed forward and dove into the fray.

34

King Red Velvet panted and struggled to keep up as they made their way through twisting hallways, up stairs, and through more doors. *If I get out of this, I'll trim down*, he thought. But he knew with a galvanizing certainty that he was not going to leave this castle alive.

Ahead of him, Kupcake trotted alongside German Chocolate Cake as he pulled her by her arm through the castle. *We were so close*, he thought. When she'd come out of the stairwell and attacked the guards, he'd been as surprised as them.

He paused, one hand on the smooth stone wall next to him, and closed his eyes. If his daughter could somehow get free and live the rest of her life, then it would all be worth it. Perhaps he could reason with Devil's Food Cake, and make some sort of bargain. Once upon a time, Devil's Food Cake had been a reasonable cake. A rough shove between Red Velvet's shoulders propelled him back into the present as one of the sour straw guards grew impatient at the old cake's slow progress.

They came to a wide doorway with a set of heavy doors flanked by two guards. German Chocolate Cake barked an order and the guards moved to push the doors open. When the gap between the doors was just wide enough, he pulled Kupcake through. King Red Velvet stepped to the threshold and, despite the swords at his back, paused to take in the Black Cake Stand Room.

The room was wide, with ceilings that spanned higher than he could see. To his right were massive windows that looked out over the mile-wide clearing and forest beyond. Sour straw and short, squat jawbreaker guards lined either side of the room, their weapons held close. In the center of the room, embedded in the floor, was a large wooden disk. But as Red Velvet approached it, he realized it wasn't a solid wooden disk at all – rather, he saw two half-moon shaped doors covering some kind of hole or recess. He gave it no more thought as he stepped over it and instead focused on the dais before him.

Devil's Food Cake's throne was a cake platter that screamed opulence and, if the king said so himself, tackiness. The dark stand was ornately carved with images of Devil's Food Cake doing what he clearly felt were very amazing and Devil's Food Cakey things, from defeating whole battalions of cookies to performing intimate acts on a bevy of ladyfingers. Based on the depiction, Devil's Food Cake had a high opinion of his... the king searched for the word... *attributes*. The carvings were outlined in gold and silver, and he noticed with disbelief that the back of the throne was a flowing chocolate fountain.

"You've got to be kidding me," he mumbled as he approached. There was a thump, and his daughter gave a cry of pain as German Chocolate Cake threw Kupcake to the floor. King Red Velvet took a quick step forward, but was stopped by a guard's rough hand on his shoulder.

"Welcome, my old friend," Devil's Food Cake boomed, his voice rumbling through the large chamber. He held his arms wide in a gesture that said both 'welcome' and 'look at my place – aren't you jealous?'

Red Velvet was prodded past his daughter. He caught her look, seeing her nod that she was fine, and then he was forced to within a few paces of the bottom step. He set his jaw and turned his face upward. "*Friend?* Really? You cakenapped my daughter. You sent a disgusting gummy pickle to deliver your message, instructing me to

come here, remove my crown, and kneel? Nobody instructs me, boy."
He pointed a finger at Devil's Food Cake. "I remember when you were
a scared little crumb, afraid to be away from the safety of your own
home."

Devil's Food Cake's face darkened. "You're not really in a position
to talk about being afraid, are you? The list of your cowardices is
longer than the Grape Jam River. I won't have a coward speak to me in
such a way."

Red Velvet felt his anger rising, his red cake growing a deeper
maroon with every incredulous word. "Unless you've forgotten, you
shitty little crumb cake, I'm the king of this land. I'm the sole ruler, by
divine province of the Great Baker Herself, and nobody—"

"Oh, do shut your mouth." The words had whipped out of Devil's
Food Cake's mouth like honey stick arrows fired point-blank. King
Red Velvet could almost feel each syllable punching him in the chest.
His adversary stood and leaned over the top step, glaring down at
him. "Do you honestly think I've forgotten our past? Do you think
that I've forgotten your lies? Your cowardice?"

"I told you then and I say to you now, I did all I could for Reggie.
Mother Baker, we were imprisoned! You remember? The torture they
inflicted on us was unimaginable. Those fig bars are insane. Pure
evil." He took a tentative step forward, ignoring the rustle of weapons
behind him as the sour straw guards tensed. "The war was so long
ago. Still not a day goes by that I don't think about what happened on
that mission. We-"

"He never should have been with you!" Devil's Food Cake spat.

Red Velvet let out a long breath. "You're right. He shouldn't have. I
told him as much, but he insisted on impressing you, his father. I
knew he was too inexperienced to go on a raid into the cookies' territory, but he wouldn't listen. So, I had him assigned to the kitchen
unit, just to keep him safe. Great Mother Baker, we were starting the
attack when I realized he'd defied my orders and snuck into our
ranks! By then, it was too late. I have to live with the thought of the
ambush, the memory of our capture, every day. Remembering our
imprisonment."

"Imprisonment!" Devil's Food Cake scoffed. Long gone were his welcoming smile and tone. Now, his cake darkened even further. "I know all about your imprisonment. That you got yourself captured means nothing to me. I didn't care then and I really don't care now. But you allowed my son, my only child, to be captured, as well. I may have been able to forgive even that, except-"

"Except that I made it back," Red Velvet finished. "I know. I've tried to tell you all this before, but you wouldn't hear of it. Grief can coat a cake's ears, I know, but I tell you again now, sincerely, I had nothing to do with his death. The opportunity to escape came, and I and the few remaining cakes took it. Reggie was with us, and I did my best to watch over him. But they seemed to have known what we were going to be attempting. Reggie was separated from us. I had told him to stay right by my side, but in the confusion... it was all too much. For Baker's sake, they had mallowmars. Mallowmars, man! The next thing I knew, the cookie who was about to skewer me was tackled by Reggie, and I was free. Your son saved my life. It haunts me that I couldn't return the favor."

"No!" Devil's Food Cake hissed. "You couldn't. Instead, you ran, you and those few crumbs who called themselves soldiers. You ran back to safety and left my boy alone to die." He raised and pointed a finger that was trembling with fury. "You're fortunate that I've allowed you to live this long. You're doubly fortunate that I've allowed that... *puff* you call a daughter to live this long. Now, you're going to shut your mouth and do as I say, or I swear to the Great Baker Herself that you'll learn what true suffering is."

Devil's Food Cake smiled wickedly and leaned back. "Let me tell you how this is going to work. You're going to remove your crown. You're going to kneel before me. You will then declare, loudly and before everyone here, that you are relinquishing power to the Land of All That's Good (But Never Goes to Your Hips or Butt) to me. Once the power has been transferred, you will be dismissed."

"To return to my castle powerless and disgraced?"

Devil's Food Cake chuckled. "Oh no, not at all. I don't know if the Lemon Icebox Castle will accept you back, having been dethroned and no longer in power. Even if they would, I'm certain you'd call the aprons, assembling any forces you could to wrest power back from me. Which, by the way, is why Kupcake will remain here for the rest of her life. Whether I make her my bride or just my midnight snack, I have yet to decide. But you will never see her again, just as I am fated to never see my own son again."

Red Velvet unleashed a growl and started to charge up the stairs, but before he made it up even two, a rough jawbreaker hand grabbed him by the collar and pulled him back to the floor. "You'll leave my daughter alone, you pathetic bathroom mint!" he screamed.

"Oh, calm down, you simpering jellybean. I haven't decided what I'll do with her. Regardless, you won't attack my palace or my army while her life hangs in the balance. And we've seen what happens when you try to send covert troops here to steal her away from me."

Red Velvet felt all the air rush out of him. The confection was right. He'd never risk Kupcake's life in that way.

Then, something flared in the back of his mind – something the Moon Pie Wizard had mentioned. A muffin. On his way here. The king's stomach turned sour at the thought of a muffin in love with his daughter and trying to rescue her. Yet, at the same time, if there was a chance.... Red Velvet sighed and decided that if what the wizard had said was true, then he had to do everything in his power to buy the worthless excuse for dough enough time to at least try.

"If I won't return to my home, what then? Will you banish me to the remote ends of the cakedom? To the Land of the Danish Wedding Cookies? West to the Breadlands? Farther south beyond even the Potato Canyons?"

"Originally, I was going to have you dunk yourself in milk and just be done with you. But then I had a better idea. After you've relinquished power to me, and while your precious daughter watches, I'm going to give you a choice. You can either be banished to one of those remote lands where you will live the rest of your miserable existence out being penniless and powerless, knowing that the entirety of All That's Good (But Never Goes To Your Hips or Butt) is firmly under my control and that your precious princess is my plaything—" he paused and a wide smile spread across his cake, "or, you can decide to go down there." He pointed over the king's shoulder towards the two wooden half-moon doors in the floor. One of the sour straw guards moved forward and, in one fluid movement, pulled the doors open. They crashed to the floor on either side of the exposed hole. King Red Velvet crept to the edge and peered down.

What he saw down there, bubbling and quietly waiting with infinite evil, nearly made his knees buckle. "Great Baker and the Holy Rolling Pin, no!" he gasped.

35

The corridor was filled with a teeming mass of candies and confections writhing together in close combat. Screams, curses, and insults of 'raisin lover' thundered throughout and seemed to hang like low storm clouds over the heads of the combatants. The clash of toothpick swords mingled with grunts of effort and cries of pain when an edge or point found its way home. Jerome struggled to stand, finding himself jostled in every direction by the bodies pressing in all around him. One minute, Maddie was next to him, and then she was gone, swallowed by the surging river of warring sweets. Jerome focused on the sour straw in front of him, the guard's eyes emotionless as he attacked. Once again, Jerome was reminded of his lack of proper training. Still, he found that what he lacked in technique, he more than made up for in luck and brute strength. He slashed diagonally and watched in grim satisfaction as the guard fell away, his gummy center exposed.

"There's too many of them!" Mopsy screamed, appearing suddenly with one arm around Balthus. The old Danish Wedding Cookie was wounded; Jerome could see dozens of places where chips had been taken out of his crusty hide. Balthus no longer carried the whisk, and instead held the jagged hilt of a red plastic toothpick sword. He swung it violently at any sour straw or jawbreaker who came within an arm's distance of him.

"Let me go, damn you!" he growled at Mopsy. "I can still fight." He twisted away and dove back into the fray, knocking down one jawbreaker who had raised his own weapon over the head of Cleetus, who sat stunned from an earlier blow. The jawbreaker rolled against the wall, and Balthus was on it before it could recover.

Mopsy looked desperately at Jerome. "Have you seen Richard?" Jerome shook his head. Once the commotion had started, Jerome had quickly lost track of most everyone. Stephen had been with him for the initial charge, but then he'd vanished in the swarming mass of animated sugar. Several confections away, Jerome heard the nasally voice of Roscoe and saw a flash of his red-pink body wielding a tooth-pick sword. Jerome tensed, ready to spring forward and kill the guard when he reached striking distance of Mopsy, but Roscoe's blade found the back of a jawbreaker guard. The jawbreaker grunted in pain and collapsed, rolling away and taking two other combatants down. Roscoe stood, chest heaving, and screamed after the dead jawbreaker, "I am better than Random Hallway Seventy-Three!" He slashed wildly at another sour straw who rushed past him. "And there was no toilet paper down in that dungeon bathroom!" Then, the sour straw was gone, vanishing into the crowded hallway, his sword hacking and slashing with spastic vengeance.

Mopsy's face bore a desperate, panicked look as she sprinted away, heading for the far end of the hall. Jerome heard her shout for her brother only once before he was again attacked. Jerome backpedaled, bringing his sword up and around. Weapons collided, the reverberations moving up Jerome's arm and into his shoulder in a single concussive wave.

Jerome swung again and saw the smile on his opponent's face as the guard realized that his foe had no real training or combat experience. Jerome's swing went wide as the guard stepped back and to one side, then raised his own weapon to bring it down on Jerome's exposed head. Jerome felt his body tense in anticipation of the blow, but when it didn't come, he looked up into the wide, shocked eyes of the sour straw. The guard's sword arm was gone, the weapon nowhere to be seen; he looked at the ragged stump of his shoulder and screamed, but only for a second before a massive green paw swiped at his head and sent it tumbling through the throngs of bodies.

"Cleetus!" Jerome gasped and threw his arms around the bear. Cleetus licked Jerome's face and turned to shamble backward, his eyes searching for another target. Jerome stood and watched the gummy bear in awe. That damned beast had hidden itself at the sight of the Moon Pie Wizard's fondant tiger not so long ago, he marveled.

He didn't have long to wonder at his friend's newfound courage, however, as two more guards were closing in. Jerome danced away, parrying their thrusts. Without thinking, he lunged forward and buried his sword in what he thought could be the neck of one of the guards. Then again, it wasn't like they had clearly defined body parts other than arms, legs, and a torso. So, he stabbed in the general direction of high torso, but well below the mouth. The guard gurgled and fell away, its companion pressing forward just as one of the tarts slashed at it. His attacker distracted, Jerome took a moment to step back. Something slapped at his thigh as he moved, and he jerked at the impact.

The Piping Bag of Ganache hung at his side, bouncing wildly as Jerome fought. *Son of a bitch*, he thought. *Of course.* He looked back up at the remaining guard engaged in a tilted battle against the macaron. Jerome sheathed his sword and brought the piping bag up, feeling the canvas swell as the bag filled. His eyes searched for a target, but he couldn't find one that wouldn't risk his hitting a tart.

He pushed through the roiling mass until he reached the edge of the battle. Ahead of him lay several feet of open corridor, and he could see what he guessed were a couple dozen new sour straw guards arriving from around the corner. Jerome squeezed the bag, and a jet of frosting shot forward and engulfed four of the guards. Instantly, they fell, screaming as their bodies were eaten away. The bag reinflated, and again he fired, and four more guards crumbled under the terrifying spray.

Silence fell in the hallway as every combatant stopped in sudden shock at what had just been unleashed. Jerome looked up and saw Maddie, leaking her own filling from dozens of cuts, staring at him in confused horror. "That's right, bitches!" Jerome yelled as the fighting resumed and Maddie was swallowed by the chaos. Jerome prepared to fire once more, but a searing pain across his upper back staggered him. He spun and saw a small amount of his cake dangling from the tip of a jawbreaker's sword. As his attacker's arm raised for the killing blow, Jerome squeezed the bag and watched as the deadly frosting turned his foe into a quivering pile of red, blue, and yellow goo.

Searching for another isolated target, Jerome growled in frustration. There was no way to fire his weapon without hitting any of his allies. All around him, the fighting raged, and he stood in the middle of it, watching in stunned wonder. How were they going to get out of this? There seemed to be—

"It's like there's hundreds of them!" Maddie screamed in his face. "They're everywhere, and more are arriving from both ends every second! We can't hold them for long."

"Let me use this!" Jerome yelled, shaking the piping bag at her. She looked at it and shook her head.

"You'll kill some of my people, and I'm losing too many of them as it is."

"What do we do?"

"You have to get out of here. You have to save Kupcake."

"How? I can't get out! There's guards on both sides of us. There's no way-" Then, he remembered. The look on his face must have registered understanding, too, because Maddie nodded.

"You have to go and do what you came here to do."

"I can't leave you guys. Stephen, Cleetus... I can't."

"You have to. We're losing people by the second, and there's not much hope of us holding what ground we have if they keep bringing reinforcements. Let me worry about what we have here." Despite the situation, one corner of Maddie's mouth twitched upwards in a smile. "I've been in worse situations, trust me. But you have to go find the princess and get her out of here. Don't argue with me, dammit!" she screamed as Jerome opened his mouth to protest again. She shoved him roughly. "Go!" Then, she was gone, swinging her sword and taking down guards left and right. Jerome watched her, a whirling dervish of furious frosting and candy death. He thanked the Great Mother Baker that she'd agreed to come with him, and then searched the melee for any signs of his friends.

There were none. All he saw were tarts engaged in close, viscous combat with minions of Devil's Food Cake.

Forcing away the pain in his heart at leaving his friends, Jerome sprinted down the hallway, leaping over dead and wounded sour straws and jawbreakers and one or two of the tarts. He hurled himself into the room where Kupcake had been held and threw the silicone mat bed to one side.

The hole yawned up at him, and he had only a brief memory of the cave he'd had to fight his way out of in order to retrieve the Bag of Never-Ending Powdered Sugar. Ignoring the thought of it, Jerome dropped to his knees and crawled into the hole.

Several yards in, he paused to gather his breath and let his eyes adjust. The sounds of battle were still present, but drastically muffled through the stone walls. Once again, he felt the urge to turn around and go back to help the others – a need so desperate that, for a second, he was helpless against it. He focused his mind on Kupcake and felt a new, deeper need fill him, wiping away all other thoughts.

He'd come to this castle for one reason. He was going to save his love, or he was going to die trying. As he crawled forward, all he could hope for was that he'd get to see her face at least once more before he took his final breath.

The tunnel Kupcake had dug turned and twisted, rose and fell, but other than the tightness of the space, it was easy to follow. Several times, he paused to catch his breath and rest before continuing steadily forward. After what felt like hours, the tunnel ahead of him filled with the glow of soft light. Jerome slowed his pace. Could there be a fire ahead? Did this tunnel end in what was now a blazing fireplace? Or was it the kitchens? How far down into the castle had she dug?

Crawling forward slowly – each movement paired with a hesitation, a readying of his body to spring backwards if he should begin to feel the heat of flames – Jerome approached a broken and jagged hole through which the light poured. Kupcake had to have dug until she'd hit this wall, and then somehow broken through it. He paused, peering through and expecting to see more guards or confections working stoves. Instead, he saw a room full of empty suits of tinfoil armor and a few scattered chairs.

Jerome considered his options. He couldn't go back the way he'd come – that much was clear. His only real option was to go forward and take his chances in the rest of the castle. Decided, he pressed through, ignoring the scrapes to his sides as he wriggled like a gummy worm.

He stood, dusted himself off, and took stock of his surroundings. The room was clearly used for storage. There were no guards other than the empty suits of armor. The room remained silent, no approaching footsteps or shouted commands to be heard.

Where the hell am I? he wondered. The shutters on a single window hung open, filling the room with the sunlight that had made its way into the tunnel. A makeshift rope made of torn curtains and tapestries threaded its way out and over the ledge. Had Kupcake gone out that way? He'd begun towards it when a thought occurred to him. The Bag of Powdered Sugar still hung from his belt. *If I'm going to continue sneaking around this castle, I should at least cover myself in it.* The thought of appearing as a sour straw or jawbreaker guard, or worse, turned his butter cold... but it did make sense. He'd already pulled the bag open and dipped his fingers into the powder within when a voice, a voice that sounded familiar despite being so muffled, cried out from beyond the door to his left.

Jerome quickly cinched the bag closed with one hand as he drew his sword with the other. Hurrying to the door, he turned the handle and peered through.

Dozens of confections, mostly sour straws and jawbreakers, were spread evenly throughout the massive room on the other side of the door. At the far end sat Devil's Food Cake himself atop his gaudy cake stand. *Is that a chocolate fountain?* Jerome thought. *You've got to be kidding me.*

Movement to the side of the dais tore his eyes away from the evil baked good. Jerome's breath caught, and his throat constricted.

Kupcake mounted the dais, led forcefully by two large guards.

Jerome lost all track of where he was. He saw his true love, and pulled the door open and stepped through.

"Kupcake!" he shouted. She stopped, pulling away from her captors as they let their grips slip with their surprise at the interruption. She stared at him, mouth agape. Everyone in the room was staring at him, in fact, shocked at the sudden appearance of the wounded and dirty muffin.

Jerome felt motion to either side of him and quickly lashed out, stabbing one guard through the heart before being grabbed roughly by several others. He felt his sword getting ripped from his hand as more guards converged on him.

"Jerome!" Kupcake shouted, and as Jerome was wrestled to the ground under a seething mass of candied bodies, he thought it was the most beautiful thing he'd ever heard in his entire life.

36

J erome fought against the hands that gripped him, but knew it was hopeless. The sour straw guards had him, and there wasn't any chance of escape. As they half-marched, half-dragged him to the Cake Stand Throne - *Who seriously has a chocolate fountain attached to their chair?* - Jerome brought his focus back around to the sole reason he had endured everything to this point. Kupcake stood next to the Cake Stand Throne. The two sour straws held her wrists.

On his throne, Devil's Food Cake smiled wickedly down at Jerome. "What is this? A muffin? *Jerome*, you called him?" He glanced over at Kupcake, who ignored him, with her wide, fearful eyes locked on the prisoner. Devil's Food Cake turned to the other side and asked, "Did you know about this?" Jerome followed his words and felt his jaw fall slack. King Red Velvet, his cake cut and scraped and battered, and with one eye swollen shut from a nasty blow, stared uncomprehendingly at Jerome. The jawbreaker guard behind him didn't flinch, keeping his toothpick sword pointed directly at King Red Velvet's back.

"I'll take it that you didn't," Devil's food Cake said with a chuckle.

Turning his attention back to Jerome, he said, "Let me guess... here to rescue the princess, are you?"

"I'm here, you pathetic shit brownie," Jerome heard himself growl, "to kill you and take her home." He struggled against the hands that held him, desperate to grip the Piping Bag of Ganache that hung across his back, but the guards' grips remained solid.

Devil's Food Cake threw back his head and laughed a deep, long, booming laugh. His mirth went on for several long moments, and Jerome felt his cheeks grow hot with embarrassment and frustration. "We'll get to the *kill me* part in a minute," he finally said. *"Take her home?* Seriously, a muffin? Red Velvet, do your subjects not know that it's against the laws of our land for muffins and cupcakes to mix? That's really telling of your abilities as a ruler, that you can't even enforce laws that have been around since the first Rolling! Just so that some random muffin with visions of reward and glory in his..." Devil's Food Cake trailed off and stopped talking, his eyes finding Jerome's own. "No," he whispered. "It's not that at all, is it? You really do love her." Throwing a glance over his shoulder, Devil's Food Cake looked at Kupcake. "Do you love him?"

Kupcake, her eyes never wavering from Jerome's, nodded. "With every crumb that I am."

Jerome felt a wave of affection crash over him. He twisted again, thrashing and hoping to break free, but they held him like the tightest springform pan. He glanced at King Red Velvet and saw despair warring with disgust on the old cake's face. Jerome said loudly, "I have loved your daughter since the day I first saw her. I will love her until I am nothing but powdered crumbs. I don't care about the laws. I fought my way across the land the moment I learned she was taken. There's nothing that could have stopped me."

"I beg to differ," Devil's Food Cake cut in. "I mean, I commend you for hauling your fat ass and unfrosted berries all the way here. You may have managed to enter my castle and, Great Baker knows how, found your way to this room. You've even killed a few of my guards – some of the weaker ones, no doubt. But you're not leaving here alive." He leaned forward, his voice dropping an octave as he went on, "Muffin boy, you're going to die here. I'm going to reduce you to nothing but dried crumbs and a few smears of blueberries. But before we do all of that, you're going to watch this decrepit cake here —" he nodded towards King Red Velvet, "declare me the uncontested ruler of All That's Good (But Never Goes to Your Hips and Butt). And just for fun-"

Jerome felt his fists clench in anticipation.

"You're going to watch me marry Kupcake. She'll give me many new cake pops, brownies, and cupcakes." Devil's Food Cake smiled. "I wanted you to have that in your mind when I sent you to your death. In fact, I may let you live long enough to watch me get started with her, if you know what I mean." Devil's Food Cake gave a quick wink that turned Jerome's stomach.

Jerome felt rage boiling up from deep within him. He screamed and bucked, throwing the guards holding him off-balance. Quickly, he brought one foot down on the leg of one of the guards and heard the tearing of jellied candy. The guard grunted in pain and surprise as he fell away. Jerome spun and pulled the toothpick sword away from his remaining guard to slash viciously across the Straw's face. It screamed and fell in a heap. Jerome turned and started up the stairs, his newly won sword raised while his other hand grasped for the piping bag.

Before he made it three steps, a heavy fist connected with the back of his head, dropping him to the floor. The sword clattered free and hands pummeled him, each blow seemingly more ferocious than the last. Jerome's world became encompassed in blinding agony, his body drowning in one solid lake of pain. Somewhere through all the blows, though, he heard Kupcake screaming his name, pleading with Devil's Food Cake to call off the guards before they beat him into a paste.

After what felt like an eternity by the baker's timer, Jerome heard Devil's Food Cake give the order to stop. The punches and kicks ceased, and he lay there gasping and blinking through the torment that racked his body.

"Stand him up." Once again, rough hands pulled him to a

standing position. Jerome blinked tears away and stared defiantly at his captor.

"Too chicken to face me alone?" he mumbled through his mangled mouth. "You gotta have these Trifle Town-rejects cake-handle me? I know peeps who have bigger chips than you."

Devil's Food Cake smiled and considered him for a moment. "You know what? How about this? I don't feel like looking at you anymore. You disgust me. You're going to die now, Jerome the Muffin. I'm a little anxious to get to the main event, as it were, but I think a little pre-show activity could really put the topper on the cake. The ice cream a la mode, if you will. Toss him in the pit."

He'd not noticed the hole in the chamber floor at first, but now, from his vantage point, the pit seemed like the giant maw of some alien worm that was ready to swallow him whole. He heard a gasp, and turned to see King Red Velvet's normally rosy cake turning white, the monarch's good eye drooping with inexplicable horror. The king even took an involuntary step backwards until he bumped against the point of the sword of the jawbreaker guard positioned behind him.

"Jerome?" He turned in the other direction and saw Kupcake staring at him with confusion and fear in her eyes. He began to speak, entirely unsure of what he was going to say, but then he was pushed roughly down the dais' stairs and found that all his attention was on not falling and breaking anything. He caught his balance as his feet hit the bottom. Immediately, he was shoved again, and this time, he didn't have time to catch himself. Jerome hit the hard floor and slid several inches, the shock and pain of the impact mingling with those pains he had from the beating he'd just taken. He'd begun struggling to lift himself, hearing Kupcake crying out his name, when a boot connected firmly with his backside and sent him sprawling once again.

This time, Jerome didn't bother attempting to stand. If they wanted him to go anywhere else, they'd either have to lift him or roll him. Hands grabbed both his arms, and he was pulled along the floor to the edge of the pit. *Dragged. Okay, didn't consider that option.* When he was near the expanse in the floor, he was lifted to his feet yet again.

The guard spun him so that he faced the Cake Stand Throne again. Devil's Food Cake's smile seemed to have grown even wider. "You, boy, will be our first round of entertainment. Once you're dead, we'll commence with the ceremony of my marrying your darling Kupcake, and of Red Velvet passing me the crown. Afterwards, I'll start to really enjoy this cupcake's frosting. Just a thought to keep you warm down there." He waggled his eyebrows, and then he nodded to the guards. They both planted a hand in Jerome's chest and pushed. Jerome's feet left the stone floor for a moment, and then there was truly nothing beneath him... only the wide chasm of the pit.

He imagined his body hanging suspended over the hole for the briefest of moments, as if it wasn't acquainted with the concept of gravity and didn't know it was supposed to plummet to the bottom. His eyes drifted towards Kupcake, and he saw the terror and sadness on her face. Then, just as he felt the inevitable pull of gravity take him, he saw her mouth move.

"I love you," she mouthed. Those words carried him down.

He hit the bottom of the pit harder than he'd thought possible. The stone ground accepted him hatefully, doing its best to greet him with as much pain and unwelcoming hospitality as it could muster. The impact screamed through him and he lay there for a long moment, stunned and struggling to catch his breath. His mouth worked so that he thought he must look like a Swedish Fish caught out of water.

All at once, breath rushed back into his lungs and, gasping, he sat up. He wriggled his extremities to ensure that everything was still intact and working. Satisfied he'd not torn or crumbled anything in the fall, he looked up. The opening he'd been pushed through seemed to be half a mile above him. Part of the light was cut off by the heads of his two guards, but only momentarily. They moved back out of sight and, in the full light - not that it was much better - Jerome turned his focus to what surrounded him.

Devil's Food Cake had said that he was going to die down here.

Had he meant Jerome would die by the fall? Jerome wondered. It was a long drop – not the half-mile it had initially appeared to be, but certainly a bit more than just a couple of feet. There was no way that kind of fall would have killed him. Which meant something else was down here.

With a grim smile, he reached behind him and pulled the Piping Bag of Ganache around, and then he turned and surveyed his surroundings. Might as well get a lay of the land before he was attacked, he thought.

The pit floor was wide, dozens of yards across. There were several boulders throughout the space. A few were large but none were high enough to give him access to the opening above. He saw no bones, no old discarded weapons, nothing on the floor for him to use in defense. In fact, the more he looked at the floor, the more he realized there was a distinct lack of anything on it. His eyes detected no small rocks, no dirt, not even animal droppings. In fact, the floor had an almost smooth sheen to it.

Across the expanse of the pit floor, he saw a wide crack extending up several feet of the wall. *That's where whatever it is will come from*, he thought. *Whenever it does come.*

"Having fun down there?" a voice called down, echoing off the thick walls.

Jerome looked up and saw Devil's Food Cake smiling down at him. "A blast. You know, it's a little bit of a brownie move, throwing me down here without a weapon. You could at least give me a fighting chance against whatever confection is coming."

Devil's Food Cake's laughter sounded thunderous as it bounced off the walls. The evil cake's head withdrew from the opening, and Jerome turned again to await his fate. As he waited, he heard Maddie's voice in his head: *"Get to higher ground – at least give yourself an elevated advantage."*

Picking the largest rock available, he began climbing. As he reached its summit, only three feet off the floor of the pit, his hands closed over the magical weapon at his side and aimed its tip forward.

Whatever came through that crack now didn't have a twinkie's chance.

The sounds of soft, liquid movement cut through his thoughts, crumbling his concentration like blown sugar. The temperature of the pit grew cold, and Jerome's cake shivered in response. His breath trickled in front of his face as faint wisps of smoke. The sounds of the approaching confection sent tendrils of fear and disgust through him. To reassure himself, he gripped the bag of Ganache and set his jaw.

He wasn't ready for what came through the crack in the stone wall, however. As it began to materialize, Jerome felt a blind panic closing in on him. This was hopeless. Nothing could save him now – not even the magical bag under his arm. He felt a level of terror he'd never known before reaching out and caressing his heart with painful, skeletal fingers as the thing pushed its way out of its lair and into the pit floor.

Yogurt had come to claim its next meal.

37

Kupcake stared down into the pit where Jerome stood on a large rock gripping what looked like... her brow furrowed. *Is that a piping bag?* He held it under one arm and pointed it ahead of him. What did he think he was going to do, pipe some swirls at whatever came for him? She didn't know what was down there that had Devil's Food Cake so excited, but she was pretty sure it wasn't a bunch of raisinettes. Could Jerome defeat raisinettes? Surely, if he'd survived the journey here, he could fight and win against most anything, but raisinettes were pretty nasty. She'd once read that they could strip a cake down to its bare ingredients in only seconds. And she'd heard stories from Old Man Nougat that, at one time, raisinettes had been used in the most extreme moments of warfare, but had been banned by the Crocker Convention because they were considered unflour-like.

She called down to Jerome, but his attention was focused elsewhere.

Daring to take her eyes off the love of her life, Kupcake looked wildly about the room for something, anything, which she could lower to allow Jerome to climb out. What she wouldn't have given for a long roll of bubble gum tape right now. Around her, sour straw guards stood chuckling, their voices like the grating of sugar across stone as they looked into the pit and mumbled wagers to one another. Devil's Food Cake was smiling, seemingly proud and pleased with himself at having tossed a simple muffin into a pit to face, unarmed - except for that stupid piping bag - whatever foul concoctions lived there.

Her eyes slid over to her father, with his shoulders slumped, his beaten and broken face downcast in defeat. All of this had practically crumbled him, she could see. What had once been a tall, proud cake king was now a softened lump of old cake. She realized that he was not going to be any help right now. The beating she'd watched him endure after his refusal to take a knee had been fierce even though the jawbreaker who'd administered it had done so with a disturbing lack of emotion in his face. To watch her father take that level of abuse had almost crumbled her, as well. She'd strained against the grip of her own guards and screamed for Devil's Food Cake to make it stop. The bitter cake had ignored her, instead watching with almost singular focus as his foe took blow after blow.

As she scanned the expansive chamber, a flash of yellow caught her eye. Kupcake hesitated, waiting for a small trio of jawbreakers to clear her field of vision. Off to one side of the room was a series of open-arched doorways that she assumed led either to more storage rooms like the one she'd found herself in earlier or else to corridors that would convey passers to deeper parts of the castle.

On the ground, near one curved wall, was... Kupcake blinked. Was that a marshmallow peep? What in the name of the Holy Rolling Pin was a peep doing here? Surely, Devil's Food Cake and German Chocolate Cake hadn't started enlisting them, she thought. She'd heard that some of them could be insanely vicious, using their soft, adorable appearances to lure victims - usually young cakelings - close enough to devour them, melting any such poor confection with burning marshmallow.

The peep blinked at her and shuffled slightly, conveying the distinct message of, "Would you get your ass over here already?" Kupcake hesitated - she didn't want to be melted, but there was something unusual about this particular peep - and looked to see if anyone else had noticed. Everyone in the room remained solely focused on whatever was happening in the pit and placing bets on the outcome. Meanwhile, the peep hadn't moved from its position. It shuffled again: "Seriously, I know you see me. Get over here or that tubby bitch down there isn't going to last very long."

Devil's Food Cake was close, certainly within grabbing distance if he saw her move away from him. Kupcake needed a distraction. A louder roar erupted from those gathered closest to the edge of the pit, and in response, her two guards loosened their holds on her, their interest and eagerness over watching Jerome die overtaking their responsibilities. A surge of hope flared in her as their hands dropped away from her arms. The guards stepped forward, and she saw that Devil's Food Cake had done the same, his body straining to see better. A plan formed in her mind.

Kupcake tensed, readying herself to leap at her captor. She focused on the evil cake's knees.

As she leapt forward, she prayed she'd be lucky enough to knock him against a stair or anything else that would knock him out. Devil's Food Cake's attention shifted - slowly, so slowly - towards her, his eyes widening in surprise as Kupcake launched herself through the air, her arms outstretched and her body aimed at his lower half.

Kupcake hit the ground hard as her target shifted backwards with a surprised cackle of laughter. She scrambled to her feet and advanced, her fists swinging wildly. Devil's Food Cake backstepped, his own hands held out defensively. He laughed nervously as he moved. Kupcake raised one fist, already aiming for her captor's left eye when a thunderous boom filled the air, this followed by shouts of confusion from those in the chamber.

Kupcake arrested her punch and instead stared across the open floor of the throne room. Her eyes widened in disbelief as a large group of confections rushed into the room, blades slashing at nearby guards who were going down with strangled cries.

Most were macarons, but at the head of the group ran an elderly and badly chipped Danish Wedding Cookie. A sour straw guard ran

close behind the Danish Wedding Cookie, too – screaming about
hallways, toilet paper, and his true purpose as he slashed and cut at
other guards. Both the Danish Wedding Cookie and the macaron
next to him appeared to be wounded from dozens of knicks and
scratches across their cookie surfaces, but they moved with an eagerness that seemed fueled by rage. They hacked and slashed their way
into the room, others behind them pouring in and spreading out as
they engaged with the jawbreakers and sour straw guards who
managed to shake off their initial shock.

A new group of guards rushed forward, and Devil's Food Cake -
the assault by Kupcake completely forgotten - screamed at them to
control the situation and dispatch those pastries who were foolish
enough to interrupt his finest hour. The guards split and surrounded
the Danish Wedding Cookie and his companion. A prayer to the
Great Baker passed quickly across Kupcake's mind as she realized this
was her only chance.

No, part of her mind screamed, *finish him now! He's not paying
attention!*

Jerome. His name cut through the swirling chaos in her mind and
brought clarity. Jerome was more important right now. Glaring one
last time at Devil's Food Cake, she spun and sprinted towards the
alcove where she'd seen the peep.

Her feet pounded against the stone floor, matching the rhythm of
her heart. Halfway across the floor, though, her progress came to a
staggering halt as a deep, pained, and hateful roar shattered the cries
and curses of fighting confections. Kupcake half-turned, terrified to
see what fresh-baked hell had entered the room.

Cleetus, Jerome's faithful green gummy bear, stood on his hind
legs and knocked Devil's Food Cake's guards aside with wide, arcing
swipes of his huge green paws. As he battered them aside, flinging
their broken bodies across the floor, his smooth eyes searched the
room. *He's looking for Jerome*, Kupcake realized, and felt sudden,
almost crippling pity for the creature. She'd only met Cleetus twice
during her courtship with Jerome, but she'd instantly loved the bear.
She knew how much the bear loved the muffin also.

Cleetus attacked several of the guards currently engaged with the Danish Wedding Cookie, and then Kupcake was away and hurrying to the alcove. She ducked behind a bend in the stone wall and pressed herself against the hard surface. The passageway stretched for several yards deeper into the castle, but was mostly pooled in deep shadows.

The peep shuffled slowly out of the darkness, its form wriggling with a fluid ease. For a brief moment, Kupcake almost screamed, but she staunched the cry. She was a princess of the land of All That's Good (But Doesn't Go To Your Hips Or Butt), and no matter what horror this peep had the potential for, she would stand tall.

"The hell took you so long?" it blinked.

"I... I'm sorry. There's a lot going on, you know," she replied. "I was... and now—"

"Yeah, now Maddie and Balthus are leading a distraction and attacking that desiccated fruitcake's men—" the peep was cut off by another roar from the gummy bear. "Mother Baker, Cleetus is really kicking their asses. Never would have thought he had it in him. You know, I saw that bear almost piss himself on a number of occasions on the way here?"

"I don't understand," Kupcake said. "Who are you?"

"Stephen. I'm friends with your boyfriend. Saved his ass dozens of times, to tell the truth. He was moments away from being swallowed whole by a congealed salad when I pulled him to safety. Been keeping his ass out of trouble ever since. Even saved him from a churro not too long ago. But it's better we don't talk about that."

"Are you saying that all of you – the macarons, that Danish Wedding Cookie, Cleetus, all of you – came to rescue me?"

"You got it, sweet crumbs," Stephen wriggled. "Now, seeing as how Jerome is down in that pit fighting the Great Baker knows what, and despite their skills, the Tempting Tarts and that old crazy-ass cookie are still outnumbered, we need to move. Here. Take this." The peep moved aside, and Kupcake's eyes fell on something leaning against the wall.

"I'm not touching that."

Stephen blinked a groan. "Are you kidding me? We don't have time for this shit. Take it."

"It's a rusty wire whisk! I'll probably get food poisoning just from touching it."

"Okay, yes, it's an old, rusty whisk. But it's also a powerful weapon. Look, we don't have time for you to argue with me. If you want to save Jerome and help us all get the hell out of here in one piece, take it and go use it."

"How? How do I use it?"

"Holy Rolling Pin, have you never seen a whisk being used?"

Kupcake felt embarrassment and anger flush her face. "I meant use it as if it's a weapon. Of course, I've seen these things used in the kitchens."

"Okay, then. Not much different. Only, you point it at your enemy rather than a bowl of flour. Crank the handle, send them to that big glass of milk in the hereafter. Think you can handle that?"

"You don't have to be so rude, you know."

"Lady, I don't have time to be deferential. My boy is in a hole fighting for his life. I've risked my yellow hide just getting here, and my other friends are out there dying. All so we can rescue you. Now, we need your help. Time to start pulling your weight. You're part of the team now." He began shuffling past her, heading out into the main chamber amid the sounds of battle. He paused. "He came here for you. We came here for him. Help us make sure he lives through this." Then, the peep was gone, moving with a speed Kupcake never would have imagined such a confection to be capable of. She looked back at the whisk. Through the patches of rust, its metal gleamed dully in the dim light of the alcove, and yet at the same time it whispered of dark and deadly possibilities.

Half-expecting the whisk to come to life and leap at her, Kupcake picked it up with trembling fingers. It was lighter than she'd expected, and she gave the crank a few solid turns. It turned easily, the tines whirring against each other, ready to blend and incorporate dry or wet goods while apparently also bringing death. *Powerful weapon, my bundt cake*, she thought. But it was better than nothing.

And besides, Stephen was right. Jerome was down in that pit fighting for his life. The least she could do was continue the fight up here.

Confident and armed, Kupcake turned and took a step towards the battle.

"Where do you think you're going, cake bitch?" a dry, eerie voice asked. German Chocolate Cake approached slowly, three guards flanking him. All four confections had their toothpick swords drawn and ready. And all were eyeing her with the steady, confident gazes of those who'd cut down other confections before.

Kupcake stared at the cake who had taken her, who had treated and teased her so cruelly on the journey to the Black Licorice Castle, who had beaten her, and who had laughed as he'd scraped that offset spatula across her.

Her confusion, her fear, and her hesitation were suddenly wiped out, replaced with a single, cold focus.

Kupcake raised the whisk, screamed, and charged.

38

J erome waited another long second, letting the yogurt slither and ooze closer. The pink slime, streaked through with clotted rivers of white, seemed to quiver in gleeful anticipation of the meal that stood on the rock. The sight of the light from above reflecting off the oily surface of the nightmare creature made Jerome's knees threaten to buckle and evaporate all resolve. This was impossible, he thought. High above, the shouts and faint sounds of battle raged. A bellowing roar cut through the din, and he felt a swelling of hope. Cleetus and the rest of his friends had somehow survived the massacre in the upstairs hallway. That meant he wasn't alone – not completely.

The yogurt slithered to within a few feet and extended a long, thin portion of itself outward like a probing tentacle sent towards Jerome. The muffin grimaced, waited only a second longer, and then gave the piping bag a hard squeeze. The recoil of the ganache erupting from the nozzle rocked him so that he slid a few inches backwards. The stream arced across the scant feet of open space and struck the tentacle and a larger section of the yogurt. High-pitched hisses and squeals erupted from the oozing mass. The tentacle percolated and dissolved. Further up the bulk, large patches of the yogurt's body sizzled and bubbled as the ganache ate away at the pink horror.

Jerome's mouth opened, and a cry of victory burst forth. Beneath his arm, the bag re-inflated and he squeezed it again, this time aiming for a larger area of the yogurt's form – over to the left of where the tentacle had formed. The ganache again splashed against the slime and began to crackle and dissolve everything it touched.

Jerome watched the yogurt liquefy. Tentacles that had formed and begun to slime their way across the rocky floor now turned and withered or simply melted into a worse and slightly fouler smelling goo than they'd originally been. He stepped down off the rock and moved forward, advancing slowly while firing well-placed shots into the quivering mass. Squealing in pain and terror, the bulk of the yogurt's mass slid backwards in a desperate attempt to reach the crack from whence it had come.

"Where you going, son?" Jerome screamed, letting loose another blast from the bag. "Thought you were king shit, did you? Thought you were the s'more?" Again, he blasted, and again the yogurt screamed. *I'm doing it!* Jerome thought excitedly. *I'm really doing it!* "You're nothing! You're not even jellybean shit!" Jerome pressed his attack, squeezing the Piping Bag of Ganache fervently, shoving it forward slightly with each blast as if he could add just a little more power to the frosting that spurted from the nozzle.

The yogurt retreated even faster, pulling itself towards the dark, wet crack in the rock wall. Jerome followed, blasting the foul substance with his frosting. Left, right, straight, and left again; the ganache sliced into the gelatinous mass and ate away. With every shot landed, the yogurt screamed, although Jerome wasn't sure how. Maybe it was simply some form of gas escaping through its thick body, but the sounds rang to him as screams of pain, anger, and panic. Jerome grinned like a cracked Danish Wedding Cookie who had just managed to offload his timeshare to an unsuspecting blondie and leapt forward, sensing his prey was near its end.

Only a small portion of the yogurt remained, slipping through the cracks of the wall and into deeper, safer recesses. Jerome considered firing a few blasts into the crack itself, but held off. Whatever was left of the yogurt would either die slowly from its wounds or would be so weakened and small as to never really bother anyone again.

Of course, this wasn't the only yogurt in the land, he knew. But knowing he'd eliminated one of them, weakened their numbers even a little, was good enough. Jerome let out a deep, long breath and allowed himself a relieved chuckle. He looked down at the piping bag and smiled. He'd have to thank the Moon Pie Wizard when he saw him next. Balthus, too, since it was the old cookie who'd led him to the storage room where the bag had been stored.

The thought of the Danish Wedding Cookie brought him back into the present, and he looked up towards the opening. He could still hear the clear sounds of battle beyond the rim of the pit. Now, all he had to do was figure out how to get up there to help. As he studied the walls of the pit for any ledges or handholds, the light - already dim – was muddied further as a large shadow fell across him.

Jerome turned and stopped, his breath dying in his throat with a pitiful wheeze. The Piping Bag of Ganache slipped from his numb fingers and thudded softly to the ground. Jerome's knees turned to water, and he sank to the stone floor.

A wall of yogurt towered over him. Twice as tall as he was and half again as wide, it quivered, only feet away. The pink and white mass was burned and singed along the edges, and he could see the wounds growing slowly as the ganache continued to eat away at the yogurt's form.

"How..." he mumbled, but then realized the answer. As he'd been charging ahead, looking only at the greater part of his enemy, the yogurt had divided itself. This large dollop had managed to flank him, allowing the repugnant concoction to strike one last time.

Jerome screamed and snatched the bag from where it had lain next to his foot. He managed to get one hand on it, squeezing with every ounce of strength he could muster. Ganache blasted out of the nozzle, striking the towering yogurt in its center and splattering outward. The yogurt let out another scream at the same time it lunged forward, one half-formed tentacle slapping at and knocking the piping bag away from the muffin.

Dying, the yogurt crashed over and onto Jerome. The slimy ooze covered his cake and bore him to the ground. Pain came immediately in a burning firestorm of agony. Never in his life had he imagined pain like this. He could feel his cake dissolving under the onslaught of the loathsome, lactose-laden enemy. His brain commanded his mouth to open and scream. By sheer force of will, Jerome managed to keep it closed – lest the yogurt find its way in.

He had a brief glimpse of the light above the rim, a sliver of freedom just beyond his reach, and then tormenting blackness crashed over him again as he was pushed down into oblivion.

39

The sour straw guard closest to her moved to meet her, his face emotionless but his eyes glimmering with a look that clearly said "What does this silly girl think she's doing?" The whisk met his outstretched hand. Kupcake never felt the impact as it chewed the guard's arm into a fine paste. The princess hesitated, stunned by the speed with which it had mutilated the sour straw. The guard himself staggered, a grunt of pain slipping past his tight lips, a look of shock in his eyes as he stared at her.

Kupcake didn't give him a chance to react. Her hand cranked and the whisk plunged forward and the rest of his upper body exploded. Without hesitation she whipped her weapon around, catching the next guard in the guts just as he closed the distance between them. She had a split second where she felt his fingers graze her chin before he too exploded into goo.

German Chocolate Cake stood transfixed, his eyes bouncing between the weapon that was reducing his soldiers to wet lumpy masses and the gummy splattered cupcake who wielded it. Kupcake stepped toward him, eyed the third guard who simply held up his hands and backed away, head shaking, "Nope." She nodded and looked back at her tormentor.

He wore an expression of pure wonder on his face, as if he were completely fascinated by what he'd seen and needed the whisk for himself. Kupcake stared at him, feeling both grounded in the moment and fully outside her body. Her head swam with a hurricane of emotions, terror and revulsion at what she'd done to the guards, embarrassment and hatred for German Chocolate Cake and what he'd done to her. Before she knew it, he'd closed the gap between them to within the length of the whisk. His mouth split wide in a grin.

"Give me that, you over-baked whore."

Kupcake shoved the whisk into his open maw, the tines pushing his jaw wide, the cake around it creasing from the pressure. German Chocolate Cake stared deep into her eyes and for a moment she thought she saw the faintest flicker of fear.

Her hand cranked.

She staggered back, stunned at the intense suddenness of the whisk's power. Kupcake felt tears welling in her eyes, trickling down her cheeks. Yes, the confections had been intent on hurting her, and yes, one had been German Chocolate Cake, one of the worst in the land, but still. Honestly, she'd expected more of a fight from him, considering he was a pretty big character in this story and given all the horrible things he'd done to her.

Her eyes remained trained on the pile of lumpy, cake-spotted frosting that had been the torturous cake. Her mind flashed images: memories of his cruelty, the looks he'd given her, the unwanted touches in the caravan on their way to the Black Licorice Castle. With every thought, she felt her guilt slough off and pool amidst his decimated remains.

The whisk began to feel more solid, more natural in her grip, and she tightened her fingers over it. She would not be mistreated any longer. She was not going to allow Jerome, her beloved Jerome who'd come all this way and fought through unnamable horrors to save her, to die down in a pit. She would not allow her own father to be dethroned, humiliated and reduced to crumbs. *No more*, she thought. *It is time to right this wrong. Time to eradicate this evil.*

Kupcake turned and moved quickly into the larger chamber, searching out Devil's Food Cake. He stood near the stairs to his dais, surrounded by three of his jawbreaker guards and slashing at the old Danish Wedding Cookie – who himself was howling with laughter as he hacked at his foe with a broken plastic toothpick sword. Devil's Food Cake pressed his attack, forcing the Danish Wedding Cookie backward. They fought, exchanging parries and shouted insults, and she saw with growing alarm that the odious cake was slowly forcing the Danish Wedding Cookie towards the open mouth of the pit.

Kupcake's feet propelled her forward a few steps in the direction of the pit before she caught herself. Her brain and her heart warred with each other over the proper course of action. Either eliminate Devil's Food Cake and end all of this now, or try to get her love out of the hole. Holy Rolling Pin, what she wouldn't give for some-

"Anyone have any bubble gum tape?" the peep shuffled loudly as it wove between the legs of sparring confections.

She scanned the expansive room, hoping to find anything with which she could fashion a rope for Jerome. The closest things were the curtains, and quick math told her that she'd need to tie several of them together. That would take time. Time she didn't have.

That left her captor. If she stopped him, the sour straws would give up the fight. Then, she could work on getting Jerome free. The thought pained her cake and made her butter curdle, but she realized that of her choices, this was the best course of action.

Kupcake pushed through the fray, making directly for the lord of the dark castle within which she'd been imprisoned for days. She was jostled as a sour straw guard bounced out of the morass of bodies, waving a sword and screaming *"I'm a special boy!"* before hacking at a nearby jawbreaker guard. Kupcake pushed him away just as other sour straw guards lunged for her, their hands slapping at her arms and shoulders in an attempt to disarm and restrain her.

Kupcake twisted the handle on the whisk and shoved the twirling tines at her attackers. The whisk seemed to barely touch its target before she felt the impact along her arms and watched as the confection was torn apart. The spinning blades sent candy shards or gummy goo splattering away, the remains – if there were any – slumping flourlessly to the ground. As she moved, decimating guards with each thrust and turn of the handle, she heard someone barking out surprised exclamations of *"Oh my!"* with each poke of the whisk. After several steps and three more obliterated guards, Kupcake realized the gasps of surprise were coming from herself.

Around her, the battle raged, and she often had to jump back or to one side as a guard or a macaron – or once, Cleetus – was pushed into her path. The bear paused and blinked at her when it was him in her way, recognition cutting through his own rage and panic, so that his features grew soft for a split second. Then, the bear's face hardened and he returned his attention to a mass of newly arrived sour straw guards. For one fleeting moment, Kupcake almost followed him, but when two guards were destroyed with a single swipe of his paw, she realized he was fine for the moment. It broke her heart, though, to see the bear looking around for Jerome in between attacks. That reunion would have to wait. Instead, she continued to move, whisking her way through throngs of confused sour straws.

She'd gotten to within a dozen feet of Devil's Food Cake and could clearly see the chunks of frosting and macaron cookie dotting his shirt, and even crusted on his toothpick sword. She didn't know how many of Stephen and Jerome's friends there were, but she did know that they couldn't hold out too much longer as more guards poured into the throne room.

Devil's Food Cake slashed at the Danish Wedding Cookie, sending it careening back into the swirling mass of bodies. The cookie bounced off a jawbreaker - the momentum sending the evil guard tumbling down into the pit with a scream that ended in a loud shattering – and then fell away from the opening and vanished between legs and writhing bodies. Briefly, she heard the cookie yell, *"Oh shut up, I'm not on my ass for the fun of it! What? Who are you calling a—"* but the words were cut off as another wave of bodies pressed past.

Turning, searching for another target, Devil's Food Cake saw her. His eyes narrowed in recognition and anger. Kupcake raised the whisk she held and nodded at her captor. This was it, she knew; she was going to destroy him, reduce him down to his basic ingredients. *He's going to be nothing but flour and scraps of butter*, she thought.

Devil's Food Cake's expression changed, and Kupcake saw confusion and... was that a small trace of fear in his eyes? Yes, she realized. He was afraid of her. With all his guards around him, high up in his own castle, even in the middle of a battle heavily pitched in his favor, he was nothing more than a weak sponge cake. He was afraid at the prospect of being confronted by someone he'd wronged and hurt. She thought of the offset spatula and the frosting he'd taken from her; the slaps and unkind words; the insults to Jerome.

Then, with a scream of rage, she lunged towards him.

The first of Devil's Food Cake's personal guards turned towards her too late. The whisk bit into him and shattered his body, throwing pieces across the room and over his companions. Kupcake brought the whisk to bear on the next guard, who could only offer up a stunned grunt as the whisk did its job.

Kupcake then faced Devil's Food Cake, and saw the near blind panic in his face. "Now, you!" she gasped, raising the whisk. But her world went upside-down as something heavy crashed into her, sending her sprawling and sliding across the floor. Random legs kicked at her as she tumbled past. When she finally stopped, Kupcake shook her head and struggled to her feet, using the whisk as a crutch.

"So sorry about that. I was trying to get at that ugly fruitcake there," the old Danish Wedding Cookie said as he picked himself up. Kupcake saw the half-dozen sour straw guards who'd thrown themselves at him, ultimately colliding with her and knocking her off her true path. "I believe we haven't met yet. I'm... oh! You have my whisk! I told that idiot peep, it is a great weapon!"

Kupcake didn't know how to react to the cookie. Instead, she turned back to her original target and raised the whisk. As she stepped to within whisking distance of Devil's Food Cake - her mind preparing a good final line for him, something along the lines of 'Gonna turn you into meringue' but definitely catchier; something which they could put on a poster maybe - the castle floor and walls began to quake, shaking her very breath. The shaking arrived at the party like any good guest, too, bringing something with it: a deep, booming rumble that grew in intensity and volume with each passing heartbeat. Kupcake paused mid-step, her legs quivering and threatening to sit out this particular dance. Throughout the room, confections gaped in shock and fear as if they expected the floor and walls to collapse at any moment.

"What in the name of the Great Baker's Oven is that?" demanded Devil's Food Cake, looking desperately at his guards for an answer.

40

"It sounds like the Great Baker Herself is coming down from the Kitchen in the Sky!" yelled one of the macarons, covering her ears. At that declaration, a new sort of pandemonium erupted in the throne room. Guards and rescuers alike threw down their weapons and clung to one another or covered their ears against the roar, many of them loudly reciting old recipes they'd learned as children.

"My lord!" screamed one sour straw guard near a window, his pink body gone pale. "It's... they're...." His jaw worked soundlessly for a moment, and then he sprinted from the room – abandoning his toothpick sword on the floor behind him.

Devil's Food Cake watched the soldier run to the doors and vanish through them, only to fly back into the Cake Stand Room a moment later. The sour straw landed heavily and slid several feet before stopping abruptly as the green gummy bear's front paw slammed down on its head. But the return of his guard wasn't what held Devil's Food Cake's attention.

That was the dozens of fresh confections - not his soldiers - who poured in through the doors waving toothpick swords and... were those kitchen implements? Yes, he saw now that several of them held spatulas and decidedly non-magical whisks.

He noticed that several of the confections who'd previously been engaged in hand to hand combat in the room were now staring dumbfoundedly out the windows at the land beyond.

"Stuart?" Red Velvet asked.

King Red Velvet stared slack-jawed at a specific peanut butter cookie who stood near the front of the group of newly arrived confections. "The last time I saw him..." his voice trailed off. He shook his head.

"Devil's Food Cake!" the cookie called Stuart yelled.

"Who are you and what do you want?" Devil's Food Cake demanded, his cake tensing at the insult of being summoned by such a common crumb.

"You are to release Princess Kupcake and her father King Red Velvet this instant!" Stuart's voice echoed loudly throughout the Cake Stand Room. "You will personally escort them out of the castle. Then, you will surrender yourself and beg King Red Velvet for mercy."

Devil's Food Cake laughed, the sound like dry pretzels breaking. "Are you serious? You and these—" he waved at the gathering of confections, "what? Simple confections think you can order me around? This is the Black Licorice Castle! I am Devil's Food Cake! I have an army of sour straws and jawbreakers ready to cut you all to pieces."

"You are correct, all of the confections and candies behind me are not battle-tested. We're all simple confections. But think about this. We made it here. To your Cake Stand Room. And, if that's not enough for you, if you need the proof in the pudding, go look for yourself." Stuart pointed towards the windows. "I'll wait."

Devil's Food Cake considered the cookie, and the shuffling dozens of cakes and pies and cookies and gummies to either side of it. Without a word, he pushed his way through the throngs and stared out the nearest window. What he saw caused the breath to die in his throat.

"What... this is impossible," Devil's Food Cake whispered. He stared at the spectacle outside the castle. He tried to wrap his mind around what he was seeing, to put it into some sort of rational perspective. But he came up with nothing. All thought and ability for rationale seemed to have fled him. In fact, they'd packed a pretty significant amount of belongings and locked the house up tight behind them. There wasn't even a note remaining to indicate where they'd gone or for how long. (In actuality, they'd left for a three-month symposium on Mary Cake-selling tips and tricks held in a timeshare by Marmalade Lake.)

Beyond the gates and walls and battlements of the Black Licorice Castle lay the mile-wide swath of clearing that Devil's Food Cake used as an early warning system, should any force try to attack his domain. Devil's Food Cake's eyes tried to focus on it, but couldn't.

Every square inch of the land, from the gate all the way to the trees a mile distant – and as far as he could see to either side – was covered by confections. He saw cookies of every kind, and cakes, pies, gummies, hard candies, and caramels. There were more sweets standing shoulder to shoulder than he'd ever seen or thought possible. Thousands. Hundreds of thousands. Some held toothpick swords, but many held rakes, shovels, or kitchen implements. All of the makeshift weapons gripped with grim determination.

"What is this?" Devil's Food Cake demanded. His voice had grown in tenor, rising to near panic.

Movement near the front gate caught his eyes. A solitary figure mounted atop an animal cracker horse pushed through the throngs and approached the gates.

The Moon Pie Wizard smiled up at the leader of the castle.

Across the room, Stuart continued, "In case you didn't notice, I have literally thousands with me. I visited every hamlet, every town, every corner of All That's Good (But Never Goes to Your Hips or Butt), and told them what you'd done. Every single one of these confections is here because they love Princess Kupcake deeply and have pledged their lives for her safety. So, yes, you do have the sour straws and jawbreakers. You have the experience. But we have our dedication and love for our princess. We will not be stopped. We will tear these walls down if we need to. You may kill many of us. But you will never kill all of us."

Devil's Food Cake saw movement as Kupcake, her face a mask of fear and worry, ran to the edge of the pit. The whisk she'd held clattered to the floor beside her as she knelt and leaned over the dark opening. "Jerome!" she screamed down into the hole.

"I believe you've been bested," King Red Velvet said calmly. "That many cakes and candies will leave this entire castle as nothing but rubble, and all your guards will just be piles of jelly on the rocks."

Devil's Food Cake's eyes shifted from the teeming masses outside to the new arrivals to the cowardly Red Velvet and beyond. Where the oven was German Chocolate? Not seeing his right-hand confection, his own cake tightened with a new emotion. *Fear.* "But I have the soldiers!" Devil's Food Cake screamed, facing the king.

"You do," Red Velvet admitted. "But they have love."

Devil's Food Cake's chest heaved as he seethed with fear and rage. His butter alternated between running cold and boiling.

"Baked, you're baked," a nagging voice sang. At first, he thought it was in his head, and then he realized it was the Danish Wedding Cookie. The cookie sang the lines over and over as it hopped from foot to foot in a strange dance.

Red Velvet opened his mouth to say more, but Devil's Food Cake spun and grabbed the king and propelled him backwards, practically carrying the monarch as he rushed towards the pit.

Kupcake pulled back and stared in shock as Devil's Food Cake skidded to a stop, holding her father at arm's length. The king's heels were only inches from the rim of the yawning shaft. Kupcake scrambled to her feet, pulling the whisk up and bringing it to bear. Her cheeks were moistened with butter tears.

"Is he giving up yet?" Stuart yelled from the other side of the room.

"Put the weapon down!" Devil's Food Cake told Kupcake. "Do it now, or he goes over. The fall may or may not kill him, but he won't come out of the pit alive."

Kupcake took a quick step forward, bringing the whisk up, her hand grasping the handle and preparing to crank. In response, Devil's Food Cake extended his arm, inching her father even further over the opening of the pit. "I'll do it. I swear to the Great Baker Herself, you take one more step, and dear old daddy goes down."

The guards and the few remaining macarons - some still holding onto their opponents' arms, frozen in the middle of grappling for survival - stared with open mouths at the spectacle. Kupcake's eyes never left her father.

"Do it now," Devil's Food Cake repeated. "I won't say it again. I'll just throw this worthless crumb cake over and into the pit and have done with it. Then, I'll have my men finish with this pathetic rescue party of yours. Those outside may kill me, but that won't matter. Your father will be dead right alongside your muffin." To emphasize his seriousness, he shook King Red Velvet in a fashion that caused the older cake's feet to shuffle unsteadily on the lip of the pit. Rocks broke loose from the rim and tumbled into the darkness below.

"You can't win like this," she said, lowering the whisk without releasing it. You can't." She gestured around him. "It's over. You saw what's out there. Even if you throw him over - and I hope to the Great Baker that you don't-"

"It's all his fault!" screamed Devil's Food Cake. "I lost my only son because of him! I lost Reggie! You've never lost someone like that, have you? No! You've lived a life in a cake carrier, protected from everything out there! You've never experienced true pain, true loss! He was my son! My only son, and he's gone. Because of this piece of shit!" He shook Red Velvet again. "You left him there – you left him to die, to be tortured by those Baker-damned cookies. He died, and it's your fault!"

"I know," Kupcake soothed as she took a step forward. She looked at her father, who stared back at her with wide eyes. "What happened to his son?"

Red Velvet stammered incoherently, his eyes squeezed tight against the impending fall. "It wasn't my fault!"

In the tension of the moment, nobody noticed the pale, burned and cut hand reaching out of the pit.

41

Jerome swam back to consciousness like an apple bobbing back to the surface of a water barrel. He floated there for a long moment – hearing nothing, seeing nothing, being nothing. Pain was all around him, inside of him, consuming him down to the smallest molecule of flour. It would have been nice to stay there, to just lie here and let himself be carried off to the cooling rack on the great windowsill in the sky. To rest at the table of the Great Mother Baker Herself.

Everything around him seemed to move as if suspended in syrup. His hands lifted before his face, turning back and forth, his eyes taking in the open wounds while his thoughts remained disconnected from them. Things fell into the pit... landing with muffled thuds around him, landing atop one another. With effort, he looked and saw that they were bodies. Sour straws, jawbreakers - those that hadn't shattered on impact - and one or two macarons.

The realization of them pressed against the sugar shell that he felt around his thoughts, cracked it, and broke through. *Bodies.* The battle above him. He gasped as reality slammed into him. He struggled, slipped, fell, tried again, and finally managed to sit up. The entire world tilted first one way and then another as pain rolled over and over and over him and then backed up, did a three-point turn, and rolled over him again.

Jerome groaned, gritted his teeth, and yelled as he fought to stand. Finally, his legs did what legs were supposed to do and supported him, but only under duress and begrudgingly. To show their unhappiness at having to be leggy, they wobbled and threatened to buckle at any moment.

He looked up and saw vague shapes and shadows at the edge of the pit, where he could hear voices and screams, but all of it was too muffled for him to make out. *I have to get up there. Kupcake is up there. But the yogurt -*

Other than the bodies, the pit was empty. Any remains of the evil that had been yogurt were long gone, either having retreated back into the crack or dead, disintegrated by the piping bag. Jerome shuffled forward a single step. His legs voiced their protests clearly, each flaring burst of pain another threat to call their union rep. Jerome ignored them and studied the bodies piled atop one another.

Above him, he heard Devil's Food Cake scream, "It's all his fault!"

Jerome placed a hand on one of the bodies, steadied himself, and then began to climb.

42

While she'd been talking to Devil's Food Cake to keep him distracted, a macaron had begun slinking through the crowds, inching closer, her sword ready to strike. However, a sour straw guard had noticed and held his own weapon up, the tip poking the macaron's meringue gently and halting her progress.

Everyone else was still too stunned by the sudden turn of events to do anything other than stare at the spectacle at the edge of the pit. Kupcake considered her options. There was a chance, if her father was away from the pit, that she could rush forward and push Devil's Food Cake down into the darkness. As much as she hated it, it seemed like her only play.

She opened her hands and let the whisk fall to the floor. It hit with a tinny crash and rolled several feet away.

"Fine," she said. "You win. Let him go, and I'll do whatever you want."

Devil's Food Cake stared at Kupcake for a long time. His expression shifted away from near blind panic, his eyes wide and fevered, to a grin of ultimate victory. To Kupcake, the smile was more horrible than the wax lips she'd used to play with as a mini-cupcake. Seeing her reflection with the lips in her mouth had always made her feel a little squeamish. But this was worse. It was a combination of victory and madness, like the milk that had helped make him had gone sour but been used anyway. In that moment, she was certain he was going to throw her father over the edge – regardless of her own actions.

Slowly, Devil's Food Cake pulled King Red Velvet away from the edge of the pit and settled his feet on more solid ground. As soon as his hand released the king's coat, Red Velvet crumpled to the floor, his head hanging low. Kupcake could see his shoulders moving as he breathed in deep, ragged breaths.

"Come here," Devil's Food Cake commanded in a husky, crumbling voice as he gestured with the hand that had held the king. Kupcake stared at her father, collapsed on the floor and helpless. She moved slowly towards her captor, gauging the distance and angle she'd need to cover in order to throw him into the pit.

Her feet stopped as she saw movement behind Devil's Food Cake. Someone screamed, and then everyone was screaming and backing away in horror. Kupcake took one final step before her brain understood what was happening.

An abomination stood on two very wobbly legs just behind the dark confection. It stared hatefully at Devil's Food Cake with one good eye, the other a wet mass of ruined cake.

Jerome's voice was distorted as he croaked, "Kupcake."

Kupcake screamed her love's name at the same time that his already precariously wobbly legs threw in the proverbial kitchen towel and buckled. Jerome - what was left of him - slumped to the floor. Kupcake rushed for him, and saw out of the corner of her eye what happened as the macaron stepped lightly around the dumbfounded sour straw guard. The macaron glanced briefly down at the collapsed form of the muffin, and then focused solely on Devil's Food Cake. She brought her toothpick sword up and placed the tip at his nose.

"Unless you want to watch everyone in the entire realm rip this castle apart," she said heavily, "I suggest you surrender."

Devil's Food Cake's eyes darted around for anything to save him, any preserver in his drowning world. For a long moment, Kupcake was certain he was going to continue to fight. However, the way the macaron held her sword, it wouldn't be much of a struggle. The mercenary looked desperate for a reason to skewer the evil cake.

Finally, Devil's Food Cake's shoulders sagged and his head bowed.

"I surrender," he whispered.

43

upcake watched, with Jerome's head cradled in her lap, as four of the remaining six Tempting Tarts escorted Devil's Food Cake out of the large chamber. They were met at the doorway by several of King Red Velvet's personal rock candy guards.

Kupcake wiped her eyes and stared down at the ruined face of her love. His remaining eye was closed, and it was only by placing her hand ever so gently on his chest and feeling the impossibly slow rise and fall there that she could tell he was alive. Around her, rock candy guards were busy disarming the remaining sour straws and jawbreakers before moving them out of the chamber. The stone-like soldiers of her father showed no emotion as they went about their duty, but she knew that every single one was ready for the slightest provocation by one of Devil's Food Cake's minions.

A soft yellow caught her attention, and she watched as the peep pushed its way through the legs of bystanders. Stephen shuffled to a stop next to Jerome and sat there, staring down at the unconscious muffin. His eyes, normally expressionless black dots, seemed to be depthless pools of sadness and worry. Looking at the peep's face, Kupcake felt a massive lump of butter catch in her throat.

Something pushed against her, hot breath washing over her arm.

With effort, Kupcake pulled her eyes away from her true love and looked at Cleetus, the large gummy bear also looking down at the broken and torn form of Jerome with his eyes filled with sadness and despair. Kupcake wrapped her arms around the bear and buried her face in his body, crying as the bear himself lifted his head to the ceiling and began howling.

"My dear," Red Velvet said. Kupcake raised her eyes and saw her father regarding her, understanding in his gaze. But then the king's eyes drifted away and focused on something across the room. Kupcake looked, and took in a breath.

The Moon Pie Wizard had stepped into the room.

He approached the still form of Jerome, concern a hard mask on his face. He moved slowly, a candy thermometer cane tapping the floor with each step. The wizard stood over Kupcake without acknowledging her or the king, who was only a step or two away. His eyes scanned Jerome's body, and she heard a soft muttering as the old, mystical cookie spoke to himself.

After a long time, he addressed Kupcake. "My dear, I need you to stand back, please."

"I'm not leaving him."

The Moon Pie Wizard turned his eyes to her, and she nearly fainted at the depth of sadness she saw reflected in them. "Sweetheart," he said, and she could tell he was struggling to keep his voice soft and even, "there is a chance I can do something for him. It's slim, thinner than a crepe, but it's a chance. Your boy here fought yogurt. There's nothing you or anyone else in this room can do."

"Why are you helping?" King Red Velvet asked. "I thought you swore to stay out of the affairs of other confections."

"I broke that vow the day I set this muffin on his path," the wizard answered. "And then did it again when I came to you that day in your home. I've spent far too long in the cupboard. I can't continue to remain there when there's a chance to save true love and - by extension - this entire cakedom. My dear?" he addressed Kupcake, giving a gentle wave of his hand to indicate she should move away.

Kupcake leaned forward and, ignoring the butter tears that

streamed along her cake, kissed Jerome before gently placing his head on the floor and backing away.

The Moon Pie Wizard cleared his throat, moved closer to the muffin, and held his open hand out. He continued mumbling to himself. With each syllable uttered, Kupcake felt a growing pressure until it seemed as if the very air in the room would crush her body. Yet, at the same time, it wasn't painful. The wizard opened his eyes, winked at her, and said loudly, "Scraggly dough!"

A brilliant flash of light blinded Kupcake and she winced, leaning away from the sudden strobe. When she could see again, her breath caught in her throat.

Jerome and the Moon Pie Wizard were gone. Confections all around the room looked about in confusion, but the two pastries were nowhere to be seen.

"Where?" she stammered.

Beside her, the king opened his mouth to say something, but suddenly there was a presence between the two of them, and a voice cutting through the conversation.

"Sir King Red Velvet, your sire," the Danish Wedding Cookie said, his voice pitched high in excitement. Kupcake took an involuntary step backwards at the sudden presence of the cookie and watched as her father regarded the intruder with disgust and anger, both of which quickly faded when he realized he was being addressed by one of the rescuers.

"Yes?" Red Velvet asked. "And who may you be?"

The cookie shifted the object he'd been holding and thrust out a hand which the king regarded for a moment before grasping. "Name's Balthus. I know you're busy, but I wanted to check with you to see if it would possibly be okay that I keep this." No sooner were the words out of his mouth than he turned his head to one side and whispered, "No, I will not. Shut up, man, I'm asking." Returning his attention to the king, he held up the item he'd been carrying. She looked at the item and saw that it was an old, yellowed kitchen timer. She doubted that it would work even under the best of circumstances, and wondered from which pile of garbage or trash bin he'd pulled it.

"I... sure?" the king stammered. "Why that? I'm sure you could find something better-suited for someone who so bravely fought to rescue my daughter and myself."

Balthus' eyes drifted to the timer. He shook his head. "No, sire. This is what I want. This is a priceless artifact to my people. We have had this in our possession for generations, and—" he lowered his voice and leaned in conspiratorially, "it's said to have been given to Drumthip the First by the Great Baker Herself on a night of holy baking, if you know what I mean." The cookie nodded and winked, cradling the timer to his chest.

Kupcake saw her father's confused expression and placed a hand on Balthus' shoulder. She cleared her throat and said, "It is yours. Take it with our deepest thanks and most sincere appreciation for your help. Tell your lord that the Danish Wedding Cookies will always be considered allies to King Red Velvet."

Balthus nodded and smiled. "I can see why he likes you so much." Then, the cookie turned and waddled away.

44

He pushed, every sugar crystal in his body straining against the pain that seemed to be everywhere. The fog in his mind dissipated, vanishing slowly... only to allow all-consuming pain to enter from where it had been waiting, growing tired of reading old copies of *Pancake Monthly* and flyers for time-share options at the bottom of the Potato Canyon. *No,* he begged of the numbing fog, *come back, I don't want this, I can't take this.*

Jerome waited, hoping the pain would recede – but it wouldn't, as it was there and it had a job to do, and if pain's daddy had taught it anything, it was do the job the best you could... unless that job was cleaning up after confections with the yeasty meringue, because that job was gross - and Jerome listened to the sounds around him, beyond the darkness of his eyes. He assumed he was on the cooling rack of the Great Baker Herself, waiting to be judged worthy or not. *Please,* he thought, *all I ever did was love Kupcake and try to rescue her. I tried so hard.*

Around him was silence, and yet at the extremities of his perception, he could hear soft mumblings like voices through thick walls. *The Great Baker's assistants,* he thought. *They will come get me and present me for judgement. Hopefully, the fact that I killed the yogurt will be enough to allow me to rest for eternity on a nice cake stand. As long as it doesn't have a chocolate fountain attached.*

The sound of voices grew closer and Jerome steeled himself, grimacing against the pain. He realized through the clouds of hurt that he was lying on something flat and smooth. His body also felt different... at least, the parts he could feel did.

There sounded a click and a rattle, and then the soft sounds of a door opening. *Here we go*, he thought, and whispered a prayer to the Great Baker Herself that She would judge him with kindness and love and anoint him with flour.

A soft hand touched his arm and sent his pain scurrying away. The hand was warm and gentle, imparting tenderness and affection.

"Jerome?"

He held his breath. He wasn't ready to be judged. He still had so much left to do; he still had to tell Kupcake one more time how much he loved her and what she meant to him. He didn't want to spend another second of life away from her. And Cleetus.... *Oh Sweet Mother Baker, please, I just have to see my bear one last time! I can't let him go on without at least a goodbye. He won't understand; he'll think I just abandoned him. I didn't want to leave that hallway, but Maddie forced me to; it was the only way to try to save-*

"Jerome, sweetheart, can you open your eyes?"

Sweetheart? The Great Baker is a little personal. I've never even met Her and She's already calling me sweetheart? What do I call her? Honeycakes? Sugarplum? Can't call her Mother... that's just gross and wrong on more levels than filo dough has.

But if She wanted him now, he had to go to Her. If this was his time, it was his time. Slowly and with great effort, Jerome opened his eyes, feeling his lids flutter against the sudden light in the room.

Kupcake sat on the bed next to him, her hand holding his forearm and her beautiful face smiling down at him. There were butter tears in her eyes, glistening in the light. Jerome felt his own breath catch, and tears of his own sprang forth both from the angelic sight of his true love and from a fresh wave of pain.

"Am... I...?"

She nodded. "You're alive. You're here, in my father's castle."

He struggled to lift a hand, pushing through the discomfort, and touched her face. "Are you okay?"

Kupcake sniffed and nodded. "I'm good. Thanks to you and your friends."

Jerome felt a panic surge at the mention of his friends. "Cleetus... Stephen?"

"They're all fine." As she settled him back, she gave him the highlights of the battle after Balthus and Maddie had led the Tempting Tarts into the throne room. Jerome listened, amazed at the acts of bravery that had been performed. All by confections who'd had no true allegiance to him or Kupcake.

"You actually used the whisk?" he croaked, a smile playing on his lips before being wiped away by a fresh round of aches.

Kupcake straightened. "I did! And I was damned ruthless with it, too, I might add." She looked around, and then lowered her voice. "I turned German Chocolate Cake into goo with it. Father doesn't like me talking about it."

They remained that way, smiling at each other, before Kupcake's smile melted away. "I can't imagine what you went through in the pit," she said. Her voice had grown thick with emotion.

"It's okay. I killed it. Yogurt. I used my bag."

"What was that thing, anyway?"

"The magical Piping Bag of Ganache. I had to go through... awfulness... to get it. But it worked. It destroyed..." his voice trailed off as a new memory came to him. Yogurt towering over him, his hand squeezing the bag one last time, and then blackness, burning, and pain. "I did destroy it, didn't I?"

Kupcake nodded. "You did. That yogurt is no more."

"But I remember falling under it. It burned. I... I don't understand."

Kupcake's tears fell freely now. She nodded. "You were buried under it. You'd blasted it and it was dying, but it crashed down on you and ate...."

He watched her struggle for the words.

"How am I here, then?" he asked. "Nobody escapes yogurt."

Kupcake nodded again. "You were... oh, Jerome, it was awful. You were almost gone, almost reduced to batter."

"What happened?" he asked, hearing the desperation in his voice.

Kupcake wiped tears away from her cheeks and took a deep breath. "The Moon Pie Wizard. When he saw you as you were, but realized you were still alive, he told us that there was still a chance. But it was extremely small. He had to get you to his home to even try. He said he'd be in touch, and then picked you up and vanished. I've never seen anything like it. He had... he looked like he was close to panic. That scared me the most, I think. Seeing your body was terrible, probably the most terrible thing I've ever seen. But seeing the panic in the Moon Pie Wizard's face almost destroyed me. Because if someone that powerful was panicking, things were really bad."

Jerome shifted slightly and winced. "What happened?"

Kupcake took a long moment, staring down at him. She smiled. "He fixed you. He had to take—" she hesitated, "drastic measures. I don't know everything he had to do, but I think it involved that Bag of Never-Ending Powdered Sugar you had with you."

"What do you mean?"

Kupcake looked across the room, and then she stood up and moved to a small table. Her delicate fingers picked up a mirror. Again, she hesitated. "I want you to know.... No. I *need* you to know that this changes nothing. I love you with every crumb of my being, and we're going to be together no matter what." Her eyes turned hard. "Do you hear me?"

"What are you talking about? What was done?" Slowly, she handed him the mirror. Jerome turned it so that he could see himself. He felt a scream pushing its way up, but bit it back, swallowing hard. "Am... am I...?"

Kupcake nodded. "The only way he could save you, the only way he could keep you alive, was to transform you, sweetheart. You're alive, though, and that's the most important thing. You're alive, and I'm never leaving your side. We can be married now."

Jerome stared at himself in the mirror. "I'm a buttermilk biscuit."

45

Jerome was cleared to leave the room three days later. The pain had subsided thanks to a butter and salt salve which the Moon Pie Wizard had administered. The wizard had stayed in Jerome's room, perched comfortably in a large plush chair and smoking candy cigarettes while prattling on about any odd thought that came to him. He'd assured Jerome that Cleetus was fine; the bear had sustained some wounds in the fighting, but nothing too serious. As soon as Jerome was able to get up and walk, he would be able to see his friend.

When the Moon Pie Wizard wasn't in the room – and oftentimes when he was – Kupcake was there, watching Jerome carefully as if afraid that he would suddenly flake or collapse. Jerome didn't mind, he was content to allow the beautiful cupcake to look at him all she wanted from these days on until the end of time.

The day he was able to leave the castle was one of the best and yet more surreal days of his life. His legs held him up just fine, and everything seemed to work as he expected, but he felt a strange sensation that the Moon Pie Wizard had called his "buttery flakiness," though he'd assured the former blueberry muffin that the discomfort would pass as he grew accustomed to his new body.

Outside, the sky was scudded with clouds, but Jerome could see flashes of blue between the white puffs and held hope that he would be able to sit in a sunny patch later. He walked out into the courtyard – a massive, sprawling expanse filled with dozens of confections going about their daily lives. Rock candy guards were positioned around the space, manning their posts beside doors or stairwells. Jerome moved slowly out into the air and breathed deeply.

It seemed surreal to him, being in the castle for the first time. He'd always assumed that he'd only be allowed to see it from the other side of the walls, believing that while those early clandestine days with Kupcake had been wonderful and true, eventually her post as Princess of All That's Good (But Never Goes to Your Hips or Butt) would take precedence and drive a wedge between them. Yet, here he was, standing in the middle of the courtyard as an honored guest - or so he'd been told - of King Red Velvet.

A shuffling noise preceded something knocking into his leg. Jerome turned and looked down to see Stephen looking up at him.

"Surreal, isn't it?" the peep blinked.

"I was just thinking that." Jerome opened his mouth to say more, but was interrupted by a hefty clap on his shoulder that nearly sent him sprawling. But he'd found that, since becoming a buttermilk biscuit, he had slightly better reflexes and balance than before.

"Jerome, my old and respected friend!" Balthus exclaimed. Jerome embraced the old cookie and noticed that Balthus was dressed for the road; he had a large bag slung over one shoulder and was followed by a small steward leading an animal cracker elephant who was also laden with bags.

"You're leaving?" Jerome asked.

"Indeed, I am! I have to return to my people and present Lord Flanta with the priceless artifact that Devil's Food Cake had stolen from the Danish Wedding Cookies long ago." He reached into his bag and showed Jerome and Stephen an old, battered kitchen timer. Jerome thought that if he looked at the thing too long, it would crumble under the weight of his gaze.

"That's pitiful," shuffled Stephen.

Balthus shoved the item back into his bag and straightened. "It will help restore our land to its former glory. And once we have, you —" he pointed at the peep, "won't be allowed in." He stuck out his tongue and then looked back at Jerome. "It has been an honor and a privilege to journey with you. You are always welcome in the Land of the Danish Wedding Cookies and will be treated as a venerated guest. No powdered sugar required." He winked.

"What if I show up?" Stephen wriggled.

"We may allow you to clean our toilets." Balthus stared hard at the peep, but then his face crumbled into a broad smile. He lifted Stephen up and hugged the marshmallow bird, laughing. "Please, both of you, come visit soon. I'll sing your praises until you arrive." He placed Stephen back on the ground and again embraced Jerome. "Best of luck to you, young Jerome, and to your future nuptials."

"Won't you attend? I couldn't imagine having the ceremony without you there."

"Wouldn't miss it for the world, my boy!" Balthus reached for the reins of the elephant and pulled himself up into the saddle. There, he paused and looked back down. "Um, would it be okay if I bring a date?"

Jerome and Stephen exchanged a look. "Date? I mean, sure. You have a little cookie back home that you didn't tell us about?"

Balthus laughed. "No, nothing like that. No. Back when we were in Trifle Town - before you set half the place on fire, that is - I met the most amazingly beautiful churro named Cinnamon. Only got to talk to her for a moment, but I thought I might swing by and bring her along next time I'm headed this way. Lovely girl... legs like you wouldn't believe."

Jerome felt his throat tighten, and then heard the shuffling laughter of Stephen. Balthus waved one last time before he spurred the animal cracker elephant towards the open gate. They watched him until he was out of sight. "Crazy son of a bitch has already forgotten that she's a siren," Stephen blinked. "So, the king is going to let you marry Kupcake now, eh?" he wriggled.

"Yeah. Well, he came to my room yesterday and thanked me for, you know. Said that even if I hadn't been turned into a biscuit, he would have made a decree changing the rule about muffins and cupcakes. So, yeah, the wedding is on."

"You really think that crazy bastard is going to bring that churro here?"

Jerome stared at the horizon where Balthus had vanished. "Great Baker, I hope not. Let's be honest – he's so cracked he'll probably forget about her. Especially if he comes across something shiny, or a rusted, broken cookie cutter that he thinks holds some religious significance to his people."

"Those cookies really are just a couple of crumbs shy."

They fell into an easy silence, watching the activity around them.

"So, what about you?" Jerome asked the peep as they drifted to a nearby bench to allow Jerome an opportunity to rest.

"I thought about heading out; maybe back to Trifle Town, maybe try my luck with the egg timer games down in the gaming halls of the French Toast people."

"It's a wide world out there," Jerome admitted, hoping the peep couldn't hear the sadness he felt at the prospect of his friend leaving the castle. Balthus was one thing, but Jerome had truly come to love the offensive peep.

"Yeah, it is. Which is why I think I'm going to stick around for a while longer."

Jerome looked down in surprise. "Really?"

"Don't tell anyone, but, I mean, you're alright to hang around with. Besides, you're a buttermilk biscuit now. You're even more of a fragile pansy than you were as a muffin. Someone has to stick around and keep you from hurting yourself. And, I heard from a few confections who arrived a couple days ago that there's an army of congealed salads roving the Red Vine woods. Probably looking for the wafer who got away from their friend. I figure you're gonna need me to stick around just to protect your delicate ass." The peep blinked a smile, and then shuffled away.

Jerome sat in the cool shade for a long while, enjoying the sounds of confections carrying out their daily chores. He felt a gentle rumbling in his stomach and realized he hadn't eaten since very early that morning. Promising himself to get a meal soon, he stood up and started for the stables.

He approached the stall that had been identified as belonging to Cleetus, suddenly nervous. He didn't want to see his friend laying there wounded, with cuts all along his large green body. Kupcake and Stephen had said that Cleetus had fought bravely, even a little wildly, and had endured several wounds from toothpick swords.

Swallowing deeply, Jerome pushed open the door and stopped, unable to move. "Are you serious?"

Cleetus lay amidst a large pile of marshmallow pillows, a short peanut butter cookie waving a large sheet of parchment paper to fan the bear. Another cookie brought a new bucket of simple syrup and poured it into a larger vat near the bear's head. Cleetus sniffed at it and blinked slowly up at Jerome.

"You're looking good, bud," Jerome said. He gazed along the length of the bear's body and saw the healing scars in the green jelly where the toothpick swords had connected. He moved closer and ran both his hands over the bear's head. Cleetus chuffed happily and licked Jerome's face. Jerome felt a wave of relief bubbling out of him, spilling down his cheeks as tears. "I love you, you big green goober," he said, and kissed the bear's nose.

"Thank you for sticking with me," Jerome said. "Thank you for never leaving me and always being there. Thank you for everything you did in the castle. I'm... I'm sorry we got separated. I'm—" he stopped as Cleetus placed a heavy paw on Jerome's chest. "I know, I'm rambling. I'm sorry. It's just—" Cleetus pushed gently, and Jerome looked at the bear. Behind him came the heavy click and squeal of the door opening. A new figure entered the stable with timid steps.

The red female gummy bear paused when she saw Jerome, and then blinked and chuffed a soft question at Cleetus. Cleetus pushed Jerome again, gently but with clear meaning. Jerome gaped at his friend, who only blinked in response. Then, laughing, Jerome left the stable, nodding in greeting at the red bear as he shut the door behind him.

He moved back towards the courtyard and paused, movement near the gate catching his eye. Maddie, Mopsy, Richard, and the few remaining Tempting Tarts stood in a loose knot, loading their own mounts and preparing to leave. Maddie, seeming to know someone was watching them, paused and looked up, catching Jerome's eye. The two held each other's gaze for a long moment. The macaron smiled and nodded. She had stopped by his room on the third day of his recovery, only spending a few moments there to make sure he was surviving and to let him know that they would be leaving soon. They needed to recruit some other confections or cookies to fill out their ranks again. Jerome had thanked her and said he hoped they'd cross paths soon. Maddie, her purse heavy with coins, had smiled and said she was sure they would.

Now, as he watched her mount up and lead the remaining tarts out of the gates, he wasn't so sure.

Jerome took a deep breath, again marveling at the clear, clean quality of it as he let his eyes wander along the battlements and high walls of the castle. He stopped, his breath catching in his chest.

Kupcake stood on a balcony, her frosting radiant in the sun that seemed to break through the clouds at just the right time. Her cheeks were rosy, and while she slumped a little, obviously tired, she still seemed brilliantly happy. Taking a break from planning the wedding, he knew. His mind flashed over all that he'd gone through in the past days to get to where he was at this moment, standing inside the castle and looking up at her. Even with Devil's Food Cake safely locked away in the lowest of the dungeons beneath his feet, Jerome knew that, if needed, he'd do all of it again in a heartbeat. There was no one else in the entire world for him, no one else in a thousand lifetimes. There was only Kupcake, and she was everything.

Smiling, Jerome took a step out into the courtyard, eager to enter the future and to do it with his soon to be wife, the beautiful Kupcake.

46

Carried by howling wind, snow streamed through the narrow mountain pass. The flakes tumbled and twisted on the currents, and slammed into the rocks only to melt and immediately freeze, adding to the treacherous surface.

A dark, gloved hand gripped one ice-crusted outcropping and steadied its grip, the owner ignoring the burning cold that seeped in through the leather to the hand within. The figure, thick cloaks layered tightly about its body, moved with careful precision through the narrow pass. Several yards later, the figure reached a widening of the rock trail and moved far to the left, where a natural curve in the mountain wall blocked the wind. Irritated at this new development, the wind howled and screamed with rage and not a little bit of jealousy.

Hands dug into the folds of the cloak and produced several items, placing each one in specific locations before the curved stone wall. Lastly, a piece of chalk was brought out and – with quick, deft strokes – the hand drew a series of symbols and arcane words on the bare stone.

The figure then stood back and bowed its head. Long minutes passed, the only sound or movement being that of the wind and snow falling. The figure began chanting softly at first, and then the words rose to be heard over the raging wind. Lips recited a specific recipe... one long forgotten to the dark baking arts.

The ceremony completed, the figure's hands rose and drew back the hood, exposing the face of the flan who stared intently at the markings on the wall. He waited several minutes before chanting the recipe again, relishing the oily feeling which each word left on his lips and tongue as it slid free and took flight on the wind.

After the sixth recital, the flan watched as the air in front of the stone wall first began to shimmer and then split apart, opening a crack darker than the blackest hole. From within the hole, the flan could hear the sounds of tortured screaming, eternal pain and suffering, and of victims forced to taste undercooked or burnt confections prepared by overeager mother-in-laws.

The flan felt a dark presence, an ancient abomination too terrible for even whispered tales, as something pushed forward from the horrifying depths. Carefully, he stepped backwards to give it room. The unholy creature, an anathema to the Great Baker Herself, oozed forth. It pooled on the ground before him, and the flan watched it all with wide-eyed excitement. The last of the creature fell from the hole and landed with a soft splat.

The flan rummaged into his cloaks again and produced a small cage that held a cherry tart. The tart clung to the cage bars as it spit insults and curses at its captor, which the flan ignored. Instead, he opened the cage door and grabbed the tart, dropping it into the pooled mass at his feet. Immediately, the tart disappeared, its pained screams cut off sharply as it was digested alive.

"Perfect," the flan said, and tossed the cage down the path. The mass was small now, but it would grow to immense proportions, becoming taller than many of the huge rocks in this very mountain range. If he cared for it properly. And he had every intention of caring for it properly. Oh, yes.

Looking at what he'd summoned, he said, "You are bound to me now. Together, we will free my father from the depths of that bastard's castle. I will have my revenge, and together my father and I will rule this land with fear and darkness. You will have all of the confections you can eat, and I will make all these lowly crumbs bow before me." The mass seemed to quiver in acknowledgement of its mission and master, and in anticipation of bringing true terror to the land.

Then, smiling and determined, the flan turned and started down the mountain with Cottage Cheese slithering close behind him.

The End.

ALSO BY JONATHAN DANIEL

The Uninvited

The Killing Tide

ABOUT THE AUTHOR

Jonathan lives in Birmingham, Alabama with his wife who occasionally finds his jokes funny, but who has also learned to tolerate the weird tangents on which his mind occasionally goes.

If you would like to communicate with Jonathan or learn about upcoming releases, you may do so at byjonathandaniel@gmail.com.

ACKNOWLEDGMENTS

I would like to extend my deepest personal thanks to the people who made this book possible. First, my wife, Kinley. Without you this book wouldn't exist at all. Thank you for your constant support and encouragement, for your patience, for the brainstorming sessions and for always pulling me out of a funk when the words weren't flowing and the characters wouldn't behave. I love you.

Thanks also to Amanda Hudson, for her insights, sharp eye and enthusiasm. Becky Johns for an amazing beta read and fantastic feedback. Allan Woodall for the wonderful cover art (find his stuff at http://www.allandoodles.com/). And last but absolutely not least, Jennifer Collins my editor for making the pile of words I threw together into something coherent and really remarkable.

Without any of you, this book would just be another file on my laptop. Your help means the world to me. Thank you.